"Dr. Cra___ we're holding your daughter."

Annie Crawford listened to the words, but for a long time they didn't register. The man's deep voice continued. "This is Lieutenant Macpherson of the twenty-third precinct. We picked up Sarah about an hour ago with a carload of teenagers and about a half ounce of marijuana."

"I'm sorry," Annie finally managed to say, "you must be mistaken. My daughter's home in bed."

There was a polite pause. "You may want to come down to the station. I could give you directions."

"That won't be necessary. I'll just call home and confirm that Sally is there." Without waiting for a response, Annie hung up and then dialed her home number. The phone rang five times before Ana Lise picked it up, her Copenhagen accent heavy with sleep.

"Ja, she's in bed, Doctor. It's after midnight." Ana Lise sounded bewildered by the question.

"Please check."

Moments later the housekeeper returned to the phone. Her voice was no longer puzzled or sleepy. "She's gone. I do not understand this. She is nowhere in the apartment."

"Damnation!" Trepidation made Annie breathless as she picked up the receiver again to dial the police station.

Dear Reader,

Maine is a place people come to for its unspoiled beauty as well as its graceful and timeless ability to heal weary souls battered by a fast-paced world.

In the innkeeping business one meets many wonderful and interesting people, and while this is a fictional story, it was born of a series of real-life encounters with people who were doing just what Lieutenant Jake Macpherson and Dr. Annie Crawford—hero and heroine of A *Full House*—seek to do.

Lily Houghton represents all elderly people faced with losing their independence. She wants to remain on the saltwater farm she loves, but after she breaks her hip in a fall, her son decides she'd be better off in an assisted living center, and lists her home with a local Realtor. Annie Caldwell rents it for the summer, and to find out the rest of the story, dear gentle reader, you must open the pages of this book.

If you've never visited the grand state of Maine, by all means put it on your list. E-mail me at www.harraseeketinn.com, and I'll help you plan a vacation you'll never forget. I'd love to hear from you.

Sincerely,

Nadia Nichols

A Full House
Nadia Nichols

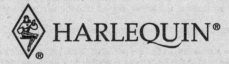
HARLEQUIN®

TORONTO • NEW YORK • LONDON
AMSTERDAM • PARIS • SYDNEY • HAMBURG
STOCKHOLM • ATHENS • TOKYO • MILAN • MADRID
PRAGUE • WARSAW • BUDAPEST • AUCKLAND

ISBN 0-373-71209-X

A FULL HOUSE

Copyright © 2004 by Penny R. Gray.

This edition published by arrangement with Harlequin Books S.A.

® and TM are trademarks of the publisher. Trademarks indicated with ® are registered in the United States Patent and Trademark Office, the Canadian Trade Marks Office and in other countries.

www.eHarlequin.com

Printed in U.S.A.

To Zilla Soriano, my much-appreciated editor.

CHAPTER ONE

THERE WAS A TIME when Annie Crawford looked forward to the unknown challenges she would face at work and the split-second, life-and-death decisions she made every day. But gradually, over the years, those feelings had changed. What she thought about now when she faced another shift was how long and stressful it would be and how desperately tired she was of holding people's lives in her hands.

These days, in those rare moments of quiet that sporadically punctuated her chaotic world, she dreamed of being someplace else. Someplace warm, where gentle winds blew all the clouds away. Someplace serene and peaceful, where tall grasses grew and where sometimes, in the midst of this lush green field, there grazed the most beautiful herd of wild—

"Horses," a man's voice said, interrupting her reverie.

She blinked, lifted her chin out of her hand and gazed up at the broad, friendly face of the man who was lowering himself into a chair across the hospital cafeteria table from her. He was dressed in casual clothes and looked wide awake despite the lateness of the hour.

"For one incredibly hopeful moment I thought you might have been dreaming about me," he continued, nudging a second cup of coffee across the table toward her. "But when I saw the sheer rhapsody of your expression, I knew it had to be that dream about the wild horses in the field of green grass."

Annie accepted the coffee with a slow smile. "There were five of them, and one was a jet-black stallion with a white star. Matt, what are you doing here on your night off? What time is it?"

"Just after midnight. I stopped by to check on Bonnie Mills on my way home from having a few beers at Gritty's." Dr. Matt Brink tasted his coffee and made a face. "So, what's shaking?"

"For a Saturday night it's been downright boring, so I checked on her myself about an hour ago. She was sleeping like a baby."

"Still is." Matt grinned. "She's going to be walking soon, I'd stake my job on it."

"That's the kind of miracle we need more of." Annie lifted her cup and stared at the black brew briefly before taking a sip. She also made a face and sighed. "Listen, I've been thinking…"

"About the beauty of the Adirondacks in spring?" Matt asked hopefully, and Annie shook her head with a rueful laugh. Matt had been prodding her for weeks to commit to a hiking and camping trip.

"Matt, how many times do I have to tell you that I can't go? I have a thirteen-year-old daughter and I can't just—"

"I know," Matt interjected, raising a placating hand. "She's going through a very difficult period in her life called adolescence and you absolutely cannot leave her without maternal supervision until she is married with several grown children of her own."

"Matt…"

He heaved a frustrated sigh. "I know," he repeated. "You're sorry."

Annie smiled. "You're impossible."

"I've been thinking, too," Matt said, leaning toward her. "Why not bring her along?"

"Bring Sally?"

"It'll get her out of the city and away from those friends of hers that you don't like. The fresh mountain air and sunshine would do her a world of good."

Annie's beeper chirped and she reached automatically to silence it, checking the extension. ER. She groaned wearily. "Let me guess. Knife wound to the abdomen inflicted by a drug dealer upon a possessive pimp who tried to talk down the price of a gram of crack for one of his girls." Annie pushed to her feet and eased a cramp in the small of her back. She smiled down at Matt. "Be seeing you around, pal, and thanks for the coffee."

"Ask Sally," Matt pleaded as she swiftly departed. "I betcha she'd love to go on a camping trip." She waved a hand at his words as she pushed through the cafeteria doors but didn't look back.

THE SIGHT OF BLOOD didn't bother her and never had, but Annie sometimes felt as though she should be wearing a full biologic suit when she dealt with some of the shady members of the knife-and-gun club that routinely passed through the ER on a Saturday night. The man she now confronted was being restrained by two uniformed policemen. Male, mid-twenties, black eyes burning with fear and hatred. Blood spurted from his upper thigh while two gloved medics tried vainly to staunch the flow. "We can't get him to hold still," one of them tersely stated the obvious, his face beaded with sweat and dark with frustration. Blood was everywhere. "Gunshot wound. Looks like it's nicked the femoral."

Annie pulled on gloves and protective glasses and leaned into the youth's face. She spoke three terse sentences in fluent Spanish, and the struggling instantly ceased. The cops looked at her in amazement as the medics quickly secured the pressure bandage. "What did you say to him?" one of them asked.

Annie smiled grimly. "I told him that if he didn't hold still I might accidentally cut off his *cojones* because I was extremely inexperienced and the bullet hole was in a very ticklish spot." She waved her hand. "Let's get him down to Number Two operating room. They're still fixing the overheads in One."

The bullet wound was just the first in a string of injuries typical on a Saturday night. Somewhere between declaring the victim of a single car accident dead on arrival and monitoring the condition of an infant admitted with severe flu symptoms, Annie fielded a call from her ex-husband. "Hello, Annie," Dr. Ryan Crawford said from some five hundred miles north in Bangor, Maine. "Sorry to bother you at work but I haven't had much luck reaching you at home, either, thanks to your hostile housekeeper. You busy?"

"It's pretty quiet now but that won't last for long, so hurry up and state your case."

"Still the same old Annie," Ryan said dryly. "It's about our daughter. I'd like her to spend the summer here, or at least part of it. Did she tell you?"

"She mentioned it," Annie said stiffly, turning her back on the nurse's station. "I'm not sure it's such a good idea. She's going through a very difficult time…"

"I know. Adolescence. Been there."

"Not as a young girl you haven't."

"Annie, why do you feel so threatened by my wanting to have Sally visit? Trudy and I would love to have her, and she told me she wants to come."

Trudy. Annie's grip tightened on the receiver. Three months after their divorce was finalized, Ryan had tied the knot with Trudy, a medical transcriptionist from his office. It was Annie who had asked for the divorce, citing irreconcilable differences that had nothing at all to do with another woman, or so she thought. Ryan's obvious involvement with Trudy had surprised the hell out of her.

"Hasn't Trudy got enough to think about with the baby? It's due pretty soon, isn't it?"

"Seven more weeks. And in case you're interested, it's a boy. Trudy wanted to know ahead of time so we could get the nursery ready. If Sally came up she'd be here for the birth. She'd get to meet her brother on day one. She'd be a part of it all, and Adam would be a part of her life."

"Adam?"

"Trudy named him. Adam Beckwith Crawford."

"Beautiful."

"Oh, come off it, Annie, don't be so bitter. Let Sally come. It'll be good for her. She'll love our place. It's on the outskirts of the city, big yard with trees, big garden, an easy drive to the ocean. It'll be a good break from New York. All kids need fresh air and sunshine, even if some doctors don't. And face it, Annie. You're so busy you're hardly ever around for her."

Annie's beeper chirped again. She checked the extension as she silenced it. ER again. "Gotta go." She hung up the phone abruptly and hurried down the corridor. He had a hell of a nerve saying something like that to her. *Even if some doctors don't.*

"Don't what?" one of the ER nurses asked as she burst through the doors. Annie felt the blood rush into her face. She hadn't realized she'd spoken out loud. She dove into her next case with grim determination. Baby girl. Four months old. Severely dehydrated from a combination of vomiting and diarrhea. *Damn* the man. *Even if some doctors don't...never around for Sally...* What did he know about being a parent, the two-timing bastard? He'd done precious little parenting with his first child.

She read the thermometer with a fierce scowl and shook her head. Well, he was about to get a second chance at fatherhood. She hoped A.B.C. was a colicky baby and that Trudy made Ryan get out of bed at least half of the time to take care of him. And that Adam Beckwith Crawford gave his parents a tough time with adolescence. *Been there.* Honestly, the *nerve* of the man.

She admitted the baby for overnight observation, and while she wrote up the orders for fluid and electrolyte therapy, she reflected on her daughter. Not a bad kid. Mouthy at times, and increasingly distracted and pressured by a chaotic world, but in spite of what her Ryan thought, Annie considered herself a good mother. Almost every morning she and Sally had breakfast together, discussed schoolwork, current events, boys, homework and future plans and dreams. Sally could talk to her about anything, though lately the girl had been too busy hanging out with her friends to talk much at all.

So why, Annie wondered with a strong twinge of anxiety, did Sally want to spend the summer in Maine? Did she really miss her father so much that she'd forsake the cute—Tom Somebody-or-other—boy she'd recently discovered, for the entire summer? Or was she unhappy living with her mother? And the real crux of the matter—if she went to visit her father in Bangor, and if he made life indescribably wonderful for her, would she want to come back?

"Dr. Crawford? Phone call." The head nurse interrupted Annie's dark thoughts and she glanced up from the clipboard, startled. She handed the orders to the nurse with a nod of thanks and took the call at the station.

"Crawford, here," she said abruptly.

"Dr. Crawford, this is Lieutenant Macpherson of the Twenty-third Precinct," a man's deep voice said. "We're holding your daughter here at the station. She's fine, but she was picked up about an hour ago with a carload of teenagers found to be in possession of about half an ounce of marijuana."

Annie heard the words spoken, but for a few long moments they didn't register. "I'm sorry," she finally managed in a haughty voice, "but you must be mistaken. My daughter's home in bed."

There was a polite pause. "You may want to come down to the station," the calm voice suggested. "I could give you directions…"

"I'm perfectly capable of finding the police station, Lieutenant," Annie snapped, "but I'm certain that won't be necessary. I'll call my housekeeper and she'll verify that my daughter is in bed. Asleep."

Without waiting for a response, Annie hung up, then picked up the receiver and dialed home.

The phone rang five times before Ana Lise answered, her Copenhagen accent heavy with sleep. "Ana Lise, is Sally home?"

"*Ja,* of course she is." Ana Lise sounded understandably bewildered by the question. "She is in bed, Doctor. It is after midnight."

"Could you please check?"

Moments later the housekeeper returned to the phone. Her voice was no longer puzzled or sleepy. "Doctor, Sally is gone!" she exclaimed. "She is nowhere in the apartment, but…she was here, I fixed her supper, she did her homework at the kitchen table, watched TV for an hour, went to bed at ten just as she always does. But now I do not understand this. She is gone!"

"Damnation," Annie said, and hung up. Trepidation made her breathless. She picked up the receiver and dialed Matt's number. His voice, too, was thick with sleep. "Matt? I'm so sorry to wake you but I have to ask you an enormous favor…"

Thirty minutes later Matt was at the hospital to cover for her, bleary-eyed and disgruntled. "You owe me a camping trip," he said gruffly when she tried to thank him. In her gratitude she nodded in agreement. "You got it," she promised.

She took a cab to the police station. It was close to 3:00 a.m. and the precinct was nearly as busy as the ER. After asking at the main desk, she was directed to the juvenile holding area where several young people were bastioned in a small room under the supervision of the juvenile officer. Her daughter was among them, looking pale, scared, and so very young. She was talking to a man whom Annie herself would have crossed a busy street to avoid—an unshaved vagrant dressed in throw-away clothes and sporting long, unkempt hair. He had one hand braced against the wall, the other on his hip, and his body was curved in a lazy slouch as he listened, head down, while Sally talked. What on earth could Sally be discussing with a bum like that?

Annie felt a surge of outrage as she marched up to the officer seated at the desk and pointed in disbelief. "Would you mind telling me why that degenerate is talking to my daughter?" she blurted angrily. "He shouldn't even be in the same room with her! I see his kind in the ER all the time, shot up and cut up, costing the taxpayers big bucks for us to patch their holes so they can go back out on the streets and sell their drugs to young innocent kids like…like these." Annie gestured to the young occupants, thinking to herself that her daughter was undoubtedly the only innocent among them.

The uniformed officer sat quietly through her angry outburst, then raised one hand in a calming gesture. "That *degenerate* is Lieutenant Macpherson, the arresting officer." The cop reached for some papers and pushed them across the desk toward her. "I assume you're here to sign for your daughter's release?"

Annie flushed at his words. She could feel the band of pain tightening in her temples as she crossed the room and regarded both her daughter and the man she'd been talking to. "I understand you're the…the *officer* who arrested my daughter," she said to Lieutenant Macpherson who had straightened out of his slouch at her approach. Up close she could see his hair was a dark tawny color and his eyes were pale.

Blue or gray, she couldn't quite tell, but they were clear, keen, intelligent eyes.

"That's right," he said. "I'd like to speak with you in private, if I may, before you take your daughter home."

"I'm sure there's been some mistake," Annie said. "Sally doesn't belong in here."

"Oh, but she does," Macpherson contradicted in a maddeningly mild voice. "She was in a vehicle full of kids smoking pot. I just happened to be working a stakeout when they stopped to ask me where they could buy some more." He shrugged. "Guess I look like the type that would know. I brought them in. They're a lot safer here than they were in that part of town."

Annie stared at him, her face burning and her heart beating loudly in her ears. She turned to Sally. "Is that true?"

Sally kept her eyes fixed on the floor. "Yes," she said in a voice scarcely above a whisper.

Annie stared at the other kids. Five of them, all older than Sally. Two girls, three boys. One of the boys was perilously close to manhood, and when he glanced at Sally, Annie frowned. "Are you Tom?" she asked. At his sullen nod, her blood pressure climbed another notch. "Sally, you told me that Tom was your age and that he was on the honor role." Aspirin. She needed a handful of aspirin...and a stiff drink.

"Dr. Crawford," Macpherson said, shoulders rounding as he shoved his hands into his jeans' pockets. "It's important that I speak with you privately."

Annie followed him reluctantly into the corridor, where he paused near the water fountain. He was tall,

she noticed, having to look up to meet his eyes, and
well built. "Once you sign for her release, you can
take Sally home. She'll need to be present at a court
hearing, and the juvenile officer will explain that to
you." He hesitated for a moment. "We'd also like
her to sign an agreement stating that she'll have no
further contact with Tom Ward. That boy's only seventeen years old but his police record spans four years
and includes shoplifting, vandalism and drug traffick-
ing on school grounds." Annie's blood pressure
soared to new heights at his words.

"Because this is Sally's first offense," Macpherson
continued, "we're recommending that she attend a
ten-hour program held at her school for two hours
every Tuesday evening. It's called Jump Start and its
purpose is to deter young people from getting into
any more trouble."

"I can assure you Sally will never step foot in a
precinct house again," Annie said grimly.

Macpherson nodded. "Probably not. She seems
like a good kid and she's pretty shaken up right now,
but this program will make her understand the reper-
cussions of bad behavior."

"All right," Annie agreed.

"I talked to Sally for a little while because she
obviously didn't belong with the rest of those kids.
Her biggest fear right now is that you'll be so mad
you won't let her visit her father this summer."

"She told you that?"

Macpherson nodded. Annie's stomach churned and
her head pounded. She drew a deep, even breath.
"Well, she's right," she said.

"I think that would be a mistake," Macpherson said.

"Really." Annie had to resist the urge to slap his arrogant, unshaved face.

"From what she told me, she misses him a great deal. Maybe I'm speaking out of place, but I have a daughter, too, Dr. Crawford. She lives with her mother in Los Angeles. I talk to her on the phone as often as I can, but it isn't the same as being there."

"Then might I suggest you move to California, Lieutenant," Annie said. "That's what any caring father would do." She turned her back on him and returned to the room where Sally waited with the other teenagers. "You," she said coolly to her daughter after signing all the appropriate release forms, "are under house arrest." She paused. "For the rest of your life."

They rode home in silence. There was nothing that Annie could say to bridge the awful void. Her thoughts were a chaos of conflicting emotions. Sally was unhurt. It could have turned out much worse. But how had she snuck out of the apartment past the night watchman? How could Ana Lise have let this happen?

Four in the morning and Ana Lise was waiting for them. She had made coffee, and the smell of it bolstered Annie's flagging spirits. Ana Lise made rich, marvelous coffee. She took the offered cup and motioned Sally into the living room. "Sit," she said wearily. "We need to talk." She sank onto the couch while Sally perched uneasily on the edge of a chair. "How did you get out of the apartment?"

Sally's eyes dropped. "I climbed into the dumbwaiter."

"You climbed into the dumbwaiter," Annie repeated woodenly. "You had prearranged plans to meet Tom and his friends and go out joyriding on a Saturday night to smoke some dope and get high.''

"Mom…"

"Sally, you're just thirteen years old."

"So what? I'm not a baby," Sally said, becoming sullen.

"Then why are you acting like one?" Annie rose from the couch and paced across the room, clutching her half-empty coffee cup. Gray hairs, she thought. Millions of them. I'm well on my way to total gray and damn close to being forty years old… "Where did you meet those kids, and how long have you been hanging around with them?"

"Tom's Melanie's brother. He's really nice…"

"*Nice?* Is that how you describe a guy who lures you out in the middle of the night and gets you arrested? A guy who has a four-year police record that includes selling drugs on school property? How can I ever trust you again? How can I ever leave here and not wonder where you are when 2:00 a.m. rolls around?"

"It's not Tom's fault. He didn't do all those things they said."

"No, of course not. Tell me something. Has he told you about the birds and the bees yet? Has he told you that girls can't get pregnant the first time they have sex? That if he can't have sex with you he'll find someone else who really cares about him?"

Sally's body language became increasingly defiant. "It's not like that."

Annie's eyes lasered her daughter's. "It had better not be. I don't want you seeing him ever again." She turned her back on her daughter and paced to the window. Looked out onto the blaze of lights that stretched out forever. Big city. Enormous city. City that never slept. She sipped coffee to steady her nerves. "Your father called tonight," she said when she could speak calmly.

"Dad?" Sally's voice was a poignant mixture of remorse and hope. "Does he know about this? Did you tell him?"

"He called before I knew myself." Annie turned to face her daughter. "He told me that he wants you to spend some time with him this summer. Trudy's going to have the baby soon, and he thought it would be good for you to be there for the birth, so you could get to know your brother right from the start."

Sally's eyes unexpectedly filled with tears. "He said that?" she said, her face working.

Annie's heart turned over. She felt breathless and turned away, wandering to the cherry highboy beside the fireplace. She trailed her fingers across the satiny finish of the old heirloom and finished her coffee. "Do you want to go?" she asked.

"I miss Dad," she said simply.

Annie nodded. The highboy was a beautiful piece, her great-grandmother's. It had begun its life in Cotswold, had been shipped to Australia for two generation's worth of family history and then had come to America when Annie had married. One day it would be Sally's. Annie pictured her mother's kind and patient face, so very far away from her now, and her eyes stung. "Someday you'll have children of your own," she said softly, turning to face her daughter. "And that, young lady, will be my revenge. Now go to bed."

Annie should have returned to work but she didn't. She phoned Matt, who told her not to bother. Everything was quiet at the hospital and only one hour remained of her shift. "Remember, you owe me that camping trip," he reminded her before hanging up. She sat out on the balcony and sipped another cup of coffee while Ana Lise worked through her guilt in the kitchen by baking. She brought Annie a big piece of apple strudel, fresh from the oven, and hovered over her.

"I am so sorry about all of this, madam," she said. Ana Lise had never called her "madam" before and it startled Annie, who raised her eyebrows at her housekeeper in surprise.

"Oh, Ana Lise. Go back to bed. It's not your fault. But from now on I think we should put a lockout on the dumbwaiter after 6:00 p.m."

"*Ja, ja.*" Ana Lise nodded vigorously, relieved. "I think so, too."

Annie watched the sun rise over the city, heard the burgeoning swell of noise gather faintly and then grow until the peace was gone, obliterated by swarms of cars, buses, trucks and people. Millions of people, all going somewhere, doing something. Alive and living for the moment...

She sighed. The camping trip with Matt suddenly appealed very strongly. She was a country girl at heart, having grown up on a big sheep station that her father managed. Her father had been a great man and a great leader of men. Quite a shock it had been to a lot of people when he had died in the Outback soon after Annie's seventeenth birthday. He hadn't come in one day from riding the fence line, that endless wire fence erected to deter the dingoes, the wild dogs of Australia, from the sheep. They had sent search parties out that night and more the following morning.

More than a hundred men had searched for three days, but he was dead when they found him, he and his horse, both.

They found the horse first, just three miles from the fence line. Broken leg. Shot. Searchers reconstructed the scenario. The horse had spooked and thrown John Gorley, then bolted three miles before the fall that fractured its cannon bone. Gorley had followed the horse, eventually finding and destroying it. He had been hurt himself in the fall, worse than he would probably have admitted, because John Gorley was not a man to admit to any sort of weakness.

Knowing where he was, he'd cut due south to intersect the fence line near the Boranga station, but had died two miles shy of his destination. The autopsy had proved his grit. Big John Gorley had walked over fifteen miles in two days of relentless heat with no food, one pint of water, a broken arm, six broken ribs and a ruptured spleen.

The Outback had killed her father, yet it had nurtured him, too. Annie had not forgotten the harsh beauty of it, the smell and the taste and the feel and the sound of it. She was born in Australia and the land of her birth was in her blood. Sally had never seen the land down under, nor had she expressed any desire to, but that might change as she matured and became more curious about her roots. About her grandmother who lived in Melbourne now and her uncles, two of whom worked at Boranga and the third who had stayed on at Dad's station.

''Daddy,'' Annie said softly, marveling at how unreal his death still seemed, how impossibly remote the idea that she would never see him again or hear his deep, humor-filled voice or feel the intense glow of pride his words of praise could evoke in her.

Sally said she missed her father, and why wouldn't she? Though he called her once a week, she rarely saw him. Perhaps she *should* spend some time with him this summer. It would be good for the both of them to get to know each other better, and it would get Sally away from those awful kids. That alone was enough to make Annie reconsider Ryan's proposal.

CHAPTER TWO

"YOU PROMISED ME, Annie," Matt reminded her two weeks later to the day. They were standing to one side of the door to X-ray. "I trust you've been packing your gear."

Annie sighed. "I know I promised, but I can't go right away, Matt," she said. "Sally's hearing is first thing Monday morning and…" She shook her head, still unable to believe she was talking about her child. "I can't just up and leave her, Matt. I was thinking that maybe we should wait until she goes to visit her father, and even then I may not be able to get a whole week off. I'll ask, but there's only an outside chance. You know how Edelstein is. He hates for anyone to have a life apart from the hospital." She gazed at Matt, then reached for his arm and gave it a sympathetic squeeze. "Come on, Matt. I said I'd go, I just can't promise you an entire week, that's all. We'll have to make the best of what we can get, and in the meantime, I'll go to court with Sally." An unexpected laugh erupted before she could quell it.

"I don't know how you can find the situation funny."

"It's not funny at all. It just sounds so strange to my ears… It's awful, it really is…" She sighed wearily and shook her head. "My daughter would never smoke pot or hang out with a seventeen-year-old juvenile delinquent named Tom or get arrested for possession of an illegal substance. Know what I mean?''

"I hope she's learned her lesson.''

"Me, too. She's been going to these special meetings on Tuesday nights that are guaranteed to put her on the straight and narrow and she seems to be taking it very seriously, which is good because I'm having a hard time with all this stuff. Court hearings, for heaven's sake. All I can picture is Sally being hauled away in handcuffs by that scruffy cop, Lieutenant Macpherson. He could easily pass for a derelict. I understand it's part of his job to look like the very people he's trying to arrest, but still…''

"I take it he's not one of your favorites?'' Matt said sympathetically.

"He arrested my daughter, didn't he?'' Annie shot over her shoulder as she pushed through the doors to X-ray.

ANNIE'S SATURDAY NIGHT in ER began with a blistering flurry of activity that only intensified as the early hours of the morning brought a rising tide of traumatic injuries. By 3:00 a.m. she was up to her elbows in other people's crises, which in a way was a blessing because she had no time to dwell on the Monday morning hearing. She was actually beginning to look forward to the camping trip with Matt, and also beginning to entertain the notion of getting out of the city once and for all. Perhaps it was time for that long-yearned-for return to the country, to a quiet, backwater place where Sally could make new friends and discover sunshine and fresh air.

"Dr. Crawford?'' Rob Bellows, a surgical resident, entered the treatment room and spoke at her elbow.

"I'll take over for you here. We've got another in-coming. Gunshot wound to the chest, EMT's report it's pretty dicey."

"They're all pretty dicey," Annie said wearily, stepping back from the table where the victim of a car accident, young and drunk, submitted docilely to having a gash on his forehead stitched. She stripped off her gloves and threw them in the waste container as she walked out. She could already hear the muted sound of the ambulance siren as it swung into the emergency entrance. Then the siren cut off and she could picture the ambulance backing up to the door. She stopped at the nurse's station and grabbed a fast drink of cool spring water and then a second as the emergency doors automatically opened and they wheeled the next patient in.

"Round three," Annie muttered under her breath as the running footsteps squeaked toward her down the polished floor. She fell into step beside the stretcher, visibly assessing the victim. The EMTs were brisk, professional and slightly out of breath. "Had a hell of a time with this one...cops said it could be a .38 caliber bullet...entry wound is on his lower left chest, no exit wound, the patient's in shock, definitely a tension pnuemo, we nearly lost him on the way in..."

There was a generous amount of blood on the vic-tim, but Annie guessed from the EMT's brief run-down that most of the hemorrhaging was internal and that a lung had collapsed. They wheeled him, half running, into the ER, where the skilled team quickly began cutting away the injured man's clothing, allow-ing Annie to make a rapid but careful examination. A scene that might have paralyzed a less experienced physician, she dealt with perfunctorily and with minimal talk. Within minutes she had established an airway and positioned a chest tube between his ribs, while at the same time the nurses, at her direction, placed two IVs in his arms and began infusing a bag of Ringer's solution as fast as possible. While Annie inserted a nasogastric tube to decompress the stomach, the nurses drew blood samples, placed a catheter and activated electronic monitors. All of their actions were so well orchestrated that scarcely five minutes had passed since the patient had been wheeled into ER.

Annie guided a large bore needle between the ribs just beneath the collarbone and, just as she had expected, pressurized air hissed out. "Okay, people," she said, "this one goes straight into OR. There's some serious abdominal bleeding going on, a collapsed lung and God only knows what else. We have a definite chest wound, but this guy's stomach is swelling up like a hot-air balloon. I think that bullet did some bouncing around inside there."

She picked up the phone and dialed OR. "Hey, Hanley, we're coming down with a gunshot wound to the left chest, in shock, definitely looks like multiple organ trauma." As she spoke, she glanced at the victim's face. There was something familiar about the guy. She drew in a deep breath as she heard Hanley say something about a kid with a hot appendix. "Bump him," she snapped. "This one can't wait."

She hung up the phone. "Who is this guy?" she asked the surgical resident, who shook his head and shrugged, but the nurse picked up the chart left behind by the EMTs.

"Macpherson," the nurse said, scanning it quickly.

"Lieutenant Jake Macpherson." Her eyebrows raised in surprise, and she glanced at Annie. "He's a cop."

"Okay, let's rock and roll, folks," Annie said, her heart rate shifting into high gear as adrenaline surged through her. "He's going to be a dead cop if we don't hustle."

FOR BREAKFAST on Sunday morning Sally always had cereal and toast and a big glass of orange juice. Her mother usually was home by 8:00 or 9:00 a.m. and Ana Lise would cook the traditional Sunday-morning breakfast of ham and eggs, but Sally was happy with her bowl of cereal. She was addicted to Cheerios. If there was a banana to slice onto it she was in heaven—except this morning. She had her Cheerios and an entire banana sliced atop, but she was about as far from heaven as she could get. She sat in the breakfast nook and watched Ana Lise bustle around the gleaming kitchen, taking a pan of pastries from the oven.

"You will have a pastry then, *ja?*" she asked over her shoulder.

Sally shook her head.

"No thanks. I'm not hungry."

Ana Lise set the pan on the counter and turned, frowning. "You would not like a pastry with butter spread over it? A cinnamon bun warm from the oven? Are you ill, then?"

Sally used the tip of her spoon to submerge the slices of banana one by one. She shook her head again. "I'm too nervous to eat," she confided miserably. "Tomorrow's my hearing…"

"*Ja*, but that is tomorrow. This is today. You must eat."

"Ana Lise, what if they put me in jail?"

"They will not put you in jail. You are only a child."

"What if they send me to juvenile hall?"

Ana Lise shook her head in exasperation. "We have talked of this before. They will not send you to juvenile hall."

"Mom might send me to private school. She might make me move away."

"That would never happen," Ana Lise said, hands on her sturdy hips. "You eat your cereal."

"Do you think she'll let me visit my dad this summer?"

Ana Lise turned back to her tasks with a shake of her head. "I am not paid to tell your fortune, young lady. Eat your breakfast. Your mother will be home soon and you can ask her yourself."

But Annie did not get home until nearly noontime, and Ana Lise had switched from breakfast mode to dinner mode, it being a Sunday. A roast was baking in the oven and she was verbally contemplating a Yorkshire pudding when Annie slumped wearily into the apartment. She dropped into a kitchen chair with a soft moan. "What a night," she said. "And what a morning."

"A hard one, *ja?*" Ana Lise said sympathetically, pouring a cup of coffee and setting it, strong and black, in front of Annie.

"Hard? Oh, Ana Lise." Annie let her head fall back and closed her eyes. She took a deep breath and released it slowly. "Where's Sally?"

"In her room listening to her music. She's worried about tomorrow. About the hearing. She didn't eat any breakfast and she says she is too nervous to eat lunch.''

They heard the door to Sally's room open and her light, quick footsteps in the hall. ''Mom? I thought I heard your voice.'' Sally paused in the kitchen doorway, her face mirroring her mother's, though for entirely different reasons. ''Mom, I'm so nervous about tomorrow that I feel sick.''

Annie opened her eyes and inhaled another deep breath, releasing it somewhere between a sigh and a moan. ''There isn't going to be a hearing tomorrow, Sally,'' she said. She raised and rotated her shoulders to ease a sudden muscle cramp. There was nothing like a long stint in surgery to trigger painful muscle spasms. ''Your arresting officer was shot last night. I spent most of the night and the better part of this morning trying to keep him alive.''

Sally's face was blank. For a moment she said nothing, just stood in the kitchen doorway and stared at her mother. ''Is he...dead?'' she finally blurted.

Annie raised her eyebrows. ''A fine question to ask. Don't you have any faith in your mother's skills?''

Sally slumped against the doorjamb. ''Then...he's still going to testify against me in court?''

''Not tomorrow, he isn't,'' Annie said flatly. She picked up her coffee cup and took a sip. ''I spoke to the big cheese at the station house. He was at the hospital, along with half a hundred other police officers. He told me the hearing would be rescheduled when Lieutenant Macpherson's health permits. So, sweet little best friend of mine, it would seem that you have been granted a temporary reprieve.''

Sally's eyes fixed gravely on her mother's face. "For how long?"

Annie took another sip of coffee. "He's young and strong. I expect an uncomplicated recovery. Let's say three weeks, four at the outside. By then he'll be able to sit in a courtroom and tell the whole world how you were out gallivanting around in the middle of the night with a bunch of pot-smoking juvenile delinquents."

"But I wasn't smoking pot..."

"Don't expect much sympathy from me right now, young lady. I'm dead tired."

Ana Lise refilled Annie's coffee cup. "What you need right now is a long soak in a hot bath, *ja?* I know how that helps you after you've spent a long time in surgery. I will get it ready."

Annie smiled wearily at her housekeeper. "That sounds lovely. I'll take you up on that offer."

Half an hour later she was immersed to her chin in deliciously hot water and lavender oil. Her eyes were blissfully closed and she was nearly asleep, her mind drifting toward that quiet, peaceful place where the wind blew all the clouds away and the horses ran free, when Ana Lise tapped on the bathroom door.

"A call for you, from the hospital," she called apologetically.

Annie moaned. "Take a message."

"He says it is an emergency."

"Okay," Annie said. The bathroom door opened and Ana Lise's arm stretched around with the cordless phone in her hand. Annie took it. "Thank you," she said as the door closed. "Yes?" she said into the phone. It was Matt.

"I'm sorry to call you, Annie, I know you just left

here, but your patient, Macpherson, went into cardiac arrest about ten minutes ago. We jump-started him, but he's not too stable. Blood pressure's 90/70.''

Annie was rising out of the tub even as Matt spoke. ''Where's Palazola?'' she asked tersely. ''Isn't he senior surgeon on call?''

''He's in OR with a little boy who was run over by a bus.''

''What about Macpherson's heart sounds? Are they muffled?''

''Yes.''

''Dammit! He was fine when I left. Okay, I'm on my way. We'll need to aspirate the blood around the heart. Can you do it?''

''I can try.'' Matt's voice mirrored his uncertainty. ''How soon can you be here?''

''Ten minutes.''

''I'd rather wait for you...''

''If you have to do it, Matt, *do it,*'' Annie said, throwing the phone onto the vanity and reaching for a towel. ''Ana Lise, call my driving service!'' she shouted out the bathroom door. Fifteen minutes later, hair still dripping, she was running down the hallway to the Intensive Care Unit. Matt was inside the cubicle watching the monitors and two nurses were with him. Annie listened to Macpherson's heart and noted the distention of his neck veins. ''People, he should already be in the OR,'' she snapped, her nerves on edge. ''I trust you've cleared it?''

Matt's face flushed. ''We're good to go.''

Aspirating the blood from around the heart was not a long procedure, but Annie blamed herself for not anticipating the complication. She had checked for cardiac tamponade several times since Macpherson had been admitted, both before, during and after the surgery. At no time did she discern a problem. Still… She exited the OR for the second time that day in a haze of exhaustion, stripping off her gloves and mask and tossing them into the disposal unit.

"I'm sorry, Annie," Matt said, hurrying out behind her. "I should've spotted the warning signs sooner."

"I shouldn't have left," Annie said. "I'll check on him when they bring him into recovery. If anything changes, I'll be in the lounge."

"Annie." She stopped and turned. Matt was holding his arms out at his sides in a gesture of surrender. "I'm sorry I messed up."

Annie shook her head wearily. "Just come and get me if there's any deterioration in his condition. He *can't* die on me, Matt. That just can't happen. They'd think I did something deliberately so he couldn't testify against my daughter."

"No one would ever think that."

Annie didn't answer.

"Get some rest. If there's the slightest change in his condition, I'll wake you."

But in spite of her exhaustion, Annie couldn't sleep. The hospital, at three o'clock in the afternoon, was bustling with life. Intercoms squawked nonstop, carts rattled, rubber-soled shoes squeaked, voices of patients, staff and visitors mingled in the corridors. She lay on the couch in the doctor's lounge, her forearm shielding her eyes, and tried to relax. Her stomach cramped painfully, reminding her she hadn't eaten for nearly twenty-four hours, yet she wasn't hungry.

She sat up and yawned. Within minutes she was in recovery, checking on Macpherson. His vital signs were good. She pulled a chair up beside his bed and sat. Matt came in quietly to adjust the IVs and returned moments later with a fresh, hot cup of coffee and a magazine for Annie. She took both with a grateful smile. The coffee was good and the magazine was a copy of *Down East,* a monthly publication full of beautiful pictures and articles about coastal Maine.

She sipped the coffee and turned the pages of the magazine, finding herself drawn to the evocative images of a world far removed from big-city life. How long she sat there, immersed in the mystique of rocky, timbered coastline, saltwater farms and quaint harbors filled with sturdy lobster boats, she didn't know. But her coffee was cold and her yawns had become more frequent when a man's voice said, "Beautiful place."

She looked up, startled to see that Macpherson had awakened. She blinked, set aside the magazine and the coffee. She checked his vital signs, relieved that they were all as good as could be expected. The cadence of his heartbeat remained clear and strong.

"My grandparents used to have a camp in Maine," he said as she straightened, easing a cramp in the small of her back.

"Don't talk, Lieutenant. You're in recovery and you're doing just fine, but you need to keep quiet."

She accompanied the orderlies when they rolled Macpherson back to ICU and saw that he was hooked up into the myriad of monitors again. "The police are everywhere," she told him as she made a few notes on his chart. "The waiting room is jammed full of them." She thought it strange that there was no significant other wringing her hands among all the badges. Surely there was a woman in his life? And what about his parents? Brothers and sisters?

"My parents sold the camp when my grandparents died," he said, still groggy from the effects of the anesthesia. "Beautiful log cabin…"

"Lieutenant Macpherson?" Annie bent over him. "Is there anyone I can call for you? Family members, close friends?"

"Those guys in the waiting room," he said. "Only family I have."

"I see. Well, you won't be able to have any visitors today. Tomorrow, perhaps." Annie paused. "And, Lieutenant, this might not be the best time to apologize, but I'm sorry I was so rude to you the night you arrested my daughter."

A vague frown furrowed his brow at her words, then cleared. "Bear clawed the door once, trying to get in. Big bear."

Annie sighed. He was still pretty dopey. "Lieutenant, no more talking. I've taped the call button right beside your hand. Can you feel it? Good. If you need anything at all, just push that button. The nurses will keep a close eye on you, and Dr. Brink will be checking in regularly. I'll be nearby, just down the hall." Annie took one last critical look at Macpherson before turning to leave, but his voice stopped her as she reached the door.

"The cabin was on a pretty little pond…"

"Lieutenant, please try to get some rest."

She turned away once again, and once again his voice halted her in her tracks. "Don't forget your magazine, Doc," he said. When she left Intensive Care Unit, the glossy periodical was tucked beneath her arm.

JAKE MACPHERSON was moved into a private room after three days in ICU. Time resumed its old dimensions and began to weigh heavily upon him. His visitors came and went in a steady stream, men and women from the department, the obligatory brotherhood of the badge. Some of them were friends, others he barely recognized, more than a few he didn't know at all. All of them came bearing get-well wishes and awkward demeanors. None of them enjoyed being in hospitals because they feared that one day, they, too, might wind up in an adjustable hospital bed with bloody tubes bristling from their bodies.

Or worse, in the hospital's morgue.

The one bright spot that moved in and out of his life was Dr. Annie Crawford, but he saw her less and less frequently as his condition improved and the regular doctors took over. And so he spent the long hours of the endless days replaying the sequence of events that had landed him in this hospital bed. Damning himself, over and over, for his carelessness. Berating himself for not listening to the skinny hooker when she'd said to Joey Mendoza, little drug runner extraordinaire, "I won't let him arrest you, Joey, I'll shoot him first." A hollow threat. Surely she didn't have a gun, and even if she did, no one would shoot a cop for Joey Mendoza.

But surprise, surprise, when he'd started to cuff Joey, she'd pulled this tiny pistol out of her purse. He'd had time to defend himself. He'd seen her move, seen the little pistol in her hand, and was pulling his own gun even as he pushed Joey away from him, out of the line of fire. He could have shot her but didn't. Couldn't bring himself to pull the trigger on a woman.

And so he lay on his back in the hospital bed, hour after hour, counting the tiny holes in the acoustic ceiling tiles, finding geometric patterns in random chaos, endlessly defining the perimeters of his life and waiting for the early mornings when Annie Crawford would walk into his room at the end of her shift, give him one of her quizzical little smiles and say, "Hey, Lieutenant. How are you feeling?"

Whenever she came he tried to engage her in conversation about her daughter. About her life. About the hospital. About the weather. About the dog-eared *Down East* magazine she'd been reading. About the camp his grandparents had owned. Anything to extend her visit. Eventually she showed him a classified ad in the real estate section, an old saltwater farm for rent for the summer in a place called Blue Harbor. "It's a wild, crazy dream, spending a summer in Maine," she admitted. "But, oh, so tempting."

He advised her to call the listing Realtor. "Live dangerously," he said. "Take the summer off and be wild."

She'd laughed at the absurdity of such a notion, but the next time she came into his room she confessed that she'd called about the rental. "It's still available and sounds wonderful, but there's just no way I can take the whole summer off, and they won't rent it by the week." Still, she was thinking about it, he could tell. She was thinking about it enough that he called the Realtor himself, remembering the name from the ad she'd shown him. An elderly sounding man answered. "I'm wondering if you carry any summer rentals in the Blue Harbor area," Jake began.

"Sure do. What exactly are you looking for, and in what price range?"

Jake told him, and after a brief pause the voice said politely, "I'm afraid you won't find anything that cheap in this area. The closest thing I have listed in your price range is a very primitive camp about twenty miles inland.'' Twenty miles wasn't that far to drive to see a woman like Annie Crawford. He logged the information, thanked the Realtor, and hung up.

Annie's visits became less and less frequent. She was always busy, whisking in and out, cheerful but impersonal, shining—like the sun—on all things equally. Nonetheless, he was secretly smitten with her, and he supposed that just about every red-blooded man she met fell under the same spell. How could they help themselves? Annie Crawford was smart, warm, compassionate and highly skilled in a very challenging profession. As if those attributes weren't enough, her eyes were a shade of marine blue that made him think of some exotic tropical paradise. Her hair was a thick, glossy mahogany, shoulder-length and pulled back in a simple twist. Annie and her daughter looked enough alike to pass as sisters, but Sally didn't have her mother's Australian accent or the bone-deep beauty that only spiritual maturity could give a woman—and Annie Crawford was a deeply beautiful woman.

CHAPTER THREE

ON THE AFTERNOON of his fifth day in the hospital, a little girl walked into Jake's room. She had pale blond hair plaited in two braids and large, dark eyes. She was wearing denim coveralls and a red-and-black plaid shirt. The sight of her rendered him momentarily speechless. He half believed she was an illusion his mind had created to while away the endless hours.

"Amanda?" He pushed himself onto his elbows, afraid she would disappear, but instead she approached the bed cautiously.

"Daddy?"

"C'mere, Pinch. Don't mind all this medical stuff. Come give your daddy a big hug." He reached out for her, and she was very real. She smelled sweet, her cheek was warm and smooth against his, and her chubby arms felt marvelous as they tightened around his neck. He tightened his own arms around her. "Amanda," he said, his voice choked with emotion. "Ah, my sweet baby girl."

"Hello, Jake." His ex-wife stood just inside the doorway, hands clasped loosely in front of her. She wore a white silk blouse, black trousers, a sage-colored linen jacket. Her hair fell in dark glossy curls upon her shoulders and she wore minimal makeup with a touch of lip gloss. She looked fresh-faced, young and beautiful. If she'd gone through the same hell as he had during and after their divorce, it certainly didn't show.

"Hello, Linda," he said, reluctantly relinquishing his embrace. Amanda squirmed out of his arms and climbed on the bed beside him, as endearingly affectionate as a puppy.

"Amanda, be careful," her mother warned.

"It's all right," Jake said. "She can't hurt anything. Thanks for bringing her."

Linda nodded. "She's your daughter. She has a right to see you."

"It's a long way for you to come. I appreciate it. I'll pay for your plane tickets."

Linda shook her head. "Your captain made all the arrangements. A police car picked us up at the airport and delivered us to the hotel and another car brought us here."

Jake thought about this for a moment. "They must have thought I was going to die," he said.

"From what I've just been told, you almost did." Linda's fingers were intertwined tightly. He could tell what a strain it was on her, just being in the same room with him.

"I had a good doctor," he said.

"Yes, I know. I met her at the nurses' station. She was the one who directed us to your room. Dr. Crawford, isn't it? She seems very nice."

Amanda tucked herself up against him, her little fingers tugging at his bandage. He took her hand in his as a sharp bolt of pain made him catch his breath. "Whoa, you with the quick fingers. Now's not the time to be pinching your dad."

"Get off the bed, Amanda," Linda ordered, frowning.

"No, really. She's fine."

"What happened to you, Daddy?" Amanda asked. "Why are you all wrapped up?"

"I got hurt, honey, but I'm going to be okay. What about you? How's my little Pinch? Still tearing up the house? How's school?"

"Miss Markham's very mean," Amanda said gravely. "She made me stand in the corner."

"What for? You didn't pinch anyone, did you?"

"I pulled Jenny Flagg's hair. Jenny said I didn't have a father. So I told her I did, and I pulled her hair, and then Miss Markham made me stand in the corner."

Jake pulled his daughter back into his arms. "You do have a father, Pinch. You have a father who loves you very much. Your teacher had no business making you stand in the corner. You're my shining angel, you know that, don't you?"

"Yes," Amanda said.

"You're the best thing that ever happened to me, and don't you ever forget it. I'm going to call that Miss Markham and tell her a thing or two."

"Jake," Linda cautioned with a disapproving look.

At that moment Annie entered the room, brisk and businesslike in a white lab coat with stethoscope draped around her neck. Jake tweaked one of Amanda's braids. "Amanda Macpherson, meet Annie Crawford, best doctor east of the Mississippi, and west of it, too. Pretty good, huh?"

"Pretty good," Amanda agreed. She smiled shyly at Annie, and Annie smiled back.

"Hello, Miss Amanda," she said. "It's nice to meet you. You look very much like your father, but I suppose lots of people tell you that. I'll let you in on a little secret, young lady. Your father's doing so well that I think we're going to have to sign him out of here pretty quick. We're going to need this room for someone who's really sick.''

"Can he come home with us?" Amanda asked with the frank directness of a child.

"You'd like that, wouldn't you? Well, he needs to stay here for a little longer. But you can visit him as much as you like.''

Amanda stared for a moment at Annie, then shifted her gaze to her mother. "Mommy, why can't Daddy come home with us? He's sick and he needs us to look after him.''

Linda's face was pale and her hands were clenched tightly together. "Amanda, your father's tired. We'd better let him rest. We can come back tomorrow morning.''

Amanda squirmed to face him. "Are you tired, Daddy? Do you want us to go?''

Jake tugged his daughter close for one last embrace. "You'd better do what your mother says,'' he said. "But come see me tomorrow, Pinch. First thing. Promise?''

"I promise, Daddy.'' Amanda's eyes filled with tears. "I want you to come home with us,'' she wept as Linda came forward and lifted her off the bed. "We could make you better. Don't you love us anymore, Daddy? Why won't you come back home?''

Linda refused to meet Jake's eyes. She carried Amanda, still crying, out of the room and down the corridor. Jake watched them go and then dropped his head into his hands with a moan of pain that had nothing to do with his injury. He took a deep, shaky breath and expelled it just as slowly. "She's five years old and Linda and I have been divorced for one year and two months.''

He pressed the heels of his hands to his burning eyes then lifted his head to look at Annie. ''I've seen Amanda twice since then. The court awarded Linda full custody. Do you know why?'' When Annie shook her head, he uttered a bitter laugh. ''Neither do I. I have visitation rights, though. I can see her every weekend, for eight hours a day. And that would be a wonderful thing except that Linda decided to move to Los Angeles to pursue her acting career.

''I thought she'd eventually come back east, but her career took off and the only thing left for me to do is to go out there. I've sent applications to every police department within a hundred-mile radius, but so far, no strong bites.'' He gazed out the window at the city skyline. ''You know, getting shot isn't much fun, but I'd go through it all again just to see Amanda. It's not fair. I'm her father and I should be a part of her life.''

ANNIE CRAWFORD sat in the hospital cafeteria drinking a lukewarm cup of coffee. She couldn't purge Lieutenant Macpherson's heartbroken visage from her mind. What if Ryan had fought for and won sole custody of Sally? What would she have done?

Macpherson seemed like such a nice man. From his chart she knew that he was the same age she was, and in the conversations she'd had with him over the past week she'd discovered that he was the only child of an astronomer and a concert pianist who'd decided on parenting somewhat late in their careers. Jake's father had died several years ago of a heart attack and his mother was nearly eighty years old, in a nursing home with Alzheimer's. She played piano for the other residents, but no longer recognized her son.

"Dr. Crawford?" Annie glanced up, surprised to see Macpherson's ex-wife standing across from her. "May I speak with you for a moment?"

"Of course." Annie looked around. "Where's Amanda?"

"We went out for lunch after we left Jake," Linda explained. "Amanda wouldn't stop crying, so I'm letting her visit her father again before we go back to the hotel. She was so upset…" Linda's eyes dropped, but not before Annie saw the bright shine of tears.

"He's going to be all right," Annie reassured her. Linda nodded, fumbling in her handbag for a Kleenex.

"I'm sorry," she said, wiping her eyes and attempting a shaky smile. "I'm not crying because I'm worried about Jake. I know he's going to be fine. It's Amanda. I feel as though I'm being cruel to her, and I suppose in a way I am. I just don't know how to make it better."

Annie nodded sympathetically. "It's obvious that they miss each other a great deal."

Linda wiped her eyes again and took a slow breath. "The divorce was nasty. We both said things we shouldn't have. Hateful things. I couldn't have stayed here. This town wasn't big enough for the two of us, and there were better opportunities for me on the west coast. I never gave much thought to what was best for Amanda, but she really misses her father."

"Yes." Annie felt a twinge of guilt as she spoke. Sally missed her father, too.

"The thing is, I've been offered the leading role in a movie that's being filmed in Europe this summer. I was going to bring Amanda along for the filming, but the director's afraid she might be too much of a distraction." Linda lifted her shoulders in a gesture of confusion. "I was planning to ask Jake if he'd like to take her for the summer, but now that he's been injured, I'm not so sure. Do you think he'd be able to take care of her?"

"Yes, I do. Lieutenant Macpherson's as strong as a horse. He'll probably be out of here in a few days and I don't foresee any problems with his recovery. He could certainly take care of a five-year-old girl. It would be a wonderful opportunity for them to spend some time together, and it would give you time to concentrate on your acting job."

Linda's expression was hopeful. "I'd have to ask him about it..."

"How about right now? I could take Amanda for a tour of the hospital if you'd like some privacy."

"Would you do that?"

"Of course. Summer's right around the corner, and you need to solidify your plans."

An hour later Annie delivered Amanda back to Macpherson's room and caught the happy gleam in his eye. Obviously everything had worked out. Jake would share the summer with his daughter.

Annie wondered if her own plans for the coming summer would fare as well.

MR. EDELSTEIN was removing his eyeglasses and massaging his closed eyes when Annie was ushered into his office two days later. It was after 9:00 p.m., late for him to still be at the hospital. He gestured to the comfortable chair opposite his desk, but she shook her head. "I received a letter from the captain at Macpherson's precinct," he said, replacing his eyeglasses and making a halfhearted attempt to locate the letter in the jumble of paperwork atop his desk. "It was mostly about what a miracle worker you were, saving the lieutenant's life. I meant to give it to you but I seem to have misplaced it..."

"Mr. Edelstein, I won't beat about the bush," Annie interrupted before she could lose her nerve. "The reason I wanted to see you is that on June twelfth I'm leaving here to take my daughter to Maine for the summer to visit with her father, and I thought it would be nice to take some time off myself."

Edelstein gave off the search for the letter with an exasperated shake of his head. "Can't find it, but when I do I'll pass it along. How much time?"

"I was thinking of taking a three-month leave of absence."

Edelstein leaned forward at his desk, staring at her over the rim of his glasses. His laugh was an incredulous bark. "Well you can stop thinking about that right now. I can spare you for a week, maybe two at the most. You know how hospitals are. They don't run well without doctors."

"Mr. Edelstein, I haven't taken any vacation time in over three years."

"I'm aware of that, and I'm sure you've been more than compensated for your dedication. Please understand. I'm not telling you you can't take a vacation, only that you can't take the entire summer off."

Annie felt a flush of anger warm her cheeks. "Three months of unpaid leave is all I'm asking for, sir, no less than what we routinely grant for maternity leave."

Edelstein stood. "If you weren't as valuable a

member of this hospital's staff, maybe I could grant it. But there's no one to replace you.''

''There are six fully competent trauma surgeons practicing at this hospital, Mr. Edelstein. The ER doesn't revolve around me.''

''Grant's the only one who comes close to your level of expertise, and he's going to be lecturing at Stamford. I'm sorry, Dr. Crawford, but I really can't let you go.''

Annie nodded, her hands clenching inside her lab coat pockets. ''I was afraid you'd say something like that,'' she said. ''I've come prepared with my resignation.'' She stepped forward and laid the envelope on top of the mountain of paperwork. ''I'm giving you four weeks' notice. I'm sorry that things didn't work out. I hope you'll come to understand that this was something I really had to do.''

Edelstein's mouth dropped open. ''I won't allow you to resign,'' he blustered. ''I won't accept it.''

''You have no choice. I've given my best efforts to this hospital for over twelve years, but I have my own life to live and right now I need some time to think things through.''

''Dr. Crawford, be reasonable. Sit down and let's talk about this,'' Edelstein said, but his plea was in vain. Annie turned on her heel and without another word departed Edelstein's office, closing the door firmly and hoping she wasn't making a huge mistake.

''You're pulling my leg, right?'' Matt Brink's face was as shocked as Edelstein's had been. ''This is some kind of sick joke, something you thought up just to get out of our camping trip.''

''I assure you it's quite real,'' Annie said, still

dazed by the sudden transformation from employed to unemployed. "I've been thinking about it a great deal lately, ever since Sally was arrested. I need some time off. I've also decided to spend the summer somewhere close to Sally, so we can still spend time together. I mean, three months is a long time not to see your daughter. But predictably, Edelstein wouldn't grant me the unpaid leave, so I resigned."

"Why don't you stay for a week or two and then come back? Sally'll be perfectly safe with her father. Annie, think about what you're doing," Matt pleaded. "You're throwing away years of work. You're at the peak of your career, the top of the ladder."

"Not any more. I threw myself off and I'm starting all over again. And you know what? I feel great. Oh, Matt, I feel young again. I feel *alive!*"

Matt Brink slumped against the ER's concrete wall. "This can't be happening."

Annie brandished the magazine she held rolled up in one hand. "I'm renting a house on a point of land overlooking the water in a place called Blue Harbor, which isn't too far from Bangor, where Sally's father lives. Listen to the description of this place." She opened the magazine to the ads in the back of the well-thumbed magazine, but Matt turned away, raising his hands to his ears.

"I don't want to hear it. You can't do this. Not only is it crazy, but you're welshing on your promise to go camping."

"Oh, Matt, don't be ridiculous. Take a week off and come up for a visit. You'll have a great time."

He dropped his hands and looked at her. "You're asking me to visit you for an entire week?"

She smiled. "This house has four bedrooms, all

with ocean views. It comes with a boathouse, a boat and its own private dock. Can you imagine such a luxury? I can hardly wait to see it.''

THAT NIGHT she visited Macpherson's room for the final time. It was late, but he was awake, reading a Clive Cussler novel. He laid it down when she came into the room and propped himself up on his elbows.

"We're kicking you out of here tomorrow," she said with a rueful smile.

"No offense intended, but I'm looking forward to it," he said. "Though I'll miss seeing you."

Annie walked to the foot of his bed. She'd come to like Lieutenant Macpherson very much during his short stay. She admired him greatly for not dying on her, and she enjoyed his laid-back, easygoing attitude and the long conversations they'd had. Since his admittance, he'd been shaving daily and, of his own volition, he'd had his long hair trimmed quite short. He looked virile and handsome. It was hospital policy for the staff to keep a professional distance from the patients, but there was no denying that had she met Jake in a context other than the hospital or the police precinct where Sally'd been arrested, their relationship might have been very different.

"No offense taken," she said. "I don't blame you a bit for wanting to get out of here. I expect you'll take some time off."

"I'm thinking of taking all the sick leave and vacation time I have coming to me, especially since I'll have Amanda for the summer while Linda's in Paris. Speaking of the summer, rumor has it you've resigned your post and rented a saltwater farm in a place called Blue Harbor."

"If there's one thing this hospital never lacks for, it's a lively rumor mill."

He grinned that brash, handsome grin she'd come to like very much. "Gotta love gossip. Keeps things interesting. When are you leaving?"

Annie felt her cheeks warm and dropped her eyes, pretending to study his chart. "I'm bringing Sally to Bangor after school lets out. I'm hoping her court appearance will be scheduled before we leave, but if not, rest assured I'll bring her back for it."

"Sally's not being summoned," he said in a puzzled voice. "Didn't you get the letter?"

Annie glanced up. "She doesn't have to go to court?"

Macpherson shook his head. "The judge decided that because it was Sarah's first misdemeanor, ten hours of community service in addition to attending the Jump Start program was adequate punishment." At Annie's skeptical look, he hitched himself higher in the bed. "The judge likes me," he explained. "I helped his daughter out once."

Annie's breath left her in a soundless sigh. She stared at the man on the bed in astonished silence, then said in a dazed voice, very softly, "Thank you, Lieutenant. Thank you very much." She paused at the door and turned back. "I won't be here when you're discharged tomorrow morning, so I'll say goodbye to you now."

That brash grin returned. "Oh, there's no need for goodbyes, Dr. Crawford," he said. "I expect we'll be seeing each other again sooner than you think."

"I certainly hope not," Annie said. "I should think you'd want to avoid guns and bullets for a while."

"I fully intend to," he replied, "but all those talks

we had about Maine brought back good memories of my grandparents' camp. Seemed like a good idea to find a cabin like the one they owned, and it just so happened that the only rental I could afford isn't more than twenty miles from yours. Inland, of course. Quite a coincidence, wouldn't you say?''

Annie gathered her startled wits and laughed. ''Actually, I doubt that it is, Lieutenant, but I hope you and Amanda have a good time there this summer. And, thanks. I owe you big-time for Sally.''

Annie was halfway down the corridor, still smiling, when it occurred to her that she didn't mind in the least the prospect of running into Lieutenant Macpherson somewhere along the rocky coast of Maine. In fact, she hoped she did. No doubt about it, a handsome good-natured man like Jake, a couple of steamed Maine lobsters and a nice bottle of wine suited her right down to the ground.

CHAPER FOUR

NEITHER ANNIE NOR SALLY had ever visited Maine before. Whenever Ryan wanted to spend time with his daughter, he simply flew to the city, using the opportunity to touch base with all his old friends and colleagues, as well. Although Sally had complained about having to leave the city and didn't say an awful lot on the long ride up, preferring to keep her headphones on and listen to her CDs, Annie was sure the girl was excited. She felt the excitement herself when they crossed into Maine. It was as if they'd embarked on a rare adventure.

Ryan's house was on the outskirts of Bangor, a modern ranch with attached garage and a lawn that looked as obsessively manicured as any golf course. Trudy was watering a circular flower garden in the middle of the lawn it when they arrived. She looked very pregnant. Annie hadn't seen her since before the divorce and couldn't help smiling as she noted how much weight Trudy had gained. Perhaps it was all attributable to the pregnancy, but Annie doubted that Trudy would ever return to her young and nubile sexiness. Trudy was seventeen years her junior, so Annie felt her satisfaction was completely justified.

Ryan was at the clinic, for which Annie was grateful. She helped unload Sally's bags and carry them to the house, and stayed just long enough to give Trudy the phone number and address of the house she was renting in Blue Harbor. Sally trailed her back out to the car, scowling.

"You're not going to dump me here when Dad's not even home."

"Honey, he'll be back in an hour or so. Trudy could probably use some help in the garden after you unpack your things and get settled in. Don't worry, sweetheart. I'll call you tonight."

Sally glanced back at the house and then lowered her voice. "Can we go back home if this doesn't work out?"

Annie gave her daughter a parting hug. "I bet you and your dad are going to have a grand old time. And you can always come and spend some time with me if you like."

Trudy came out of the house and walked down to the car. She laid a hand on Sally's shoulder and to Annie's grateful surprise she said, "Your father's coming home early today. He wants you to help him pick out a golden retriever puppy. Think you can do that?"

An hour later Annie was cruising along Route 1, entering the village of Steuben. The driving was slower than she expected and she amended the travel time between Blue Harbor and Bangor by an additional forty minutes. The drive was lovely, the afternoon sunny and cool, and the air that gusted through the open window was clean, salty and delicious.

Blue Harbor was like a place out of the past. Annie felt the tranquility flowing into her as she drove slowly through the coastal New England village. She found the Realtor's office with no problem and met the agent who'd arranged the house rental. His name was Jim Hinkley and he was a spry, lean, seventy-nine years of age with piercing blue eyes and a lively interest in just about everything.

"I hope you like the old place," he said, grabbing the key out of his desk drawer. "It's one of my all-time favorite saltwater farms. I've known Lily Houghton, the owner, since she was a young girl. Used to court her back in high school, when she was still a Curtis. We were sweethearts for a time, but then she took a shine to that fancy-talkin' Ruel Houghton.

"The only good thing Ruel ever gave her was his grandparents' house, and Lily loved it. She was an artist, you see. She made a studio out of the old boathouse and did her painting there. She was good, too. Made quite a name for herself. It broke her heart when her son put her into the nursing home this spring, but he thought staying out there all by herself after she fell and broke her hip was just too risky." He shrugged into his jacket. "I'll take you out to the old place. It's a ten-minute drive, just follow me and you won't get turned around."

The farm lay at the end of a mile-long dirt road on a high point of land overlooking the Atlantic. They passed through a gate at the entrance of the drive and Jim unlocked it. "It's all Houghton land from here on in, all five hundred acres of it. Prime for development and worth a fortune, but Lily would never sell. Of course, now that she's in that nursing home, I don't know what her son will do. I'm not sure Lily has any say. I guess she gave Lester power of attorney. She hates developers, though. I do know that. They've been after this peninsula since Ruel died, and she's refused to sell even the littlest piece of it."

The first half mile of road wound through tall pine

woods that gave way abruptly to a bright, greening sweep of field. Massive stone walls ran along both sides of the road, protectively enclosing an orchard on one side, rolling pasture on the other. Annie tried hard to take it all in but her senses were overwhelmed. The blue sky, the green pasture laced with wildflowers bending in the sea breeze, the gnarly old apple trees, some still blossoming, the great drifts of lupine blowing blue, purple and pink along the stone walls, the sharp ping of gravel against the undercarriage of the Explorer, all served to heighten her keen sense of anticipation as she craned for her first glimpse of the farmhouse.

She was not disappointed when at last it came into view. The stalwart boat-roofed Cape Cod was connected to a long, rambling ell, which was connected to a big old ark of a barn in a perfect example of classic New England architecture. All the buildings, including the barn, were painted white. The house and its attached string of outbuildings were oriented east to west, as most old farmhouses were, to take advantage of the sun. It was also positioned on the point of land so that it faced the magnificent harbor views to the south.

Unkempt but vigorous flower gardens flanking the south side of the house and the ell were a riotous bloom of color. Annie parked beside Jim's car and joined him on the porch while he fished in his pocket for the key. "Wow," she said, holding her hair away from her face in the stiff breeze and gazing out across the sparkling harbor.

"The view's great, but if you recall, I warned you that the house was rustic," Jim said, turning the key in the lock.

Annie drank in the spectacular scenery a few moments longer before following Jim inside. He paused for a moment to let her appreciate the kitchen. There was big cast-iron combination wood-and-gas cookstove with warming ovens above and a water jacket on the left hand side, a deep soapstone sink big enough to float a small boat, and a pitcher pump mounted to the counter beside it. The wide pumpkin-pine floorboards, the deep-silled windows with their plain cotton-tab curtains, the old farm table flanked by six sturdy chairs, the wall cupboard with its old blue paint and the kerosene lamps in their wall sconces completed the country feel of the room.

"Rustic," Jim repeated as if bracing for some negative reaction. "I warned you."

"It's lovely," Annie said with a smile. "I grew up in a house without electricity, and as far as I can tell it didn't hurt me a bit."

Jim cast a surprised glance at her. "England?" he said.

"Australia. A sheep station in the Outback, and I adored every moment of it. I suppose there's a backhouse here. A loo."

Jim laughed, relaxing. "Two, actually. One in the woodshed, the other in the barn. But Lily had a conventional bathroom installed at her son's insistence. Flush toilet, shower, tub, sink. There's a diesel generator in the woodshed that powers all the modern extravagances. Come on, I'll show you."

The tour continued, and the more she saw, the more Annie fell in love with the old homestead. Memories of her childhood home in Australia came flooding back, the sounds of children thundering down the back stairs into the kitchen, the squeak and clank of the hand pump as her mother drew water at the kitchen sink, the tang of wood smoke from the stove, the soft glow of oil lamps in the evening and the smell of good food cooking.

The entire farmhouse had a warm, friendly feel. The bedrooms were wallpapered in old-fashioned prints, the curtains were plain cotton muslin hung on wooden dowels and the floors were covered with handmade rugs of braided wool. The place was simple and clean, and Annie couldn't believe her good fortune in being able to rent it for the summer. "Mrs. Houghton must have hated to leave here," she said softly as Jim showed her what had been Lily's bedroom, the queen four-poster angled so that she could prop herself up against the headboard and gaze out at the harbor as the sun rose on a Maine morning.

"Lily always hoped that she could live out her life here."

There was a phone in the back hallway off the pantry. "It works," Jim said as she lifted the receiver, "but no guarantees. The line just sort of lies on the ground and runs through tree branches for over a mile. Lily never wanted electricity in here, but her son insisted on a phone. Lester means well, but he can be overbearing at times. Still, he was right about the phone. Lily used it to call for help when she fell and broke her hip."

"Where does Lester live?"

"Oh, he's a hotshot lawyer. Went to Bowdoin College on a scholarship and took a position with one of those big Boston law firms. Makes a ton of money. Married a woman who doesn't like Maine, so Lester doesn't come north much. He wants to move Lily to a nursing home down near him, but she's having none of it. Said if she couldn't die at her farm, the very least she could do is die in Maine.''

"How sad.''

"Yes,'' Jim said. "Strange, how things turn out. If she'd married me, she'd never have gone into that nursing home. But then again, she wouldn't have had this place, either. Hard to know which would've made Lily happier in the long run…'' Jim shrugged philosophically. "Now, about groceries…''

"I shopped in Bangor after dropping my daughter off at her father's,'' Annie said.

"Well, there's a good store right here in town if you forgot anything. The refrigerator and stove in the kitchen run on gas. I'll arrange for monthly propane deliveries, if you like.''

"That would be wonderful.''

"There are lots of staples in the pantry. Things like spices and sugar and flour. Some canned goods. Lily loved to cook. You're welcome to use anything in the cupboards.''

"Thank you.''

"Well then, I guess you're on your own.''

"I'll be fine, Jim. And thank you so much for the tour.''

"I'll leave my card by the phone, just in case. My home number's on it, too. If you need anything, just give me a ring. And I'll leave you the key to the gate. I don't think there'll be many busybodies driving down, but it's summertime, after all, lots of tourists cruising about, so if you want to lock it…''

"Thank you, Jim. You can leave it open.''

She stood on the porch that spanned the south side of the ell and listened until the sound of his vehicle was drowned out by the steady rumble of the wind in

the stunted pines that stood at the peninsula's edge.
The sun was hovering just above the horizon and the
colors of sunset painted the granite outcroppings and
the sparkling Atlantic waters.

Annie retrieved several grocery bags from the Explorer and found the one with the bottle of Australian
pinot noir. She opened it, poured herself a glass and
carried it outside, following the overgrown path
through the grass that led toward the water. After a
roundabout descending journey she came upon the
boathouse, sturdily bolted to a projection of granite.

The boathouse was locked, its windows tightly
shuttered, so she sat on the edge of the walkway that
ran alongside it. She sipped her wine and watched the
waves roll against the pier, rhythmically raising and
lowering great fluxing beards of seaweed that clung
to the sides of the old stones. She watched the seagulls hover in the stiff breeze and the plovers explore
the tidal pools along the rocky shoreline.

For a long time she sat there, feeling the briny wind
pushing cool and strong against her. Suddenly, for no
reason she could have explained, she began to weep.
She wept until she was exhausted, then she blew her
nose, wiped her eyes, let her head tip back against
the old silvery dock post, inhaled a deep, shaky
breath—and smiled.

JAKE MACPHERSON used the full weight of his body
in an attempt to open the unlocked but badly jammed
door of the cabin after several manly kicks with his
booted foot had failed. Amanda watched in silence.
One heave did nothing at all to budge the door. In
the movies, the door always gave on the second
heave, but Jake reconsidered as he rubbed his of-

fended shoulder and took several tentative breaths around the dull ache in his chest. It would be unwise to aggravate his wound. He never, ever, wanted to see the interior of a hospital again.

"The door's stuck," he reported to Amanda in case she hadn't noticed.

His daughter nodded somberly.

The sun sank lower, the woods grew darker around them and the logs of the cabin looked solid, stoic and impenetrable. He began to doubt the wisdom of renting a place that hadn't been used for more than three years. The Realtor had offered to drive out and open it up for them, but Jake had declined. After seeing how old Jim Hinkley was, it seemed too much to ask that he drive twenty miles just to unlock and show them a simple little cabin. So Jim had drawn them a map, given them the keys and wished them well. "Oh, one thing," Hinkley had cautioned before they'd embarked. "If any repairs need be made, you'll have to do them yourself or hire the job out, and the owners'll deduct the repair bills from the rent. They're too old to handle that stuff themselves."

"Well, what do you think?" Jake asked Amanda. "Should I give it another try?"

Another somber nod. His stomach tightened. She was counting on him. He'd better make good. He picked up a two-by-six that someone had tucked beneath the cabin and used it to tap the edges of the door, hoping that would be enough. But it wasn't. He took a breath, raised the two-by-six again and struck the door in the places that appeared to be bound tight. He put more muscle into it, and in the end was using the timber as a battering ram. When the door finally gave, it burst abruptly inward, spilling him into the dark interior with an undignified bellow. He tripped on something and landed in a face-down sprawl.

In the startled silence that followed, he heard small musical sounds behind him. Amanda, giggling behind her hands. He rolled onto his back and glared up at her. "What's so funny, Pinch?"

"You, Daddy," she said, convulsed in mirth.

He sat up and took stock. Not much to see through the light of the door. Two bunks against the far wall. Small gas stove on the left, along with a short run of countertop and a sink. Woodstove dead center, stovepipe rising straight up. Table and two chairs to the right of the door; squeezed in between them and the stove, nearly spanning the length of the little cabin, the promised canoe.

The first thing he did was haul the canoe outside and leave it beneath the big pines at the edge of the pond. Then he rummaged in the toolbox in the back of his truck, found a hammer and pried open the shutters while Amanda explored the cabin's interior. "Daddy?" she asked as he worked on the last shutter. "Where's the bathroom?"

Jake nodded toward a little structure behind the cabin. "Out back, Pinch." He fastened the shutters back with the eye hooks and was putting the hammer away when he heard Amanda scream in fright.

"Daddy!" She had opened the outhouse door and recoiled in horror. He came up beside her and peered inside. "Spiders," she pointed. "*Big* ones."

He stared. "You're right, Pinch, they're huge."

"I have to pee," she whimpered.

"Not in here. Not until we evict these giants. C'mon. Let's go find a handy tree."

He took her hand and inhaled a deep breath of the

woodsy air. It had been a long time. Too long. His daughter should have spent time in the outdoors the way he had as a boy. He'd been lucky. His parents were older, but they'd loved the woods and had brought him often to his grandparents' camp. They'd taught him to appreciate the cry of the loons at dusk, the splash of a moose ambling along the shoreline, the deep authoritative hoot of a great horned owl in the midst of a moonlit night. They'd shown him how to paddle a canoe, how to tie the proper fly onto the proper weight leader, how to release a brook trout unharmed into the dark cold waters from which it came.

He needed to teach these things to Amanda. Instead he'd forgotten it all. It had been years since he'd last visited Maine. *Maine.* The name rolled off his tongue, sounding solid and big and just a little bit wild. It sounded like a place of tall trees, rugged mountains and rocky coastline. It sounded *good.*

How had he ever wound up in a place like New York City? He'd been so in love. Linda had been so beautiful, so in control, so sure of her future. Sophisticated and sharp, and so very kind to take any interest in a blue-collar boy such as himself.

He'd met her at a U-Maine party in Orono. She'd been visiting one of her friends, a girl in Jake's physics class. They'd been introduced and the next thing he'd known he'd transferred to NYU just to be near her. While she'd studied acting at Juliard, he'd gotten his degree in political science and then picked up another degree in criminal justice, figuring that a cop could always get a job in New York City.

Linda had started making commercials, he'd walked a foot patrol and written parking tickets.

They'd moved in together, a tiny studio apartment in Brooklyn. She'd won a small but steady role in a soap opera, he'd gotten his own patrol car. They'd married. When she'd landed her first movie role, he'd been working as a plainclothes detective, Amanda had been two years old and things had been looking good. But Hollywood changed Linda; the long separations had been difficult. By the time he'd made lieutenant, Linda had been nominated for an Oscar for best supporting actress in one of the most popular films of the year and their marriage was on the rocks.

Amanda was the one bright light that remained. Spending the summer with her was a gift beyond price. This place wasn't quite as grand as his grandparents' camp, but the important thing was that they were together. After Amanda had found the proper tree, which took some time because she wasn't all that excited about the idea, Jake looked around the yard. "Well, Pinch, we've got our work cut out for us. This old cabin needs some tender loving care."

"I'm hungry," Amanda said.

"Me, too. That hamburger wore off a long time ago. Let's get the truck unloaded and I'll cook you something you won't believe, it'll be so good."

"Can I watch?"

"You can supervise."

Unfortunately, there was no propane in the tank outside the cabin, and Jake hadn't thought to bring a jug of kerosene for the empty lamps. It was growing dark. He was about to suggest that they beat a hasty retreat to the nearest town for the night when he heard the cry of a loon wavering across the pond.

"Daddy," Amanda breathed in awe, her hand reaching out for his. "What was that?"

"That's a loon, Pinch. Sounds kind of crazy, doesn't it? They can sound sad, too."

"It's scary," she said.

"C'mon. Walk down to the dock with me and let's listen for a while." She stepped cautiously beside him and they stood on the thick cedar planking. The cry came again, long and mournful. "It's definitely lonely this time."

"What's that splashing noise?" she whispered, pressing against him.

"Trout rising to a hatch of insects. See the ripples when one comes to the surface?"

Hard to see anything in the thick gloaming. A branch snapped in the woods nearby and he felt Amanda shiver. "Daddy?"

"Probably a moose coming down to the pond to drink. Sometimes they wade right out into the water and put their heads under to eat pond lily roots and grasses. We'll see lots of moose while we're here."

"Are they big?" she whispered.

"As big as horses, with longer legs."

"Daddy, I'm scared."

"There's nothing to be scared of. Let's go back inside. I bet I can cook us some toasted cheese sandwiches on the woodstove. It's getting kind of cool, and a little fire will warm the chill off the cabin. I think there are some candles, too. We'll light a few and it'll be real cozy, just like camping out."

ANNIE CALLED her ex-husband that night. Ryan answered the phone himself and his voice was weary. "Sally's fine, Annie. She picked out a cute puppy today, and between the two of them they've worn me out. Trudy's been having some bad back pains and

I'm a little worried about her, but she doesn't want to call her doctor..." He rambled on distractedly for a few more minutes and then asked, "So, where are you staying? Sally told us you were renting a farmhouse up the coast."

She gave him the phone number and address. "I told Sally she could spend some time here if she got lonely for her old mum."

"Sure. I think it's a good idea, you spending the summer nearby. It'll be as good for you as it is for her, getting away from the big city. Sounds like you're enjoying yourself already."

"I am, actually. Very much," she conceded.

"Annie, gotta go. Trudy just came downstairs and she looks pretty wrung out. Talk to you later." Loud click. Dead line.

Annie replaced the receiver gently and sighed.

The old farmhouse creaked in the night the way old houses do, telling their own stories, and she sat in the kitchen for a while, reading the local paper by the light of the oil lamp. The muted thunder of the waves crashing up against the granite ledge was a constant lulling undercurrent of sound. When she looked out the window down the dark narrow bay, she could see the periodic flash from the Nash Island light. She had opened several of the old double hung windows in the kitchen and the curtains moved gently in a faint night wind. The only outdoor sounds were those of the ocean, of the light breeze through the wind-stunted evergreens that clung tenaciously to the shoreline and the distant clang of a buoy.

A far, far cry from the constant cacophony of human noise generated by a city the size of New York. It was only 9:00 p.m. and Annie thought that maybe she'd make some popcorn and curl up with one of the novels she'd brought to read, but instead she went to bed and slept better than she had in many months.

AMANDA HAD CHOSEN THE TOP bunk and just past midnight let out a shriek that woke Jake from a sound sleep and stopped his heart for a few beats. He sat up, slamming his head into the bottom of her bunk. "Amanda, what is it?" he gasped, holding his head.

"A mouse just ran across my bed," she said, her voice quavering with fear.

"A mouse? You mean, one of those cute little creatures you were admiring while we ate supper?"

"Yes." She sounded very close to tears.

"Amanda, that mouse isn't going to hurt you. Go back to sleep."

"I can't," she said, small-voiced. "I'm afraid it will come back."

"Are you kidding? The way you just screamed?"

"Daddy, can I come down and sleep with you?"

"It's a mighty narrow bunk, Pinch."

"Please, Daddy."

He wondered what the child experts would say about such business. Amanda was, after all, five years old. Still, she'd put up with a lot in the past twenty-four hours without complaining. She'd even eaten the burnt cheese sandwich outside on the porch while they'd waited for the smoke to clear from the cabin. "Okay," he relented. "But just for tonight. Tomorrow we'll get a trap for the mice so they won't bother you anymore, and you can sleep in your own bed."

Moments later she was snuggled up against him and almost instantly asleep. He lay in contemplative

silence, listening to the loons on the pond and wondering about a certain doctor by the name of Annie
Crawford. Wondering how long it would be before
their paths crossed.

CHAPTER FIVE

ANNIE WOKE to a morning more beautiful than she'd seen in nearly two decades. She sipped her coffee sitting on the porch in an old rocker, nudging the weathered planks with her bare toes to move herself ever so gently back and forth. Watching the sun rise over Dyer Island and the bay, she realized with sudden and poignant clarity that she could stay in this place forever.

Moments later she heard the chugging throb of a boat engine and her attention turned toward the harbor. A lobster boat had passed the point and was nosing its way into the channel, close enough that she could read the name on the stern. *Glory B.* She was still watching when the boat turned abruptly toward the stone wharf, engine throttling up as it approached, then easing off and slipping into reverse as it pulled alongside. She frowned. Was this normal procedure or could there be something wrong?

The engine cut out as a man jumped onto the pier, rope in hand, and made a quick dally around one of the pilings. Then he started up the long, steep steps, taking them two at a time in gear that could only be described as cumbersome. Annie rose to her feet as the man crossed the intervening space between them. He took big steps, moving with great urgency. What on earth? She was in her nightgown, for heaven's

sake. She crossed her arms in front of herself protectively, still holding the mug of coffee.

Close enough now, she could see that the man was
smiling. Coming toward her at a gallop in tall, dark,
rubber boots and yellow, waterproof overalls, he was
grinning ear-to-ear. He was bare-headed, his hair thin-
ning, gray and wind-tousled. When he got closer his
reaction was startling. He skidded to a stop, arms
thrown out for balance at first and then lifted shoulder
high in a gesture of apology.

"You're not Lily," he said from fifty feet away.

"No," Annie said.

His arms dropped to his sides. "I saw the smoke
from the kitchen chimney and thought…" He turned
and looked at his boat as if he could wish himself
back onto it. "Well, I thought Lily'd come back
home."

"I'm Annie Crawford. I'm renting the place for the
summer. I arrived yesterday."

He glanced back at her. "Joe Storey," he said.
"Welcome to the peninsula. Sorry to bust in on you
like this, but good to meet you, all the same." He
paused for an awkward moment before adding, "If
you need anything, just do like Lily did and run the
white flag up the pole down by the boathouse."

He turned to go and Annie said, "Thank you. I'll
remember that."

Joe glanced at the rocking chair Annie had been
using. "Lily was always watching right there, rain or
shine, every morning when we headed out. She'd
wave one of her dish towels to us. It was a tradition.
Somehow the days aren't quite the same anymore,
with her gone and this old house of hers sitting
empty." His eyes turned back to her. "Well. Got my

traps to check.'' He turned away again and Annie watched him hurry back toward the wharf steps.

''It was nice to meet you, Mr. Storey,'' Annie called after him. She sat in the rocker and watched until the *Glory B* dwindled into the distance, wondering about Lily Houghton, and then wondering if Jake Macpherson and his daughter Amanda were in Maine yet. She might have sat there all morning if the phone hadn't rung. Annie rose from the rocker and went inside to answer it.

''Mom?'' Sally's voice was choked with tears. ''Can you come get me?''

''Of course I can, Sally. What's wrong?''

''Trudy had the baby last night,'' Sally blurted, and then sobbed convulsively, causing Annie to clench up tight.

''Sally,'' Annie said in a calming voice. ''Sally, are you at the house?''

''I'm at the hospital. It all happened so fast, Mom. Trudy's really sick, and Dad says the baby might not live.'' She began to cry again. Annie waited for a moment. ''Sally, listen to me. You stay right where you are and I'll come get you. It'll take me an hour to get there, maybe a little longer. Okay?''

After a period of sniffs and gulps, she replied, ''Okay.''

''I love you, Sally. I'm on my way.''

Ten minutes later she was headed for the hospital in Bangor. The first full day of her summer in Maine had begun.

JAKE BURNED THE EGGS the same way he'd burned the cheese sandwich, but Amanda never complained. They ate out on the porch for two reasons. The first was that the cabin was once again filled with smoke. The second was that it was a real pretty place to sit to look out over the pond. He drank his coffee, not burned but not strong the way he preferred it. He hadn't boiled the water long enough. But if Amanda wasn't going to complain, neither was he.

"The first thing we need to do this morning is head back into town and get stocked up on supplies. We'd better make a list."

"A mousetrap," Amanda said.

"Propane tanks filled."

"Lights for at night."

"You didn't like the candles?"

"Daddy." She gave him a reproving glance.

"Okay, then. Kerosene for the lamps."

"Can we get a TV?"

"A television? There's no electricity here, Pinch. We could get some books. I'll read to you, you read to me."

"I don't read good."

"Practice makes perfect. What else do we need?"

"Peanut butter and jelly."

"Don't know how I ever forgot that stuff."

"Soda."

"No soda. Bad for your teeth."

"Juice."

"Juice." He wrote it on the list. "Milk. Lemonade?"

"Lemonade," she nodded.

"Window cleaner. You any good at washing windows?"

She frowned. "Are they dirty?"

"Good answer. What about lunch. Hot dogs?"

"Hot dogs."

Jake made note of the items between bites of burnt egg and charcoal toast, sips of weak coffee and hopes of running into Annie Crawford.

Not a bad beginning to the day, all things considered.

"HE WAS FOUR WEEKS premature and he has a transpositional heart defect that for some reason they didn't find in the prenatal testing," Ryan said, as he sat slumped on the waiting room couch, Sally slumbering beside him. His face was haggard and he looked much older than his forty-two years. "But he's hanging on and they're trying to stabilize him enough to fly him to Boston Children's Hospital for surgery in two weeks. They're trying, but—" His voice broke and he dropped his head into his hands.

"Of course they are," Annie said.

"I should have known something was wrong," he said. "I should have brought her to the hospital when she first started having those pains and that terrible swelling. I should have known."

"Ryan, every woman who bears a child has all kinds of pains and swells up," Annie said gently. "You should know that. You went through it with me."

"I do know that. But she was so filled with fluid. I should have insisted they look at her. Her doctor said…"

"Ryan." Annie reached out and touched his shoulder. "Don't do this to yourself. Trudy and the baby need you to be strong right now."

He nodded and wiped at his eyes, blotting tears. "I'm sorry."

"Don't be sorry. You're a good father and good

fathers care. But listen to me. I want you to eat the sandwich I brought you and drink this tea. You have to take care of yourself.'' Annie squeezed his shoulder reassuringly. "I'll take Sally home with me."

Ryan nodded and lifted his eyes. "I'll need to stay at the hospital until…"

"I know."

"Can you take the puppy, too?"

"Of course."

He reached for her hand and squeezed it. "Thanks, Annie."

"No prob." Annie rumpled his hair the way she used to and then turned and walked out of the waiting room. She couldn't wait to leave the hospital. The last thing she wanted to do on her summer vacation was to spend time inside a hospital.

"Mom!" Annie stopped her headlong rush down the corridor and waited for Sally to catch up with her. "You weren't going to leave without me, were you?" she said.

"Of course not. I'm just in a hurry to get going. We have to pick the puppy up at your dad's. I promised him we'd look after it."

"Okay," Sally said. "Nelly's about the only neat thing about being here."

Annie reached for her daughter's hand but Sally moved ahead of her. Suddenly the sunny Maine day wasn't looking so bright.

NELLY WAS ALL big paws, liquid eyes and soft, golden fur. Annie's heart melted as the fat little puppy licked her face with a vigor that matched its enthusiasm for chewing on her fingers. "Oh, my goodness, look at you," Annie said. She handed the pup back to her daughter. "You're in charge of her on the ride home. She'll probably get carsick."

"No, she won't," Sally said. "She didn't the first time and she won't this time, either."

Nelly was perfectly content to ride in Sally's arms, sleeping part of the time and part of the time looking around at her new environment. "Not only is she adorable," Annie announced as she parked the Explorer beside the old farmhouse, "she's well behaved."

Sally deposited the puppy on the lawn and did a slow three-sixty of the old farm. "Wow," she said.

"Like it?" Annie said.

"It's kind of isolated. I mean, you know, empty."

"Quite a change from Manhattan, isn't it?" Annie chose to ignore the critical tone of Sally's question. "There's supposed to be a boat locked up in the boathouse. I haven't explored that building yet. You can just see it, down there where the stone wharf sticks out. Maybe we can peek inside after lunch. Hungry?"

"A little. I didn't eat supper last night, or breakfast, either. Nobody did."

Annie nodded sympathetically. "I'll fix you something. Better bring Nelly inside."

Sally scooped the puppy up and followed her mother onto the porch and into the big farm kitchen, looking around again in dismay. "No microwave?"

"Wait till you see the outhouse, my girl," Annie said, opening the refrigerator and snagging the makings of a summer lunch. Shortly thereafter they were sitting out on the porch eating cucumber sandwiches and sipping tall, cool glasses of iced tea.

"You're really going to live out here all by yourself for the whole summer?'' Sally asked while Nelly chewed on the toe of her sneaker.

''There's a bedroom for you here, too, as long as you want it. I think your father might be tied up for a while, but eventually the two of you will want to spend some time together.''

Sally took a bite of sandwich. Her brow furrowed. ''What if the baby lives and Trudy dies?''

''That's not going to happen.''

''But if it does.'' Sally paused for a moment. ''Do you think you and Dad would ever get back together?''

Annie looked at her daughter. ''Sally, I'll always have a great deal of respect for your father, but we've both changed too much to ever be husband and wife again.''

Sally was quiet for a while. She sighed, looking out across the harbor. ''I know,'' she shrugged. ''I was just thinking, that's all.''

''Well, think about this. We'll be spending some time here together so let's plan some fun things to do, and please don't suggest shopping for clothes.''

''Mom,'' Sally protested. ''Can't I just take the bus back to New York? There's nothing to do here if Dad's going to be at the hospital all the time...''

Annie gave her daughter a sharp look. ''That's out of the question. Ana Lise is visiting her sister in Copenhagen. Besides, your father and Trudy won't be at the hospital forever. So, young lady, while you're staying with me, we're going to be doing outdoorsy things.''

''Like what?'' Sally's expression was guarded.

''We'll explore the countryside, shop for great food, check out antique stores, read good books, bake gingersnap cookies and eat them while they're still warm.'' Annie stretched her legs out in front of her and crossed them at the ankles. ''Maybe we could even take sailing lessons.''

''Whoopee.'' Sally slouched deeper in her chair.

Annie ignored the sarcasm. ''Then maybe we could take out the little sailboat that supposedly came with the rent. I'll phone the Realtor and find out who gives lessons…'' Annie paused. She sat up in her chair and stared across the parking area. ''Sally, is that a dog coming down the drive?'' Nelly spotted the intruder and let out a puppy bark at the same time.

The dog didn't pause at this challenge but continued its weary trot. When it reached the old farmhouse it climbed the porch steps, passed them by without so much as a sidelong glance and, with a quick nudge of its sharp, pointy nose, opened the screen door and went into the kitchen.

''Well,'' Annie said, meeting Sally's surprised look. ''We have a visitor, and a hungry-looking one at that.''

''A stray?'' Sally said as they both stood.

''Maybe,'' Annie said, ''except it doesn't act like one, does it?''

They followed the dog into the kitchen and were not surprised to see it ravenously bolting kibble from the puppy's dish. It was a border collie cross, tricolored, a good five pounds underweight and wearing no collar. When the puppy tried to nose into the dish, the dog froze and growled, and Sally quickly picked up Nelly. ''What'll we do?''

''Feed it, for starters.''

The stray didn't eat very long before trotting in a very businesslike fashion through every single room in the house, repeatedly going into Lily's bedroom and once even jumping up onto the bed, as if searching for her. Finally, Annie knelt and called the dog to her. "Hello, you poor old thing. I have a feeling this is your home." Annie let the dog sniff her fingers before she let them slide along the collie's cheek and neck, until her fingers were gently rubbing the chafed place where the collar used to be. "Lily's not here," she spoke gently. "But you know that now, don't you?"

At her gentle touch and the sound of her soothing words, the skinny dog let his haunches drop to the floor. Annie picked up one of his front paws and felt the rawness of the pad. Her vision blurred as she looked into the animal's bright, burning gaze. "We'll have to take care of you, won't we? And find out your story."

"Mom?" Sally frowned from the doorway, the pup cradled in her arms. "Is that dog staying?"

"For now he is," Annie said. "Let's find him a blanket to sleep on."

JAKE COULD HAVE gotten all his supplies in Danfield, but chose instead to travel the extra miles to Blue Harbor on the pretext of showing Amanda the beautiful harbor. In fact, he was hoping to catch a glimpse of Annie Crawford, but he knew luck would have to be on his side, for as small as Blue Harbor was, timing was still everything.

First they stopped at the hardware store to get the necessary supplies for repairing the cabin door, fixing a broken pane of glass, replacing a window screen, and of course, eliminating a family of rodents. "Are

you sure these will catch the mice?'' Amanda asked
the man as he rang up the mousetraps.

"Oh, you betcha. Simple but effective." The pro-
prietor, a heavy-set man with a broad, friendly face,
proceeded to demonstrate to Amanda just how the
mousetrap worked. He showed her where to put the
little piece of cheese and then he used a pencil to trip
the pan. Amanda flinched when the metal bar snapped
down on the pencil.

"But won't that hurt them?" she said.

"It's too quick to hurt 'em, sweetie," the propri-
etor of the store beamed. "It just kills 'em dead."

Amanda turned her stricken eyes on her father.
"But, Daddy, we don't want to kill them. We just
want to catch them so they don't run across my bed."

And so instead of paying a couple bucks for a common mousetrap, Jake shelled out thirty-odd dollars for
a dainty little wire cage that caught the mice un-
harméd to be released "in the woods where they belong."

The next stop was the grocery store, where he
pushed a cart up and down the cramped aisles while
Amanda filled it with all sorts of dry, canned and
fresh goods.

"Whoa," he cautioned her when she came to the
ice-cream freezer and pounced on a half gallon of
chocolate. "We don't even know if the refrigerator
works. We have to refill the propane tank first, remember?"

"We can eat the ice cream now, Daddy. If we eat
really fast we can do it."

"Pinch, we'd have to inhale it. How about getting
a couple of ice-cream bars instead?"

After the grocery store, they filled the propane

tanks at the marina. Since there was a lobster pound that also sold hot dogs on the wharf, with a great view of the harbor, they ate lunch there. They were still sitting with their legs draped over the edge of the dock, watching the boats come and go, when Amanda said in a voice that brooked no argument, "Daddy, I have to pee."

So he took her to the nearest gas station and then they headed back to camp, his dreams of running into Annie Crawford unfulfilled.

ANNIE PHONED the real estate agent, Jim Hinkley, to tell him about their unexpected visitor. "A stray dog, you say?" he said. "Is it a collie cross?"

"Yes. Somewhat reserved but gentle-natured, and he acts like he belongs here."

"Well, I'll be. That sounds like Lily's dog, Rebel. Lester put him in the pound when they took Lily to the nursing home. I thought for sure he'd be put to sleep, he's not a young dog anymore, but someone must have adopted him. And by God, you say he found his way back home?"

"Well, he's a bit the worse for wear, but he's been through the entire house several times, looking for her."

"I'm not surprised. The two of them were awfully close. He went everywhere she did."

"I believe it."

"I guess I could call the shelter and find out who adopted him, have them come out there and pick him up," Jim said.

Annie glanced into the kitchen where Sally sat at the table reading, Nelly gnawing a chew toy at her feet. Rebel was lying on the braided rug by the woodstove, sound asleep. "Thank you, that would be nice. I hate to think about his owners worrying…" She bit her lower lip. "But Rebel's obviously made a huge effort to get back home. It would be equally nice if he could at least spend at least one night here."

There was a pause, and then Jim cleared his throat gruffly. "That's good of you. Meanwhile I'll make a few calls to see what I can find out."

While Rebel slept on the kitchen rug, Annie and Sally took the boathouse key and walked down the path, Nelly at heel. The late-afternoon light was glorious, dancing off the harbor waters. They descended onto the stone wharf and Annie fitted the old skeleton key into the keyhole and turned it. The lock rasped back with a snap and she opened the door.

The boathouse windows were shuttered from within and the room was dark and cool and smelled of oakum, tar and turpentine—sharp smells evoking images of tall sailing ships and gnarly silver-haired men smoking pipes, sitting on upended barrels and mending fishing nets. "Open the shutters," Sally urged, hugging Nelly close. "It's spooky in here."

There were six windows. One flanked each side of the door and there were two on each side wall. The end wall had none. It was not truly a boathouse, in that boats had never been able to motor inside it. The building sat up on the stone wharf and the closest it came to being a boathouse was when boats were winched up and stored inside. With all the shutters open, light streamed through the old glass panes and revealed a little ketch on a wood cradle in the center. It was painted a dark Nantucket green and the name on the stern pronounced the *Dash* in gilt-edged maroon letters.

"Pretty, isn't it?" Annie said, running her finger-tips along the gunwale. She looked around the room, noticing the easels, the shelves neatly holding all sorts of essentials from cans of paint to jars of nails and other assorted hardware. She recalled Jim telling her that Lily was an artist. Canvases leaned against the back wall and there was one on each of the easels, as if Lily might return any day to take up where she left off.

The paintings were almost all seascapes of the harbor, the boats, the buildings. Several were different views of the old farmhouse. There was one that Annie particularly admired of three children sailing the little green ketch. A girl was at the tiller. She had the snowy hair and rosy cheeks of youth and she was obviously laughing at something one of the two boys had said. There was a rough chop on the water and she was holding the tiller with both hands, bare feet braced on the opposite gunwale. The painting was full of motion and exuberance.

Lily Houghton was a very talented artist, but most of the oils in the boathouse were unfinished, as if she'd lost interest in them. Even the upper left-hand corner of the painting of the children in the ketch was unfinished.

"It's cold in here," Sally said. "I'm going out-side."

Annie followed her and locked the door behind them. She'd spend more time down here later, when Sally and Nell were gone. They stood for a while at the end of the stone pier and faced the harbor, the strong warm wind blowing in their faces and the waves of high tide rolling up against the pier with a dull, rhythmic rumble. Then they walked back up to the old farmhouse.

"Maybe I'll work on weeding the flower garden," Annie said when they reached the porch. "It's obviously been a long time since Lily was able to care for it properly. Will you be all right?"

"Sure," Sally said with a shrug. "I'll listen to CDs. Nothing else to do around here."

Annie donned the pair of gardening gloves and broad-brimmed straw hat she'd found lying side by side on a bench in the shed and spent the next two hours liberating the weed-choked perennials that grew along the south side of the house. She hadn't worked in a real garden since leaving Australia and it was immensely satisfying to sit back on her heels to look at the progress she'd made.

"Mom?" Sally called from the porch. "Telephone. It's the Realtor about the dog."

Jim had been successful in contacting the shelter and finding the name and phone number of Rebel's adoptive family. "But they didn't keep him," Jim said. "Rebel kept running away, so they gave him to someone who lived just outside of Ellsworth. They gave me the phone number and I called. The woman who answered told me Rebel has been missing for nearly a week." There was a brief pause. "The thing is, Dr. Crawford, they don't want him back, and they asked if you would be kind enough to return him to the shelter."

Annie glanced at Rebel, who was still sleeping. "That dog traveled at least sixty miles to get back home. Probably quite a bit farther, considering he didn't come in a straight line."

"Probably," Jim said.

"Well, that's quite a journey, and it seems like he should be allowed to enjoy the place for a while."

Another pause, and then Jim cleared his throat. "Look, to be honest, I think Rebel should be laid away. It would be much kinder than parceling him out to someone else. He's too old to adjust to life without Lily. I'll take him to the vet and pay for it myself. It's the least I can do after all that poor dog has been through."

Annie turned away from the sight of the sleeping dog. "I don't even like to think about that sort of thing."

"Well, when the time comes..."

"Thank you, Jim. I'll keep it in mind." Searching for some way to change the subject, she asked, "Do you think Lily would be interested in selling any of the paintings she has down in the boathouse?"

"I don't see why not," he replied. "She made her living as an artist."

After hanging up, Annie walked slowly into the kitchen and poured herself a glass of iced tea. At the sound, the old dog raised his head and looked at her. "It's all right, old boy," she said. After a few moments he heaved a big sigh and went back to sleep. She went out onto the porch where Sally sat.

"Did he find Rebel's owners?"

"Yes, honey, but they don't want him back, so he's going to hang out here for a while. Why don't you go call your dad, see how things are going?"

Sally looked at her, alarmed. "What'll I say to him? What if the baby's dead? What if he starts crying again?"

"Just tell him hello. Tell him you love him."

"But he *cried*, Mom," Sally said.

"Of course he cried. His wife and his newborn son are very sick. I know it's hard to see your parents cry, but they do sometimes, just like you. And they need to be comforted sometimes, just like you."

Sally looked down at the puppy who slept at her feet. "I guess."

"I'll call him, if you want."

Sally stood. "No, that's all right. I'll do it."

Annie followed her daughter into the farmhouse kitchen and glanced at the clock, surprised to see that it was already suppertime. She thought maybe she'd fix a picnic supper and they could eat it down on the pier, watching the sun set. She began putting the makings together while Sally called her father. From what Annie could make out, Ryan was at the hospital, the baby was holding his own and Trudy was doing okay. When Sally hung up, she headed out of the room without a word to her mother.

THERE WERE CERTAIN basic issues involved in cabin maintenance that had been woefully neglected by the current owners, Jake discovered. It was suppertime and he was no closer to getting the propane stove to work in spite of the fact that the tanks were now filled and properly hooked up.

And Amanda was hungry. She'd spent much of the afternoon setting the live trap for her mice, baiting it with cheese, and checking it every five minutes to see if she'd caught anything. Busy work for a five-year-old.

"Pinch," Jake said, laying the wrench aside in defeat. "Looks like we're going to be cooking on the woodstove again tonight. I'll try not to burn everything."

Hot dogs should be easy. If he steamed them in a pan of water there was no way they'd burn. He fired up the woodstove with a big stack of kindling and newspaper and soon the flames were roaring up the metal chimney.

"Wow, Daddy," Amanda said. "That's pretty."

He followed her gaze and was dismayed to see that the chimney pipe itself was so rusted out that he could see the flames through several fair-size holes. "Jeez, why didn't we notice that last night?"

"Too much smoke," Amanda said.

Jake watched a few sparks stray out the largest of the holes, then threw a coffee can full of water into the fire box. He couldn't risk burning down the cabin. Steam and smoke hissed, and the fire was promptly extinguished. Jake gathered up all the supper fixings and put them inside a plastic grocery bag. "C'mon, Pinch. Fortunately for us, hot dogs and marshmallows always taste best over an open campfire."

He built a little campfire at the edge of the pond, and they roasted their hot dogs on long birch sticks, laying the rolls to toast on a fireside stone. They ate the entire package of hot dogs and afterward cooked marshmallows over the glowing coals while darkness settled so gradually that Jake was startled to see the moon's reflection in the still waters. At the sound of a trout rising, Amanda moved closer to him.

"What was that?" she whispered.

"A trout getting his own supper. Maybe tomorrow night we'll have time to do a little fishing before bed. Sleepy?"

She nodded and he put his arm around her and pulled her close. "Me, too. Let's put out this fire and go to bed. We've got a big day ahead of us. We'll have to go to town again, pick up some stovepipe and the stuff to fix the gas stove.''

"And some more hot dogs,'' Amanda said sleepily.

"Yup." Jake figured at the rate things were going he'd have to make a daily trip into town, and a daily trip into town greatly increased the odds of running into Annie Crawford. Maybe having these continual problems with the old cabin would turn out to be a good thing.

CHAPTER SIX

ANNIE TREASURED the foggy quiet of the harbor in the hour before sunrise. She sat out on the porch, wrapped in a warm flannel robe, sipping her first cup of coffee and reveling in the great good fortune of simply being in this beautiful place. "I wonder what the rest of the world is doing," she murmured smugly, and Rebel raised his head from his paws to gaze up at her. He was much improved after a good night's rest and had already devoured a big bowl of puppy food for breakfast. "We'll have to get you some adult dog food today," she told him. "And some special treats. You've certainly earned them."

Rebel's eyes mirrored complete understanding of everything she said. His tail flagged ever so slightly.

"You miss Lily, don't you?"

The tail twitched again.

"I bet they'd let you into the nursing home to visit her. Most places allow pets to visit." Annie took another sip of coffee. The muted hoot of the whistle buoy in the harbor was a steady accompaniment to the thick fog. "I think she'd like to see you, and know that you were safe. If you were my dog, I'd want to know." Rebel pushed himself into a sitting position, watching her steadily. "Well, we can only try, right? I mean, all they can say is 'no, you can't come inside.' And if that's the case, Lily can come out."

Annie raised her coffee cup for another sip. "I could bring her a bouquet of her own flowers. She'd like that, too, don't you think? And I can ask her about the painting of the three children sailing the ketch."

Rebel cocked his ears, tilted his head and flagged his tail approvingly.

"Sounding better and better, isn't it? Now all we have to do is get Sally out of bed before noon. You know how teenage girls are. They don't know there are two seven o'clocks in one day."

But Annie hadn't figured on Nell. In fact, Annie hadn't even started on her second cup of coffee when Sally stumbled bleary-eyed to the kitchen door and came out onto the porch, Nelly gamboling happily at her heels. "She peed on the floor before I could get her downstairs," Sally grumbled.

"Well, puppies have accidents. Did you clean it up?"

"I will, as soon as I'm awake."

"There's plenty of newspaper in the back shed. Want a cup of hot cocoa?"

Sally scowled at her mother. "If I say yes, does that mean I'm up for good?"

"It's going to be another beautiful day when this fog burns off, my girl."

Sally's scowl deepened. "Another long *boring* day, with nothing to do." She followed Nell down into the wet grass and they left two dark trails through the thick morning dew.

REBEL REFUSED to get into the Explorer. The moment Annie called him and opened the vehicle's door, he took one look and bolted back inside the old farmhouse. Annie watched him, and then realization struck. Rebel was afraid she was going to take him away from here.

She closed the car door with a sigh. "All right, old boy. You guard the house while we're gone. Sally?" she called. "You ready?"

"Coming," Sally responded, and Annie heard the clatter of feet on the back stairs. She burst out onto the porch, looking coltish and leggy in a pair of cut-offs, her hair flying loose, wearing a tie-dyed halter top. It had surprised Annie that Sally had been almost eager to come along. Undoubtedly, she was looking forward to any kind of contact with the outside world. Sally picked up the puppy and deposited her in the back seat before climbing into the passenger seat herself. Nelly promptly jumped into her lap.

Annie locked the farmhouse door and, moments later, with the puppy, Sally and a big vase of freshly cut garden flowers, they were headed for Blue Harbor. They stopped at the real estate office, where Annie took some flowers from the vase and presented Jim with a small bouquet. "They're from Lily's garden," she said. "I have more that I'm hoping to bring her. Can you tell me where the nursing home is?"

"Not far from here, in Danfield." He hesitated and his eyes became reflective. "She's not doing very well there. She's been…difficult." He paused. "Truth is, I haven't seen her myself for three weeks now. I used to take her for a drive two or three times a week, but once she got put in that place she always asked me to take her back home. Lester said if I did that she'd never leave, and that's why he decided to rent the farm. He thought if Lily knew someone else was living there, she'd give up the fight. Lily sent me away when she found out I was the listing Realtor. Now she won't even take my phone calls. She considers me a traitor. I'm not sure how she'd receive you."

"I understand, but I'd really like to meet her and ask about possibly purchasing one of the paintings I discovered in the boathouse."

In spite of Jim's reservations, Annie was in good spirits as she drove toward Danfield. The nursing home wasn't hard to find. It was on the main drag, an industrial-looking brick building with an equally industrial sign proclaiming it to be the Danfield Rehabilitation and Living Center.

Annie parked in the lot out back. Sally jumped out, Nelly in her arms, and Annie took out the vase. They proceeded to the front entrance, which was locked. Annie tried to open the door again and then glanced at Sally. "Maybe they're not accepting visitors?"

Suddenly a buzzer sounded and a mechanism clicked within the door itself. Annie gave another tentative pull and this time the door opened. An overweight nurse was walking toward them.

"Oh, no," she said with a disapproving frown when she saw caught sight of the golden retriever puppy squirming in Sally's arms. "No pets allowed."

"But she's just a puppy," Annie said, feeling foolish as she stated the obvious. "We thought some of your residents might like to pet her. She's very gentle…"

"I'm sorry," the nurse said with a firm head shake, "but no pets. It's the policy here. Allergies and all, you understand."

"I'll wait out in the car, Mom," Sally said, her expression matching that of Attila the Hun's.

Annie handed the keys to Sally and braced herself for the next round. "My name is Annie Crawford and I'm here to visit Lily Houghton. I'm renting her house for the summer and I brought her a bouquet from her garden. I trust you allow flowers inside."

The woman's mouth tightened. "Let me see if Lily is up for company," she said, and squeaked off on soft-soled shoes.

While she was gone, Annie looked around. The foyer was a sunroom where the residents could sit in chairs at tables or on couches along the walls. There were several elderly people in the room, but few seemed aware that Annie was there. The room reeked of pine-scented cleaning solution. A TV was blaring but nobody was watching it. One woman sat in a wheelchair, an Afghan draped across her knees, eyes fixed on some point between here and eternity. Many others had that same look.

"Ms. Crawford?" The nurse's voice startled her. "I'm sorry, but Lily says she's not feeling up to having visitors." Grim-mouthed, the woman delivered this information and then went back to her paperwork.

"Excuse me," Annie interrupted, leaning over the desk. "But I really wanted to talk to Lily about possibly purchasing one of her paintings. Could you please tell her that?"

The woman looked up, weighed Annie's request, and sighed. "All right," she said, and walked off again. This time, at a safe distance, Annie followed. The corridor branched. They turned left. It branched again. They turned right. Room after dreary room, doors all wedged open, residents in various stages of their morning routines. The nurse paused outside one of the doors and leaned in. "Lily?" Her voice was raised as if Lily was hard of hearing. "Lily, your visitor's asking about a painting of yours that she'd like to buy."

Annie walked up to the door on silent feet and looked over the nurse's shoulder into the room. An elderly woman sat in a chair by the window. Her head was turned away and she was gazing out at whatever view her window afforded. She was very slight, her white hair drawn back in a neat bun at the nape of her neck. She wore a red cardigan over a white pullover and a pair of dark slacks. Her black Reebok sneakers looked well worn.

"Mrs. Houghton?" Annie said, stepping around the nurse and moving into the room. "I'm Annie Crawford. I've brought some flowers from your garden. They're beautiful right now, as you know. The delphinium are the most wonderful shade of blue, and I can't even begin to describe the peonies, so I brought a blossom from each plant. They smell lovely, don't they?"

Lily Houghton turned her head slowly to look at her. Her face was wrinkled and speckled with liver spots, but the bone structure beneath was proud and regal. Her eyes were dark and there was nothing vacant about her stare. She looked first at Annie, and then dropped her gaze to the flowers that Annie held. Annie stepped forward and placed the vase on a table beside her chair. Lily bent forward ever so slightly to breathe the essence of the peonies. She closed her eyes and remained that way for several silent moments. "You're renting my farm," she said, opening her eyes and reaching her fingers to gently brush one of the flowers.

"Yes, for the summer. Jim Hinkley told me something about the place, and about you." Annie paused for a moment. "I thought you'd want to know that Rebel is back home. He found his way back to the farm just yesterday, and I would have brought him with us today but he wouldn't get in the car."

Lily's hand stilled. "Rebel's *alive?*"

"He's a bit thin and lame, but when I left him this morning he was looking ever so much better. He got loose from the people who had him and traveled over sixty miles to get back home."

Lily clasped her hands in her lap and looked out the window. She sat in absolute stillness for so long that Annie took another step forward. "There's a painting I found down in the boathouse," she said. "I was wondering if you'd be interested in selling it. It's of three children sailing a ketch—"

Lily looked at her fully for the first time. "They don't allow pets here," she interrupted.

"Yes, I know. I was told," Annie said, glancing behind to where the nurse still stood, her mouth pressed into a thin line. "I think Mrs. Houghton and I will be all right now," she said pointedly, and the woman departed.

"Are you sure it's Rebel?" Lily said.

"Well, the dog's a border collie mix and he certainly knows his way around the farmhouse. He went right up to your room and jumped on the bed as if he was used to sleeping there."

The old woman looked back out the window, and her mouth firmed around a tremble. After a few moments she cleared her throat and lifted her chin. "I'm not sure I know the painting you're asking about."

"There are three children in it, and they're sailing a boat…"

Lily shook her head.

"I could bring it here," Annie offered.

"There are a lot of paintings in the boathouse. I used it as my studio."

"Yes, Jim told me."

"I should look them all over and sell the ones I can. They're doing me no good where they are." Lily looked at her and her expression became more determined. "I'll need to see them in order to price them and it would be much easier if I went there to do it. We could go right now."

Annie hesitated and glanced around the bleak room. "Do they let you leave here when someone comes to visit?"

She nodded. "Jim used to come by quite a bit and take me for short drives, but we had a falling out. I haven't been for a drive in over three weeks."

"Well," Annie said slowly, wondering if she were making a big mistake. "If you like, I suppose I could take you there and we could look over your paintings. I'm sure Rebel would be overjoyed to see you."

Hope swept over Lily's face and to Annie's surprise she rose to her feet unassisted and retrieved a cane that rested against her chair. "Good. I'll just need to tell them where I'm going and when I'm coming back," she said, her voice gaining strength with each word she spoke. "Living here is like being in prison, but as long as I behave myself, they allow me certain freedoms."

Ten minutes later they were leaving Danfield and heading for Blue Harbor.

"DADDY, why are we going this way?" Amanda asked after he'd picked up all the supplies they'd needed at the stores in Danfield.

"Well, it's getting close to lunchtime and I thought we could eat at the pretty spot we found yesterday, the one overlooking the harbor," Jake explained.

"Okay," she said agreeably. "Can I feed the gulls again?"

"Sure, after we eat. We don't want them hovering over us for too long. Could be hazardous."

They ate hamburgers at the lobster pound, sitting as they had before on the edge of the dock, watching the tide come in. Jake ate slowly, aware that it was still early, too early, really, for Annie to be getting lunch. Sophisticated women like her probably ate closer to midafternoon, not 11:00 a.m. Still, he kept his eyes peeled, turning around at every slam of a car door, at every footstep, until Amanda said, "Daddy, what are you looking for?"

"A miracle, Pinch," he said. "I'm staking this place out hoping that we'll see someone we both know. Remember that lady doctor who took care of me when I was sick?" Amanda nodded. "Well, she's living somewhere in this town, and I figure that sooner or later we'll run into each other."

"Why don't you just call her on the phone?" Amanda said.

Jake hesitated. "Well, she's come here to get away from the city. I don't think she'd be very interested in hearing from me."

"Yes, she would. She made you better, didn't she?"

"That's her job. She tries to make everyone who's sick better."

"Do you know where she lives?"

Jake had done that research long before heading for Maine. "I know where she's living and I know her phone number, but I don't want her to think I'm being too pushy. Know what I mean?"

Amanda shook her head and then her eyes shifted to something over his shoulder. "Look, Daddy," she said around a mouthful of hamburger, pointing toward the lobster pound. "Isn't that her?"

Jake whipped his head around and stared. "Thank you, God," he muttered under his breath, unable to believe his good fortune. He stood, finished the rest of his burger in one gulp and pulled Amanda to her feet. "Let's go say hi, Pinch."

Amanda walked ahead of him into the lobster pound, marched up to where Annie Crawford stood looking at a tank full of live lobsters and tugged on her shirt tail. "Hi, Dr. Annie. Remember me?" she said.

Annie turned and looked down. "Why, Amanda Macpherson," she said with a wide, beautiful smile. "I most certainly do." And then she raised her eyes and spotted him standing just inside the door. "Hello, Lieutenant. As I recall, you did say that Blue Harbor was a very small town."

"That I did," he said, straightening off the door-jamb and approaching in what he hoped was a nonchalant manner. "Picking out dinner?"

"Trying," she said with a rueful laugh. "Lily Houghton, the owner of the farm I'm renting, is coming home with us for a visit. She's a grand sort, and when I asked what she'd like for lunch, she said it had been a dog's age since she'd had a steamed lobster."

"In Maine?" Jake was near enough now that he

could smell the light fragrance of her hair. He moved closer on the pretense of studying the lobsters in the tank and wondered if he were the only one that felt the electrical charge that filled the gap between them.

"She's living in a nursing home now, and I doubt steamed lobster is their regular bill of fare."

"Well, you came to the right place. Freshest and best, right here. What's your preference? One-pounders or two?"

Annie looked back at the tank and bit her lower lip. She shook her head. "To tell the truth, I don't know anything about lobsters, other than ordering them in a restaurant and eating them with drawn butter." She raised her eyes to his and grimaced. "Lily really craves a steamed lobster, so I suggested eating here, but she's so anxious to see the farm and her dog that she can hardly sit still." Annie shrugged helplessly. "I honestly don't know what to do. You see, I've never cooked a lobster before."

He grinned, unable to believe his good fortune. "Tell you what. *I'll* buy the lobsters and cook them for you, too. I've done it plenty of times. You can introduce me to Lily as your personal caterer."

Annie laughed and then glanced down at Amanda, who was tugging at her shirt again.

"Can we come with you, Dr. Annie?" she said.

"Yes, of course," she said, kneeling to bring herself down to Amanda's level. "I'd love that."

"JUST THINK OF THEM as giant bugs," Jake advised Annie less than an hour later, after he'd fired up the propane cookstove at the farmhouse and was waiting for the water in the big pot to come to a rolling boil. Outside on the porch the girls played with the puppy while Lily sat in the rocker with Rebel's head in her lap, overcome with joy at being home again, reunited with her dearest friend.

"I can't," Annie confessed, turning away from the wraiths of steam rising from the pot.

"Then, dear, gentle lady, I suggest you go outside and enjoy that incredible view and let me take care of everything."

"Thanks, Jake," she said. "I really appreciate this." She turned to go and then glanced back when she reached the door. "I have a nice bottle of Australian red…"

"Sounds perfect," he said with that brash grin.

"I'll ask Lily if she'd like a glass," Annie said, her cheeks warming under his bold stare.

"Careful. She won't want to go back to that home if you keep this up."

"If you'd seen the place, you wouldn't want to take her back," Annie said dryly. She walked out onto the porch and sat beside Lily with a contented sigh, watching the girls on the lawn below play with the puppy. "Look at them," she said. "If only I had a fraction of their energy."

"You did, once," Lily said, dabbing her eyes with a white lace handkerchief. "It's their turn now."

"How long have you had Rebel?"

"My husband Ruel didn't like dogs, but when he died, I saw an ad in the paper for border collie pups. I didn't know Rebel wasn't a purebred, and after I saw him I didn't care. I paid the money, brought him home, and until the day I broke my hip, he stayed beside me night and day. Ten years of loyal companionship." Lily gently stroked Rebel's head as she talked. "Lester told me I couldn't go home again to live. He sold my car, put me in the nursing home and Rebel in the pound. Lester loves me, I know he does, but he just doesn't understand how much I love this place and how much I love this old dog..."

Annie sat quietly, pondering the complex issues of caring for an elderly parent. Suddenly a piercing scream broke the peaceful silence. Annie jumped to her feet and charged through the screen door, fearing savage lobster bites and scalding burns, only to find Amanda standing, unharmed, beside the stove. She'd apparently come into the kitchen just as her father was about to plunge one of the lobsters headfirst into the pot of boiling water. "No Daddy, stop," she begged. "You'll *kill* her if you put her in there."

Jake caught Annie's eyes as he held the lobster above the plume of steam. His own expression was as stricken as his daughter's. He looked down at Amanda. "Why don't you go outside with Dr. Annie, Pinch?" he said.

"You're going to kill Lucy!" Amanda said, her big eyes flooding with tears.

"Lucy?"

"You said one of the lobsters was mine, and I named her Lucy."

"Oh." Jake gave Annie a mute "help me" look, and Annie moved to Amanda and gently gripped the little girl's shoulders.

"Amanda, honey, come sit with Lily and me."

"No!" She twisted out of Annie's grasp. "Please, Dr. Annie, don't let him do it."

Lily with the help of her cane, limped into the kitchen with Rebel at heel, took in the situation at a glance, and stared down at the little girl. "You don't want your lobster to be cooked, is that it?" she said.

The tears filling Amanda's eyes spilled over and her lower lip trembled. "No, I don't."

"Humph! Well, it just so happens that I don't want mine cooked, either." Lily fixed her most forbidding gaze upon Jake Macpherson. "I'm afraid I must request that you set aside Amanda's lobster, Lucy, and mine, as well, whom I shall call Leticia."

Jake stared for a moment at the lobster he held in his hand and then obediently returned it to the cardboard box. He looked at Annie, who returned his gaze with a silent plea of her own. "Please, Jake, I'll have to ask you to spare my lobster, as well," Annie said. "Her name is...Lorena."

"I can see how this is shaping up," Jake said, eyes narrowing.

The screen door slammed and Sally came into the kitchen, the sleeping pup draped in her arms. "Oh, yuck," she said, coming to an abrupt halt. "Is it true that lobsters scream when you put them in boiling water?"

"I'm only cooking two. Yours and mine," Jake said, inclining his head. "With your permission, of course."

Sally studied Amanda's tear-streaked face for a moment and shrugged. "I don't even like lobster that much." Her face brightened with sudden inspiration. "Hey, why don't we take them down to the water and let them go?"

"I think that's a fine idea," Lily said, thumping the floor with her cane. "I happen to know that a lot of happy lobsters live in this very harbor."

Amanda sniffed and wiped her cheeks, hope filling her eyes. "I think Lucy would like to live there, too," she said.

Jake shrugged with amiable defeat. "All right. You ladies win. We'll set them free." He shut off the propane burner beneath the big lobster cooker, found a pair of scissors in the kitchen drawer, and picked up the box of two-pound lobsters for which he'd just paid very dearly. "Okay," he said. "Lead the way."

"Are you letting yours go, too, Daddy?" Amanda said.

"Of course. I can't let all those beautiful female lobsters go unattended, so I guess Leroy'll have to look after them."

"And Leonard," Sally said. "Don't forget my lobster."

Lily walked slowly with the use of a cane. She took the arm Annie offered and, with Rebel flanking her, the three of them trailed the procession to the stone pier, where Jake set the box down and took the scissors from the back pocket of his jeans.

"What are you going to do with those?" Sally said, frowning.

"Remove their handcuffs," Jake said. "Can't turn 'em loose all tied up. They'd never make it. Now, you girls stand back. These lobsters are apt to be a little ugly from being trussed up for so long, and they can pinch really hard with their claws."

"Do you think they'd bite us, Daddy?" Amanda said.

"I think they'd bite your little fingers off if they could," he said. "That doesn't mean Lucy doesn't care for you. I'm sure she appreciates very much the gift you're about to give her." That said, he lifted the first lobster, deftly snipped the rubber bands off the front claws and tossed it into the deep cold water off the stone pier. The girls bent over and watched it scoot rapidly out of sight.

"Goodbye, Lucy," Amanda said, beaming happily.

"Good luck, Leonard," Sally called after the next freed prisoner.

Lily leaned over when the third one was dropped into the water. "Bon voyage, Leticia. May we meet again someday very soon." She directed a somber sidelong stare at Annie, who couldn't help laughing.

"Stay safe, Lorena," Annie called after her lobster. And finally, Jake held up Leroy.

"Well, Leroy," he said just before snipping the heavy rubber bands. "Today's your lucky day. Make the best of it, buddy."

Splash. The fifth lobster disappeared from sight. Amanda reached up and took her father's hand. "Thank you, Daddy," she said. "You, too, Miss Lily."

Lily smiled. "Thank *you,* Miss Amanda. I don't know when I've ever felt quite so virtuous."

"And hungry, too, no doubt," Jake said. "We have some groceries in the truck. How does a chili dog sound, with big crunchy deli dills and some potato chips? There's lemonade, too, and Dr. Annie promised to produce a bottle of red wine."

"My goodness," Lily said. "It's a party."

And it felt that way to Annie, as well. They sat on the porch talking and laughing, eating Jake's most excellent chili dogs. Lily fed bits of her food to Rebel and Sally followed suit, sneaking pieces of hot dog to the pup. Annie sighed and leaned over to lift Nelly's chin. "You're going to be spoiled rotten," she announced.

"Children and dogs *should* be spoiled," Lily said,

handing down a piece of bun to Rebel, who took it delicately from her fingers. "That's the whole purpose of having children and dogs."

"How many children did you have, Lily?" Annie asked.

"Just the one. Lester. Not that we didn't try. I wanted to fill this house with children, but it simply wasn't meant to be."

"That painting of three children sailing a little ketch…"

"Ah, yes." Lily nodded. "I never finished it. The kids are Joe Storey's. He's my nearest neighbor, lives about a mile from here. Lobsterman. He and his father built that ketch for me. I painted that picture, oh, maybe ten years ago."

"Do you intend to finish it?"

"In another life, maybe. I haven't painted in well over a year."

"You could start again."

"They don't like the smell of the oils and the turpentine at the nursing home." Lily lifted her shoulders in a shrug. "I have no real inspiration there, anyway. What would I paint? Old man Howard slumped in his wheelchair?"

"If you don't mind my saying so," Jake said, "you don't seem to belong in a home."

Lily snorted. "I don't mind your saying so at all. It was my son and my doctor who decided I was no longer able to care for myself."

"But you've recovered from your fall," Annie said.

"You'll get no argument from me," Lily said. "I'd like nothing better than to come back home again, but Lester never liked the idea of me living out here by myself after my husband died. I think putting me in that nursing home was his way of not having to worry about me anymore." Lily gave the last morsel of her chili dog to Rebel and sighed. "Well, the charge nurse informed me several times that I was to be back by 5:00 p.m."

"I can take you," Jake volunteered, "and save Annie the trip. Amanda and I go right past that place on the way to our cabin."

"Why don't you just stay the night?" Annie offered impulsively, warmed by Jake's sweet offer. "I'll phone the nursing home and tell them we're having a sleepover."

"You've all been so kind," Lily said, "but I can't impose, and I didn't come prepared." She smiled. "It's been wonderful to spend the afternoon here, and seeing Rebel again was..." Her voice broke. She picked up her cane and pushed out of her chair, shaking her head when Jake rose to help. "Your young lady was quite right," she said to him. "I'm fully recovered from my broken hip."

"But not so independent-minded, I hope, that you plan to walk back to Danfield," Jake said.

"No, young man. I'll gratefully accept your offer of a ride." She looked at Annie. "He's brash, but I'd say your chef de cuisine's a keeper," she said.

Annie flushed as Jake grinned. He carried dishes back into the kitchen, pried Amanda away from the puppy, and herded her out toward the truck. Annie turned to Lily. "I really do wish you'd stay."

Lily shook her head. "Thank you for that offer, dear, but I have little say in the matter. You'd have to talk with my son, and Lester can be somewhat difficult."

"I'll phone him," Annie promised. "I'm sure we can work something out."

When Jake helped Lily into the truck, Rebel tried to climb in after her. "No, old fella," Jake said, gently prying the dog away from the truck so he could close the door.

"I'll take good care of Rebel," Annie said, lacing her fingers through his collar. "And I'll phone you tomorrow to tell you what kind of conversation I had with your son. Either way, I expect you'll be visiting again very soon. We never did get around to looking over your paintings."

Lily nodded. Her firm chin trembled as she fixed her gaze stoically out the windshield. Annie saw Amanda take Lily's gnarled hand in her own as Jake started the truck.

"I owe you a bottle of wine, Doc," he said.

"And I owe you five two-pound lobsters, Lieutenant," she returned with a smile.

"Come visit us sometime. Anytime. Our cabin's on Round Pond. Take a left where the old road forks a couple miles in and keep driving till you can't anymore. I'll take you fishing." He was looking at her in a way that made her blush like a schoolgirl.

"'Bye, Dr. Annie," Amanda said.

With a farewell wave and mixed emotions, Annie watched them leave. Sally came to stand beside her. Annie held Rebel's collar to keep him from running after the truck. Her eyes suddenly stung with tears, and she knelt beside the dog. "It's all right," she said to him, but she knew that it wasn't all right at all. This was Lily's home and she belonged here.

"Will she be coming back, do you think?" Sally said, watching after the truck.

"Yes," Annie said.

"I liked her, even though she's really old," Sally conceded, then added grudgingly, "And *he's* not that bad, either, even though he did arrest me."

Annie stood, still holding Rebel's collar. "No, he's not," she said, the realization softening her, reawakening a feeling she'd believed long dead within herself. "He's not bad at all."

CHAPTER SEVEN

RYAN SOUNDED TIRED when Annie spoke with him that evening. "Trudy's coming home tomorrow," he told her. "The baby's scheduled for surgery at the end of next week, but I'm worried about Trudy. She's really depressed. I don't think she should be alone right now, and I've already taken a lot of time away from my practice. Do you think Sally could come stay with us?"

"Why don't you ask her yourself?" Annie handed the phone over to her daughter and wandered back into the kitchen to pour herself a glass of iced tea. She carried it out onto the porch and stood looking out across the harbor. She watched the lobster boats returning with the day's haul and made a mental note to find out about sailing lessons for Sally...

And then she thought about Jake Macpherson, and a tingly feeling swept through her. She had enjoyed his company this afternoon. There was no denying his incredible magnetism. She'd found it hard to resist moving closer to him, touching him. He'd invited her to visit them at his cabin on the pond. Maybe she would...

"Mom?" Sally came out onto the porch, the screen door banging behind her. "Dad wants me to go back to his place. What do you think?"

"What do *you* think? You're the one who has to decide. You're welcome to stay here, you know that."

"Well, I'd still like to go back to New York, but Dad says he needs me right now. He says Trudy's pretty sick."

"Yes, I know. She's worried about the baby. She probably doesn't want to be alone."

Sally dropped into a chair with a brooding frown. "I don't know."

"Maybe you could stay for a day or two, see how it goes."

"I told Dad that's what I'd do."

"That's my girl."

"He's picking me up tomorrow and bringing Trudy along for the ride."

Annie nodded. "It'll be good for her."

"Will you be okay here by yourself?"

"I'll be fine. I've got Rebel to keep me company."

"Oh, yeah. I forgot." Sally looked to where Rebel lay, head on his paws, his gaze fixed steadily on the drive. "He's waiting for Lily to come back home," she said. "That's sad, isn't it?"

IT WAS SO INDESCRIBABLY delicious to wake to the wild cry of gulls and the muted clang of a buoy. It was so sinfully decadent to lie in bed and think about all the things she didn't have to do now that she was here in Maine, and to plan the things she really wanted to do. Annie couldn't remember when she'd last felt so at peace, so relaxed. It was only her fifth morning in Maine but she felt as though she'd been here much longer.

Ryan, looking drawn and fatigued, had picked Sally up the day before. Trudy hadn't gotten out of the car. Annie had walked out to speak with her, and had been shocked at Trudy's appearance. "Trudy, if there's anything at all I can do..." Annie had begun.

Trudy had lifted sunken eyes and nodded, voicing a wooden, "Thank you."

Annie had hugged Sally fiercely before the girl climbed into the car. "Call me every night," she'd said to her daughter.

After they'd left, Annie had gone inside to call Lily's son. She was put on hold by his secretary for several minutes, before Lester Houghton had finally come on the line.

"My mother can't live by herself any longer—" he said bluntly "—and quite frankly I can't live my life worrying about her falling and dying all alone out there, with no one to look after her."

"I understand your concerns," Annie said, "but there are alternatives to a nursing home. She could have a companion here at the farm, a live-in caregiver. It would cost far less than the nursing home she's in now, and she could live here, where she wants to be, with her dog."

"Her dog was put in the humane shelter when she went into the nursing home. Rebel was so old I doubt anyone took him. I'm sure he was put to sleep."

"No, he wasn't. They were able to find a home for him, but Rebel ran away and came back here, looking for your mother." She gripped the receiver tightly. "He traveled over *sixty miles* to find Lily. I think that's extraordinary. I only wish you could have seen the reunion between the two of them."

She heard him sigh. "That's going to make it all the harder for her," he said.

Annie took a deep breath. "Mr. Houghton, why

don't you let her spend the summer here with me? I'm a competent physician and I'd look after her. It would do her a world of good.''

"Because she'll want to stay there after you leave," the terse voice came right back at her, "and she can't. She's not capable of living alone anymore, I have her doctor's written statement to that effect. Furthermore, there isn't a chance of convincing a home health aide to live in or to make daily visits to such a remote place, especially when winter rolls around. No, the property is going on the market just as soon as I get the legalities out of the way. With the money from the sale I can set her up very comfortably in a very exclusive assisted-living center down here, close to my wife and me.''

"But…''

"I appreciate your concern for my mother, Dr. Crawford, but in this instance I believe I know what's in her best interest. Once she sees how nice this place is down here, she'll give up any notion of returning to Maine.''

"And what about her dog? Will they take him at this assisted-living center?''

Lester hesitated. "Rebel's old. It isn't as if he has a lot of years left.''

"I take that as a no," Annie said. "Do you have any objections to your mother being a frequent visitor here this summer?''

"I think that would just make the transition more difficult for her, and for me, as well. It's better if she stays at the nursing home until I can get her moved down here. Now excuse me, but I have to go. I have a client waiting.''

After he'd hung up Annie had sat on the kitchen

stairs for a moment and then picked up the phone once again. "Matt?" she said when she heard the familiar voice from another lifetime. "It's Annie. Listen, I need a big favor, but there are big rewards. *Huge* rewards. A week in Maine at one of the most beautiful places you could ever imagine. But Matt, I need this favor right away."

THE PHONE CALL to Matt had been made just yesterday, yet tomorrow morning Matt Brink would arrive at Bangor International Airport, along with Dr. Elsa Morrow, his cousin and one of the country's most renowned geriatric specialists. Annie would pick them up and they would proceed to the nursing home in Danfield. Arrangements had been made for Dr. Morrow to examine Lily. Annie's conversation with Lester Houghton had troubled her to the point of persuading the older woman to allow Annie to pay for a second opinion on Lily's present state of health. Tomorrow they'd find out just what Lily's situation was.

But today? Today belonged exclusively to her. And she had decided that she would very much like to visit Lieutenant Jake Macpherson and his daughter at their cabin on Round Pond.

And so she rose, made coffee, carried it out onto the porch, and was sipping it when she heard the chug of a lobster boat and the *Glory B* appeared out of the thick morning mist. This time Annie was prepared. She remained seated while the pilot of the boat docked, and climbed the stairs and headed toward her.

"Mornin'," Joe Storey said as he came to a halt at the bottom of the porch steps. "Jim called last night, said you were interested in sailing lessons."

"Morning, Joe." Annie smiled. "Yes, I am.

There's a ketch in the boathouse, and my daughter and I would like to learn how to sail it."

"I know the boat." Joe nodded. "I helped my father build the *Dash* for Lily. I teach sailing Tuesday and Thursday afternoons, from three to five, at the town wharf."

Annie ran her fingers through her hair and frowned.

"Today's Wednesday, right?" she asked. When he nodded, she added, "I'm not sure if we can make it tomorrow."

"Come when you can," he said. "I have five students signed on and there's always room for a couple more."

He turned and began the descent to the *Glory B*. She settled back into her chair with her coffee and planned her day. The general store in Blue Harbor had a good deli where she could pick up something fun for lunch at the cabin on Round Pond.

Not lobsters, that's for sure.

"PINCH?" Jake rose to his feet after spending a long time crouched at the front of the propane refrigerator, trying to figure out why the thing wouldn't work. "Amanda?"

No response. He dropped the flashlight onto the table and stepped out onto the porch with a lurch of anxiety.

"Here, Daddy." He heard her voice. "Look! A bird's eating out of my hand. Watch."

She was standing just off the end of the porch, holding a piece of bread out in one outstretched arm. On the branch of a nearby pine sat a Canada jay. They were close cousins to the blue jay but a world apart, personality wise. Jake slouched against the doorjamb and grinned.

"Hold still, Pinch. It'll come right to you. That's a camp robber, and he wants your food."

"Daddy, he ate a piece of bread right out of my hand." Amanda's voice was high and excited. She turned to look at her father. "Just like he was tame!"

"He's hungry. How about you? It's time for lunch."

"Wait, Daddy. Watch." The jay made a sudden swoop toward Amanda's hand, landed neatly on her wrist, took the piece of bread she offered and then sprang back into the air to seek the safety of the pine branch to eat its bounty. "Wow," Amanda said. "Did you see?"

"I saw. Pretty neat, huh?"

"Coooool." Amanda's face was lit from within and the smile she gave her father wrenched his heart. In two short months Linda would take her back to Los Angeles, and unless he landed a job out there, it would be months until he saw her again. "C'mon, Pinch," he said. "You've fed the bird, now it's time to feed yourself."

He heard the vehicle at the same time she did. She called, "Daddy, it's Dr. Annie!" as she ran to the parking spot behind the cabin. Jake followed more slowly, rounding the corner in time to see Annie scoop his little girl into a big hug. She caught his eye over Amanda's head and smiled. "I brought lunch. Hope the two of you are hungry."

Jake carried the basket up onto the porch, arranged the chairs, fetched paper cups and plates and silverware. Then he sat to enjoy the sight of this extraordinary woman laughing with his daughter, pouring lemonade into paper cups, catching his glance with those clear, beautiful eyes of hers that were so bright with laughter and love of life.

Her nearness triggered something primitive and powerful inside him and made him afraid. He was steering his course toward the west coast to be near his daughter, and Annie was just as strongly tied to the east. Unfortunately, it was too late for him to suppress the feelings he had for this woman. He was already more than a little smitten.

"You're not eating," she accused him halfway through lunch, and he dutifully bent to the task, but tasted none of the food. The sense of panic built within him until he had to leave. He walked through the big pines that graced the shore and stepped onto the dock. Several moments passed before he heard her footsteps lightly tracing his own path.

"Jake?" she said, coming to stand beside him. "You okay?"

"Never better." He shifted his gaze to look down at her. "Thanks for coming."

"You don't like pasta salad?"

"It was great. I loved it."

"Perhaps you would have preferred a steamed lobster," she said with a teasing smile. "I never got a chance to properly thank you for the other afternoon. You exercised great forbearance, considering the amount of money those giant bugs cost you."

He couldn't suppress a rueful grin. "I'm learning a lot about my daughter. Last night just before bed she caught a mouse in her trap and she made me walk outside with her to set it free."

"Obviously it's not the kind of mouse trap I'm thinking of."

"It's this little cage contraption. She doesn't want to kill them, she just doesn't want them running over her bed at night."

Annie laughed. "She reminds me of myself when I was her age, and I guess in some ways I haven't changed much. I have to confess that I was as happy as she was to set my lobster free."

"Does that mean we'll never share a lobster dinner?"

"Perhaps we could visit a lobster shack?"

"Hypocrite."

"Oh, absolutely." Annie raised her hands in a gesture of surrender. "No argument there." She looked out over the pond. "What a lovely spot this is. Totally different from Lily's place, but beautiful. Peaceful. Is this the only cabin on the pond?"

"There's one other, but you can't see it from here. It's set back in that cove. All the rest of the land around the pond is part of a Maine Public Reserve, so there can't be any more camps. That makes this pretty special."

"There must be all sorts of wildlife wandering about."

"It's a nonstop show." He was intoxicated by her nearness as she stood beside him. "Loons, deer, moose…" The graceful curve of her neck was so sensuous he could scarcely breathe.

"Hmm. I'll bet it's nice."

"Annie…" he began.

"Daddy?" Amanda tripped down onto the dock, barefoot, her overalls rolled up to midcalf. "Can I catch some frogs?"

"Stay right here by the dock, where I can see you."

"Wanna help?" she asked Annie.

"I'll watch." Annie smiled. "I've never been much good at frog catching."

She and Jake sat side by side on the dock, feet dangling over the water. The sun westered enough to shine on them and the golden warmth felt good. Annie told him about her conversation with Lily's son.

"You're something else," he said. "Going to bat for an old woman you just met."

"I know Lester thinks he's doing the right thing, but someone has to fight for Lily's rights."

"Hey, I'm on your side, and if push comes to shove, I'm a pretty good fighting man."

She cocked her head at him. "Really? The last fight you were in you didn't fare so well. Whatever happened to that woman who shot you, anyway?"

"She's awaiting trial, probably thanking her lucky stars every day that you're such a good doctor, or she might be locked up for a long, long time."

"Hmm. How are you healing up, by the way? Any problems?"

Jake shook his head. "My pride was hurt more than my body."

Annie pulled back. "Not quite, Lieutenant. As I recall, you were more dead than alive when they hauled you into ER."

Jake shrugged. "I'll have to take your word for that. Anyhow, it's over, and I learned my lesson."

"What was that?"

"Never doubt anything a woman says. I didn't believe that hooker really had a gun."

"Why do you do it, Jake? Why don't you find another line of work?"

"Hell, Annie, it isn't all life-and-death, blood-and-guts stuff. And I like to think my job makes a difference. Same as you, I guess.''

Annie swung her sneakered feet above the water, back and forth, back and forth. ''Sally's been behaving herself since the night you dragged her into the police station, so I guess I can't argue with you there, Jake,'' she admitted. ''You may have changed the whole direction her life was heading in. She's a good kid, even if she's not thrilled to be in Maine for the summer. But hooking up with the wrong bunch has ruined lots of good kids. I had no idea she was running around with them. I mean, I thought Sally and I kept no secrets, but I guess I was wrong.''

''She still in touch with them?''

''No way. I laid down the law after you arrested her, and to my knowledge she hasn't had any contact with them since. Thank you.''

''Welcome.'' He bumped her gently with his shoulder. ''And thank you.''

''Welcome,'' she said, leaning into him with a sigh of contentment. ''I wasn't sure I'd ever look at another man again after my divorce,'' she said, ''but I gotta tell you, Lieutenant, you're beginning to convince me otherwise.''

''Guess that makes two of us, Doc,'' he replied, draping his arm casually over her shoulders.

She glanced up at him, and just as he threw all caution to the wind and bent his head to kiss her, Amanda's shrill, excited voice startled all the wildlife in a one-mile radius.

''Daddy, Dr. Annie, look at my frog!''

ANNIE STOPPED at the Blue Harbor store on the way home and picked up some dog food, a newspaper and a couple bags of groceries. She drove down the mile-long winding gravel road that ended at the most beautiful place in the world. She parked, then sat for a few moments, listening to the shifting press of the ocean wind against the car and the muted lap of the waves against the granite ledges below.

Jake had kissed her goodbye. Oh, it hadn't been the world's most passionate kiss, not with Amanda looking on. Annie smiled and recalled the scene.

"Can we go back with you, Dr. Annie?" the child had asked. "And can I bring my frog?"

"Your frog would be lonely without all its friends in the pond," Annie had replied. "Besides, you and your father have a lot of work to do here. He told me so." Annie had noted the crestfallen face and knelt beside the little girl. "Amanda, you know you're welcome to visit me anytime. Do you like ice-cream cones? Ah, I thought so. Well, I have my first sailing lesson tomorrow at 3:00 p.m. at the town landing in Blue Harbor, and guess what's right near the town landing?"

Amanda looked up at her father, eyes alight. "Can we go watch, Daddy, and get an ice-cream cone? And can I go sailing, too?"

"I'm pretty sure you're too young," Jake had said.

"But Dr. Annie will be there."

"Sailing's serious business, Amanda." Annie had spoken softly. "And you have to know how to swim."

"I can swim," Amanda had said. "Tell her, Daddy." Just then the frog had twisted its way out of her grasp and landed at her feet. Two great leaps had launched the amphibian into the safety of the pond.

Amanda looked after it, her eyes filled with tears and lower lip quivering. "He got away."

"Don't be sad. Your frog was lonely and its family was calling it," Annie had said, stroking the little girl's hair. "Hear them?"

Amanda had nodded, wiping her tears. She'd listened for a moment and sunshine had swept across her face again as she'd looked up at Annie. "Please, can I come sailing with you, Dr. Annie?"

"You can come watch if you like, but I think your father's right. You're probably too young to take lessons. We could still get an ice cream, though."

Both Annie and Amanda had looked at Jake, who'd lifted his shoulders and let them fall. "Fair enough," he'd said. "Three o'clock tomorrow at the town landing. Shiver me timbers, hard a'port and stern a'bow, I'm kinda lookin' forward to it, Doc."

As she'd prepared to depart, Jake had touched her arm and then let his fingers slide down to grasp her hand. "Thanks again, Annie," he'd said as he'd ducked his head to kiss her. It was so unexpected that she hadn't had time to react. His lips had brushed hers, and that was all. It had been brief, sweet, and had left her aching deep inside. One kiss and she was adrift in a sea of conflicting emotions. One kiss and she could hardly think straight. One kiss and all she knew was that she couldn't wait to see him again.

CHAPTER EIGHT

MATT BRINK didn't like to fly, but he would have taken a rocketship to the moon if Annie Crawford asked him to. It was with great relief that he left the plane in Bangor and entered the airport terminal. He dropped his bag when he saw her and swept her into his arms in a great bear hug. "You look great," he said, holding her at arm's length.

She smiled. "So do you."

"It feels like you've been gone a million years. The hospital's not the same without you. Don't you miss it?"

She laughed. "No, not at all. Oh, don't look like that. I miss *you*. I just don't miss the rest of it." She glanced questioningly over his shoulder. "Where's Elsa?"

"She had a last-minute emergency and said she'd hop the earliest flight tomorrow and meet us at the nursing home around 11:00 a.m. Looks like I have you all to myself, for a little while, at least."

Matt picked up his bag and linked his arm through hers as they walked out to the parking garage. He couldn't help staring at her. "I'm jealous," he said as they reached her vehicle. "I can't wait to see this place. If summering in Maine has made this much of a change in you, then I'm quitting my job and heading north."

"Oh, Matt, I can't begin to explain it," she told him as they drove out of Bangor and headed due east down Route 1. "I know I've only been here a little while, but God help me, it's such a wonderful place I don't ever want to leave."

Matt watched the countryside roll past. Quaint, parochial and suffocatingly static. She'd tire of it quickly. "So tell me about things. How's Sally doing?"

"She's doing pretty well. Poor kid only spent one night with Trudy and Ryan, and then Trudy went into labor and the baby was born premature with a transposition of the great vessels of the heart. Sally stayed with me until Trudy came home from the hospital the day before yesterday. Now she's back with Ryan, helping Trudy out. The baby's scheduled for surgery next week. Trudy's pretty depressed and Ryan works twelve, fourteen hours a day. It's a lot for a thirteen-year-old to handle."

Matt nodded.

"I'm going to call Ryan tonight to ask him whether Sally can spend at least a couple nights a week with me. And you won't believe this, but you remember the cop who arrested Sally?"

"The one who got shot?"

Annie nodded. "Well, he's here. He's spending a month or so in Maine with his little daughter. Isn't that just the wildest coincidence?"

"I don't know," Matt said coolly. "Is it?"

Annie laughed. "It wasn't planned, it just worked out that way. His ex-wife's over in Europe filming a movie and she asked him if he'd take their child for the summer. He had some sick leave and vacation time coming, so he said yes and rented the cheapest place in Maine, which happens to be this old log cabin on a pond not twenty miles from Blue Harbor. Anyhow, I have a sailing lesson this afternoon, and Amanda's coming to watch. She's such a sweetie.''

Matt slumped in his seat. ''So how does Sally like having her arresting officer at the scene of her summer vacation?''

''Sally can be hard to read, sometimes, but I think she actually *likes* him.''

''Great.'' Matt slumped lower. ''I guess this means you're not going to marry me,'' he said glumly.

Annie laughed again, flashing him another sidelong glance as she drove. ''You're crazy.''

''I'm crazy about you, Annie Crawford, but otherwise I'm perfectly sane.''

''Matt…'' Annie swept her windblown hair out of her face and held it back with one hand as she drove. ''We've always been good friends.''

''The best.''

''And I want to believe we always will be. I count on you.''

''So is this your way of saying you're not going to marry me?''

''Half the time I don't know if you're teasing or serious.''

''Half the time I am.''

''Teasing or serious?''

''Both.''

She took a deep breath and firmly gripped the wheel with both hands. ''Matt, I'm not in love with you.''

''I know. I've known that for years now.''

A troubled frown furrowed Annie's brow. ''Then why are you talking like this?''

"Because I'm not ready to give up on you."

She glanced at him briefly, then turned her attention back to the road. "Oh, Matt," she said softly, and then a short while later, "Why don't you take a sailing lesson with us this afternoon?"

"No, thanks. I can't swim, and nothing appeals to me less than deep cold water." He shifted in his seat to study her frankly. "So tell me about this little old lady you've adopted."

"Lily Houghton. She's a spark. She wants to come back home and she'd be perfectly happy and safe there with a live-in companion, but her son wants to sell the place and put her in an assisted-living center. The farm's no doubt worth millions of dollars in development potential, and Lester has power of attorney. So unless we can prove that Lily still has all her marbles and she's physically capable of independent living, he could make things difficult. That's why I thought Elsa might be a good person to have on our side."

"You'll need a good lawyer, too, if push comes to shove," Matt said.

"I know. I hate the thought of it, but you're right."

"So am I staying at this rustic farm with you?"

"Of course. There are four bedrooms. Three over the main house, one over the ell. One bathroom, unless you don't mind using the backhouse."

"Backhouse." Matt took pause. "Is that what I think it is?"

"Primitive, but not too very long ago we all used them, to no ill effect."

"Annie, does this place have electricity?" He held up his hand on the tail end of the question. "Wait. I'm not sure I really want to know the answer to that, but I'm beginning to feel that maybe I shouldn't have packed that electric razor.''

JOE STORY, the lobsterman, looked quite different dressed in a T-shirt, blue jeans and sneakers. He was wearing a Boston Red Sox baseball cap and shepherding five young people toward the end of the town landing, where several small sunfish sailboats were tethered.

"Now, this stick here is called the tiller and it controls the rudder,'' Annie heard him drawling in a broad flat twang as she led Matt down the steep ramp. "When you're seated in the stern, the tiller will be in your right hand. Push it away from you and the boat'll turn in the opposite d'rection, to the left. Pull it toward you and the boat'll turn to the right. Right and left have different words when you're speakin' boat language. Any of you know what they might be?''

Five somber young faces stared blankly. Annie came to a stop at the end of the wharf and raised her hand. Joe nodded to her. "Port and starboard,'' Annie said primly.

"Yes, ma'am, them's the words, but which is which?''

Annie grinned. "I've no idea.''

"Port is left. Remember it this way. The word 'left' has four letters. So does the word 'port.' Starboard has a whole lot more letters. Starboard is right. Right is a longer word than left, was you to spell it out. Got it?''

Everyone nodded. Port and starboard were committed to memory.

Joe stepped toward her. He glanced at Matt, then back at Annie. "I may never have gotten off the island," he said, without the least little bit of down east accent, "but I doubt this is your daughter."

Annie laughed. "Joe, this is Matt Brink, a friend of mine visiting from New York. Sally couldn't make it today. I didn't know how many you could take in your class or the minimum age."

"Well, your friend meets the age requirement, if the two of you don't mind sharing one of the sail-boats."

"Count me out," Matt said. "I'm not getting into one of those tiny boats."

"Actually, a friend of mine might be bringing his daughter," Annie said, "but she's only five years old."

"Ten's the minimum age," Joe said. "Sorry. It's an insurance thing."

"Dr. Annie!" a young voice cried from the parking area. Moments later Amanda was racing down the ramp. "Am I too late?"

"No, honey, you're not," Annie said, sweeping her into her arms. "But Joe says you're too young to go sailing. I'm sorry your dad had to drive you all this way for nothing."

"Nothing?" a voice at her elbow said. Jake stood with his thumbs hooked in the rear pockets of his jeans and gave her an appreciative up-and-down that made her blush. "I wouldn't exactly call seeing you nothing. Besides, I'm old enough to go sailing with you, if you're shopping for a partner, and your friend can watch Amanda."

"Hello," Matt said at Annie's other elbow, thrust-ing out his hand. "I'm Matt Brink. I believe we met at the hospital."

"Yeah, I remember you," Jake said with a calculating squint, shaking his hand briefly. "Seemed like there was always some sort of emergency in progress when you were around."

"It's always tense when someone's heart stops beating," Matt said stiffly. "I'm surprised you remember any of that."

"Oh, sure. I was floating above my body in this most amazing out-of-body experience, watching you panic, over and over again."

"Gentlemen," Annie interrupted, "since sailing is out, perhaps we could find some other diversion that doesn't involve two grown men acting foolish?"

"There's a recital this afternoon up at the church," Joe suggested. "The Ladies Aid Society is putting on a play to raise money for the library."

"That sounds good," Annie said.

"And, ma'am, if you like, I could help you get the ketch out of the boathouse and give you a lesson right there at Lily's place. Wouldn't take long to teach you the fundamentals. I have this coming Sunday afternoon free."

Annie smiled. It seemed fitting that she should be taught to sail the *Dash* by the man who had helped build her. "Thank you, Joe," she said. "That would be lovely." And then to Amanda she said, "What do you think? Want to see a play?"

"What's a play?" Amanda asked. As Annie began to explain, she led the little girl by the hand up the ramp toward the place where she'd parked. She could hear voices and the trundling footsteps of Matt Brink and Jake Macpherson behind her and wondered what they were discussing.

"Dr. Annie?" Amanda tugged on her hand. "Didn't you hear me?"

"What's that?" Annie stopped and looked down at Amanda's bright countenance.

"I said," Amanda began, and then lowered her voice to a whisper, "he likes you, doesn't he?" She glanced at her father and Matt.

"Who?" Annie whispered.

"That man. He likes you the way my father likes you."

Annie straightened, her heart skipping a beat. She tightened her hand on Amanda's and led the little girl briskly up the ramp to increase the distance between them and the men. "You think your father likes me?" she asked, bending close as they walked side by side.

Amanda, tripping along beside her, nodded vigorously. "A whole lot. And so does that other man."

THE PLAY was called *The Lobsterman's Daughter* and it was about a girl torn between leaving the island of her birth to go to college or staying and marrying the boy she loved and becoming a lobsterman's wife. It was a comedy of sorts, and was thoroughly enjoyed by everyone. Afterward, they went for ice cream at the little parlor on Main Street. They sat outside at a picnic table in the warm, buoyant air of an early July evening.

Jake finished off the last of his sugar cone and eyed Matt with an inscrutable expression. Annie was beginning to feel uneasy about what he might be about to say when a wail from Amanda galvanized them. Jake looked at the blob of ice cream that had toppled from Amanda's cone onto the warm pavement.

"It's okay, Pinch," he said standing. "I'll get you another."

"Pinch?" Matt said. "That's quite a nickname. How'd you come by it?"

Amanda raised her eyes from her ice cream melting on the asphalt and looked after her father who was walking toward the take-out window. "Daddy just calls me that. He says when I was little, I was no bigger than a pinch. And he said I pinched him, too."

"Well, I've never heard a nickname like that," Matt said.

"Mommy says it's a silly name, but I like it."

"I do, too," Annie said. "Your father loves you very much."

"I love him, too," Amanda said. "Do you love him, Dr. Annie?"

Annie froze, allowing ice cream to melt down the cone and onto her fingers. "I think your father's a very special man, Amanda," she said when she found the words to respond.

Matt was wiping his hands on a paper napkin. He rolled the napkin up into a tiny ball and tossed it into the waste receptacle. "Yeah," he said sarcastically. "He's special, all right."

"Matt," Annie admonished.

Jake returned, handed Amanda a fresh ice-cream cone, and grinned at Annie. "They didn't charge me," he said. "That'd never happen in the city."

"Oh, I don't know," Matt said. "It's not like New Yorkers don't have a heart."

"Oh, I *do* know," Jake said.

"I think it's time we called it a day," Annie interrupted. "And a very pleasant one, I might add."

"Indeed," Matt muttered.

"Hey, Pinch." Jake tweaked his daughter's pigtail. "Think you caught any mice today?"

Amanda licked her ice-cream cone studiously. "Yes," she said. "The little one. The baby."

"Ah." Jake nodded. "The last of the Mohicans. I guess we'd better get back so we can turn it out with the rest of its family. Don't want it to spend the night alone."

Amanda shook her head. "No, that wouldn't be good. We'd better go, Daddy. 'Bye, Dr. Annie. 'Bye Dr. Matt. I hope you and Dr. Annie have a good visit, but I hope you don't stay too long."

Jake reached for his daughter's hand and gave Annie an apologetic grin. "See you," he said. He nodded to Matt. "C'mon, Pinch, let's hit the road."

Annie watched the two of them walk off hand in hand and felt a lonely pang. She gave herself a mental shake. What was the matter with her? Why did watching Jake Macpherson walk away in that easy saunter of his trigger a lonely ache deep down inside?

ANNIE TREATED MATT to a lobster dinner at the wharf before they headed home, and it was getting dark when finally she drove down the long private road. The headlights swept across the farmhouse yard and came to rest upon the kitchen door. Annie jumped out of the vehicle, ran up the porch steps, unlocked the door, stood aside while Rebel exited, and went into the kitchen to light the oil lamps. Matt followed her and stood watching, hands shoved in his jacket pockets, as she moved with easy familiarity around the room. "You like this sort of life, don't you?" he asked suddenly after she had pumped water to refill Rebel's water bowl.

"Pardon?" she said, pausing in the act of lifting

the water bowl out of the sink to set it back on the floor.

"You like living like this, primitive and low tech."

Annie smiled. "I grew up this way, Matt. To me, it's comforting."

"A lot more work, though."

"Yes, but it's *comforting* work." Annie set the water bowl on the floor and prepared Rebel's supper. As soon as she'd finished mixing it, she heard the scratch at the kitchen door and opened it. Rebel trotted in, looking expectantly at the dish she held in her hand. She put it beside the water bowl, and the skinny little collie wolfed it down. "Poor thing, he's still rundown from his long journey home." She glanced up at him. "You must be rundown, too. Long day, and it's getting late. Come on. I'll show you where you'll be sleeping."

Matt retrieved his duffel bag and followed her up the steep, narrow kitchen stairs to the bedroom directly overhead. Annie lit the oil lamp on the bedside table and the warm glow gave the little room a cozy, homey look.

"Your window looks out over the harbor," she said, raising the dormer sash and letting a stream of cool, salty air into the warm room. "Wait till you see the sunrise, Matt. You won't believe how beautiful the mornings are, even when it's foggy."

He dropped his duffel to the floor and sat on the edge of the bed. "I'll take your word for it," he said glumly. "In case I sleep in."

She gave him a puzzled smile, bade him good-night and left, closing the door gently behind her. Matt flopped back onto the bed with a heartfelt moan. One week. He had just one week to win Annie's heart

away from Jake Macpherson and to convince her to
return to New York City, because the way she was
behaving, she was going to marry the cop and live
out the rest of her life in the boonies.

CHAPTER NINE

LILY HOUGHTON took the extensive physical and psychological exams, which lasted the better part of the day, like a trooper. Elsa, having completed the tests, was heading back to the Bangor airport to catch a late flight to New York. Annie thanked her profusely.

"Not at all," Elsa said, climbing into her rental car in the nursing home parking lot. "I can see why you're on her side. She's a great lady. I'll get my report to you within the week."

When Annie went to say goodbye to Lily, the older woman patted her hand. "Don't look so worried, dear. I'll be just fine."

"I know you will," Annie said. "But it was a long day for you. I'll have the staff bring your dinner to your room if you like."

"Supper," Lily corrected. "In Maine, dinner is the noon meal. Supper is served at precisely five o'clock."

Annie smiled and squeezed the elderly woman's hands gently in her own. "Supper, then. Are you hungry?"

"Famished. I could eat a horse, or half a hundred Leticia lobsters, if I should ever be so lucky."

They laughed together and then hugged impulsively. "I'll have them fix you something. You did great today. It'll take a week or so for all the results to be compiled.''

"No matter what that doctor says, my son will fight this," Lily said matter-of-factly. "He has his mind made up about how things will be."

"The question is, are you prepared to fight *him?*" Annie said.

Lily hesitated. "I know he means well, but I have rights, too, even if I am an old lady."

"Then we'll do our best to get you back home. But, Lily, Lester's right about not wanting you to live there alone. When I leave, you'll need to have live-in help. Will you agree to that?"

Lily hesitated again before giving a reluctant nod. "All right."

Matt was waiting patiently in the parking lot. He started the engine as Annie climbed into the passenger seat and fastened her seat belt. "How's she doing?" he said, backing out of the parking space and turning onto the road.

"Lily's a rock," Annie said, letting her head fall back against the headrest. "She has more stamina than I do. But I'm afraid that if she loses the farm, she won't last long."

JAKE SLOUCHED inside the phone booth and unfolded the piece of paper he'd pulled out of his jeans' pocket. The telephone number had been scrawled in his own untidy hand, but miracle of miracles, he could read it. He glanced up to where he'd parked his vehicle. Amanda met his eyes through the windshield and grinned at him, giving him a rakish thumbs-up.

Jake fed the coin into the phone, waited for the dial tone and dialed. He heard a series of clicks and then the ringing at the other end of the line. Having stacked a pile of quarters neatly on the metal shelf in advance of dialing, he picked the first one up. "Please answer," he said softly into the receiver. "Pick up the phone, Annie. Pick it up." He let it ring and ring and ring. He glanced back at Amanda, and she waved encouragingly.

"Hello?"

Relief flooded through him, weakening his knees. "Damn, I miss you, woman," he said.

"Jake? I just got home..." She sounded out of breath. "You okay? Everything all right? Amanda...?"

"Fine," he said. "I just... Well, I finished washing the supper dishes and..."

"Supper dishes. Ah, yes, today I learned that dinner and supper are two totally different things here in Maine," Annie said in a voice full of humor.

"Anyhow," Jake continued lamely, "I finished the dishes and then Pinch said, 'Why don't you just call her up, Daddy?' but because my cell phone doesn't work at the cabin, we drove into town and now I'm..."

"Calling me," Annie said. Her voice held a warm smile. He could picture her sitting on the stool in the kitchen, glossy hair tousled, her cheeks warmed by the sun.

"Calling you," he said.

"I miss you, too," she said, lowering her voice several notches as if someone else might be listening.

"Is Matt still there?"

"Yes."

"Keep your bedroom door locked at night," he said. Her resulting laughter was full of all kinds of things he couldn't fathom. "And keep Rebel with you," he added.

"Think that old dog would defend me?"

"I think after a few days in your company, that old dog would die for you. I know I would."

"I hope you never do," she said, the mirth leaving her voice.

"When can I see you again?"

He heard her take a deep breath. "I have a sailing lesson here at the farm on Sunday," she said. "You could bring Amanda..."

"Sunday? That's three days from now. I'll never last that long. I'm in agony now."

"My daughter's coming back to the farm tomorrow. Trudy's not doing very well, and Sally wants to stay with me until after the baby's surgery. Matt's here for the week, but Dr. Morrow is flying back to the city even as we speak. She spent most of the day with Lily and before she left she told me Lily is as capable of independent thought and logical actions as you or I. Dr. Morrow's one of the finest geriatric doctors in the nation and her report will go a long way toward getting Lily back home again even if Lester puts up a fight, which I'm hoping he won't."

Jake slumped against the phone booth wall. Matt Brink was there with her in that farmhouse for a whole week. It was ludicrous to think that he stood a chance against that big-city doctor when it came to winning Annie's heart. Time to wake up and get real. Keep what little dignity he still had. "You're lucky to have such good connections. Well, I guess seeing you will have to wait. Sounds like you're pretty busy entertaining."

"Jake, that doesn't mean—"

"Listen," he interrupted. "Amanda's waving at me like she has to pee. Gotta go, Doc. Good luck with Lily. She's one hell of a lady."

He hung up before Annie could respond, gently replacing the phone in its cradle and gazing out to where Amanda watched him from the passenger seat, her face beaming with anticipation.

"Did you talk to her, Daddy?" she said as Jake levered himself back behind the wheel.

"I sure did, Pinch. She's just fine."

"Was she glad to talk to you?"

"She sounded happy."

"Does she love you, Daddy?"

Jake quelled the surprise at his young daughter's words. "She's a very caring kind of person, Pinch," he said, reaching out a hand to smooth the hair back from Amanda's forehead. "She cares a great deal about everyone."

Amanda gazed up at him with wide serious eyes and then shook her head. "No, Daddy. She cares about some people a whole lot more than others. I think Dr. Annie *loves* you. I really think she does."

"ABOUT THAT PICNIC you promised me for getting Elsa here so quick," Matt said to Annie the following morning over an early cup of coffee. They were sitting on the porch, watching the lobster boats head out of the harbor.

"Did I mention a picnic?"

"Actually you said we'd charter a sailboat and have a lobster bake in some private cove. Remember?"

"Ah, yes. The lobster bake. Well, Matt, the thing is…"

"I'm not particular. If you'd rather have a hamburger, that's fine with me."

Annie smiled apologetically. "Sally's coming back today. Her father's dropping her off sometime this afternoon."

"We could have the picnic down on the stone wharf. Charter the boat some other time." He looked at her hopefully. "Annie, we only have a few days together…"

"And we'll have fun, just like I promised. There are some great antique shops in the village, and we can have our lobster bake at the town dock. They cook the lobsters right there, fresh out of the ocean. We'll be back in time for Sally's arrival…"

"But…"

She heard the phone ring in the kitchen and a look of relief swept across her face even as she ran to pick it up. Matt trailed dejectedly after her and poured himself another cup of coffee, not meaning to eavesdrop, but unable to ignore the sudden gasp and the cry of outrage. He glanced at her. She stood rigidly, one hand gripping the phone to her ear, the other palm pressed against her forehead.

"But I signed the rental agreement for the entire summer and Lester Houghton signed that paper, too."

There was a long pause while someone on the other end spoke. Then her words tumbled out in a rush of anger. "Oh, Jim, that just can't happen. Lily belongs here. This is her home. I'll fight this. I'll hire a lawyer. And I'd like to see that legal piece of paper he sent you. He has one hell of a nerve to think he can bring prospective clients out to view this place while I'm renting it, and then sell it right out from under Lily against her wishes!"

After she hung up, she paced to the kitchen door and looked out at the harbor, her face flushed with anger.

"Lily's son?" Matt guessed.

"He's listed the farm with a Boston realty group and the agent wants to bring several prospective buyers to view it this week."

"Does he have the right to do that?"

"No. And I intend to stop him, one way or the other."

Matt had never seen Annie in a true fury before, but she was close to it now. He stood back in deference to her anger as she paced the confines of the kitchen and couldn't help but feel a twinge of pity for Lily's son.

Lester Houghton had no idea what he was up against when he took on Annie Crawford.

"DADDY," Amanda said. He could hear her voice clearly but all he could see of her were her bare toes. Covered with dirt and pine duff, they looked thoroughly woodsy.

"What is it, Pinch?" he asked, wriggling under the cabin. He adjusted the flashlight by propping it on a stick of firewood.

"I'm hungry."

"Me, too. What's for lunch?"

"You said we were going to catch a fish for lunch. Remember?"

"I sure do, and instead I've spent most of the morning under the cabin fiddling with this propane line. But, Pinch," he added, "be honest. If you caught a fish, would you eat it?"

Long pause. "I don't know. I've never caught one before."

"We should have gone out at dawn to fish. We'll do that tomorrow morning. Or maybe we can fish tonight, but that still leaves us with a lunch dilemma, doesn't it?" He took the section of tubing that he'd cut and tossed it out beside her bare feet. "That's why the refrigerator and the stove don't work," he said. "Look at that gas valve. It must have come across on the *Mayflower,* and why they put it so far under the cabin is beyond me. Give me a couple more minutes and I'll have it fixed up as good as new."

"Daddy, can we go see Dr. Annie today?"

"I don't know, honey. She has a lot of company right now." Jake felt a surge of anxiety as he adjusted the flashlight on the piece of wood to illuminate the end of the tubing. He worked for a few seconds, then said, "There. Now I'll turn on the gas and test this job with a little soapy water."

Amanda crouched to peer beneath the cabin. "Why do you need soapy water?"

"If there's a leak, the soapy water bubbles up and tells you. If it doesn't bubble, there's no leak."

"If you fixed it, Daddy, there won't be a leak," Amanda said.

"Let's hope so," Jake said, squirming out from under the cabin. He pushed to his feet and rumpled her hair. "So. You fixin' lunch?"

"Sure," she said. "Sandwiches?"

"Go for it, Pinch."

"Then can we go visit Dr. Annie?"

He shook his head regretfully. "Not today. She's really busy."

He mixed up some dish soap in a cup of water,

turned on the propane at the tank, and crawled back under the cabin, daubing great quantities of the mix over the newly spliced copper tubing and shining the flashlight beam intently on the suspect couplings. He waited and watched. No bubbles. No leaks. He breathed a sigh of relief.

Dr. Annie. He wondered if she missed him half as much as he missed her. He scowled, thinking about Matt Brink and the two of them sleeping under the same roof. For all he knew, they shared the same apartment in New York City. In spite of their long conversations and their deepening feelings, much of Annie remained a mystery to him, an uncharted territory. She—

"Daddy!" Amanda shrieked his name at the top of her lungs and terror filled the word. He lunged up off the ground and bolted into the cabin. She was standing on top of an upended five-gallon bucket at the counter, loaf of bread, jars of peanut butter and jelly, plates, paper towels all strewn about. She held a big carving knife in one little hand and with one smooth movement he wrested it away. "Pinch, what the hell are you doing with that knife?"

"I'm bleeding, Daddy. That's my blood!" she wailed.

He uncurled her clenched fist, pried the tiny fingers back, saw the great gash in her palm and felt his gut tighten. "It's all right, sweetheart. It's just a little cut. Daddy'll clean and bandage it. You keep your eyes closed and let me take care of it, okay?"

"Daddy," she sobbed. "It hurts."

"I know, Pinch," he said, scooping her into the curve of his arm and pulling the first-aid kit down from the shelf. "But it's only a little cut. And it's a long way from your heart."

Five minutes later he was driving like a mad man down the dirt road, bouncing wildly through potholes, swerving to avoid rocks and ruts, while Amanda sat with tears streaming down her cheeks. Her hand was cradled in her lap and swathed in reams of red-stained gauze pads and a clean kitchen towel. Oh, God, he thought, will she lose the use of her fingers? Why had he let her make lunch? His fault. This was all his fault. Amanda was going to be crippled for life and it was *all his fault!*

"WILL HER HAND be all right?" Jake asked the physician at the clinic in Danfield who had stitched the cut. Amanda had been so brave, allowing the elderly doctor at the clinic to flush the wound, examine it, stitch it closed and wrap it in sterile bandaging.

The doctor nodded and pushed his glasses back up on his nose. "Oh, sure. She'll be right as rain. Keep it dry for a couple of days, then you'll need to change the dressing. Bring her back in a week for me to have a look, unless you notice anything unusual in the meantime."

"Unusual?" Jake said, picking Amanda up off the examining table and holding her in his arms. "What do you mean?"

"Any signs of infection, abnormal swelling, extreme pain, numbness or inability to move her fingers." He reached out and gave Amanda's pigtail a gentle tug. "Be a good girl," he said. "And no frog-catching for a while."

Amanda nodded gravely and cuddled close to her father. When they were out in Jake's truck she allowed her father to buckle her in and then said, "Daddy, can we please go see Dr. Annie?"

"I think we should try to call your mom. She'll want to know about this."

Amanda forgot her hand for a moment and glanced up at him as he pulled out of the clinic parking lot. "We just talked to her yesterday."

"We promised we'd call every day, remember? Right now's probably a good time to catch her."

"I want to see Dr. Annie," Amanda said tearfully.

Jake faced forward, puzzled by his daughter's response. "She's busy, Pinch. She has a full house. We can't just drive out there uninvited."

"She won't mind, I know she won't. My hand hurts."

"I know it does, honey. Maybe we should just go back to the cabin. We can call your mom tomorrow, first thing..."

"But, Daddy, my hand *hurts,*" she whimpered.

Jake inhaled a deep, even breath as he approached the intersection at U.S. Route 1 and hesitated only briefly before turning toward Blue Harbor.

CHAPTER TEN

RYAN ARRIVED at the farm just before lunch, and Sally leaped from her father's car, raced up the porch steps with Nelly at her heels to give her mother a big hug. "Hey," Annie said, startled by this rare display of affection. "You okay?" She smoothed a stray wisp of hair from her daughter's flushed forehead.

"Oh, Mom," Sally said, a world of pathos in those two quiet words, and then Annie heard the car door slam and glanced up as her ex-husband approached the foot of the porch steps. She caught a glimpse of Trudy's pale face in the passenger's seat and lifted her hand in a wave to which there was no response. Ryan looked exhausted. He paused at the bottom of the steps.

"Annie," he said. "Thanks for taking Sally. Things'll be a lot better after the baby's operation, but right now…"

Annie nodded. "Is there anything I can do to help?"

For a moment Annie thought Ryan might break down, but his mouth firmed and he shook his head. "The waiting's the worst part."

"I know," Annie said. "We'll keep good thoughts and take it day by day. Have you had lunch? We're having a cold picnic. Deviled eggs, potato salad…"

Ryan looked grateful. "That sounds good."

"Bring Trudy in." *Poor thing, she needs some mothering herself. Though I'm hardly the one who should be providing it,* Annie thought as Ryan turned to get his young wife from the vehicle.

Matt had obviously overheard the conversation from inside the kitchen and had set three more places at the kitchen table. "We could eat outside," he said as they filed in, "but it's clouding over. It looks like it might rain."

Annie guided Trudy into the kitchen and into the closest chair. Trudy's complexion was pasty, she wore no makeup and her hair was mussed. "Sit here," Annie said gently. "I'll get you a glass of iced tea. Do you like lemon?" Trudy's eyes flickered at the question, coming to life briefly and meeting Annie's. She made no verbal response, but Annie straightened and gently squeezed Trudy's shoulder.

"Mom?" Sally whispered in her ear as Annie prepared the light lunch. "I'm so glad to be back, even if this is a boring place."

"HEY, PINCH," Jake said as they drove through Danfield en route to Blue Harbor. "How's this for an idea. Let's pick up Lily and bring her with us. That way we'll be killing two birds with one stone." Surely with Lily in tow, Annie would look more favorably upon their unannounced visit.

Amanda gave him a puzzled look. "Why would we want to kill two birds, Daddy?"

"It's just an expression of speech," Jake explained. "It means that we'd be accomplishing two things at the same time. We'd get to see Annie and Lily would get to spend some time at home with her dog."

"Oh," Amanda said, nodding her understanding

and wiping her wet cheeks on the back of her arm.
"All right. Let's kill 'em, then."

Jake stopped at the grocery store first to pick up a
cardboard box full of offerings. "Can't visit Dr. Annie without bringing something," he told his daughter. This time he picked out several bottles of nice
wine, a pound of fresh-ground Blue Mountain coffee,
an assortment of deli meats and cheeses, two fresh
loaves of crusty peasant bread and a box of dog biscuits. He also bought an Italian sandwich and two
cartons of chocolate milk, which he and Amanda
shared on the way to the nursing home.

Lily was surprised to see them and more than willing to take a spur-of-the-moment drive out to the
farm. By 3:00 p.m. the tires of Jake's truck were
crunching down the long gravel road that led to the
old cape overlooking the Atlantic. As they approached the farm Jake was surprised and a little dismayed to see that Annie had more company than he'd
expected. A strange vehicle with a Maine license
plate was parked alongside Annie's. Annie must have
heard their approach. She was watching from the
porch, a welcoming smile on her face.

"Sorry about dropping in unannounced," Jake
apologized as he guided Lily up the steps to greet the
old border collie waiting at the top. "But we just
happened to be out for an afternoon drive and I
thought Rebel might like a chance to say hello to
Lily."

Annie's smile broadened with just a hint of something he couldn't quite read. "That was a very good
idea, Jake." Then she froze, smile fading. "Amanda,
what on earth happened to your hand?"

Amanda held up her arm to exhibit her injured

hand, impressively swathed in fresh white bandaging. "I cut myself on a *huge* knife," she said.

Annie caught Jake's eye, eyebrows raised.

"Huge," he conceded. "Big cut, too. Six stitches."

"But I didn't cry much, did I, Daddy?"

"No, Pinch, you were a brave girl."

"Sometimes it's not a bad thing to cry," Lily said as Annie settled her into her rocker on the porch. She smiled and squeezed Annie's hand in thanks. "We won't stay long, dear."

"As far as I'm concerned, you can stay the entire summer if you like," Annie said. "I'm so glad you came." She turned to the three people who had stepped out onto the porch. "I'd like to introduce my ex-husband, Ryan, and his wife Trudy. They dropped Sally off this afternoon. And you've already met Matt Brink."

Jake nodded at Matt, then shook Ryan Crawford's hand, sizing him up in one keen glance. Good-looking in a soft way. Soft hand. Soft body. Soft personality. Certainly no match for Annie's strength and passion. His new wife was half his age and looked as though she hadn't slept in weeks. Annie had told him about the premature baby, and it looked as though Ryan's wife would be a long time recovering from the stress of it all.

Lily sat with Rebel's head in her lap and gazed toward the open water. "The wind's making up out of the northeast." She took a deep, satisfied breath of salty air into her lungs. "I love a good storm, and there's no better place to watch them come in than right here."

"We'd better get going before it starts to rain,"

Ryan said, much to Jake's relief. While he went to fetch the supplies from his car, Ryan hugged his daughter and guided his young wife down the steps. They departed minutes before the rain arrived, and it came down hard, in wind-driven sheets that gusted and rattled against the roof and walls of the stalwart cape. Jake ran back up the steps and deposited the goodies on the kitchen counter, dripping rainwater and grinning at Annie's surprised expression.

"Just some stuff," he said, ignoring Matt's scowl.

"Why, thank you," Annie said, peering into the box. "Stuff is always nice, especially stuff like nice wines and gourmet foods."

The two girls were divvying dog biscuits between Nelly, who was cavorting around their feet, and Rebel, who sat with Lily out on the porch watching the storm come in. A sudden gust of wind slammed the screen door shut behind them and Jake said, "Maybe we'd better get going, too. I didn't know it was supposed to storm."

"Can't you stay for supper, at least? You only just got here and…" Annie looked up at him with an expression that made his heart race.

"He's right, Annie," Matt said, walking to the screen door. "Driving could get treacherous if they wait much longer. The weather forecast was predicting…" He stopped in midsentence and pushed open the screen door. "Hey, look at that boat. Think it could be in some kind of trouble? It's heading right for your dock."

MATT'S WORDS BROKE through Annie's thoughts and she tore her eyes from Jake's as they stared through the rain at the lobster boat that struggled through the

stiff chop and high winds to maneuver around to the
leeward side of the pier.

"That's Joe's boat," Lily said, leaning forward intently. "That's the *Glory B.*"

"Why would he be visiting now?" Annie said.

They watched as the figure of a man dabbed a loop
around a piling and jumped onto the pier. He raised
his arm in a vigorous wave and in unison they all
waved back as he moved toward the boathouse.

"There's all kinds of gear inside there," Lily said.
"Joe must need something."

"The door's locked," Annie said. "I'll get the
keys." She turned back inside, quickly donning her
raincoat and reaching for the bunch of keys hanging
on a coat hook beside the door, but a much larger
hand beat her to it. She glanced up at Jake and felt
her heart skip a beat.

"I'll go," he said.

"Jake, wait…" He ignored her protest and ran
down the porch steps bareheaded, no raincoat, trotting
through the wall of wind-driven rain with his head
turned and shoulder rounded against the lash of it.
"You'll get drenched," Annie finished lamely.

Matt stood at the edge of the porch, hands jammed
into his pockets, scowl furrowing his forehead. "He'll
be okay," he said. "It's just a little rain."

Annie watched Jake descend the long series of
steps that led down to the boathouse and the next
thing she knew she was off the porch and racing after
him. She ran, not caring that the wind tore the hood
of her raincoat or that she was getting soaked. Not
caring about anything at all except catching up with
Jake. She was breathless and laughing when she
gained the solid footing of the stone pier. The boat-

house door was ajar and she heard men's voices as she stepped inside.

"Must've been a freak wave," Joe was saying. "Knocked the old girl onto her side and blew out a sea cock. My pump quit and we started going down in the stern. I have a manual pump but, dammit, my shoulders're sore... Now, where'd Lily stash that oakum?"

"Can you get the pump going again?" Jake asked. He was staring at the shelves and hooks that held all kinds of boating paraphernalia.

"Tried," Joe said. "Couldn't." He reached for something. "Ah, got it."

"Can I help?" Annie said. Both men turned toward her; it was hard to read their expressions in the dim light.

"Know how to fix a bilge pump?" Joe asked.

"Nope," Annie admitted, "but I know how to bail." She snatched an empty pail and turned back into the rain. She could see immediately that water had risen above the bilge and was swamping the rear cockpit. The *Glory B* was in serious danger of sinking. She clambered aboard, dipped the bucket into the icy water and flung it over the side, bent again, flung again. After a few minutes she got into the rhythm and urgency of it and forgot everything else. There was just the immediacy of the moment and the need to save the *Glory B.*

Out of the corner of her eye she was aware of Joe and Jake working together, lifting something aside, some part of the boat, to get at the sturdy hull. She bent, dipped, flung. Bent, dipped, flung. But it seemed the water was coming in as fast as she could bail it out. She could see Jake operating a manual bilge pump, bending over and putting his upper body and the strength of his shoulders into the work of it while Joe was working in the flooded bilge.

It seemed to take a very long while, but in retrospect it probably wasn't more than fifteen minutes before Jake wrested the bucket out of her hand. "Enough, Annie," he said over the buffeting of the wind. "She'll be okay now."

She straightened, bracing her legs against the roll of the boat and the push of the wind against her. Jake's hand on her upper arm steadied her as she moved to the side of the boat and climbed onto the pier. Matt stood there, wrapped in a raincoat and clutching an umbrella, with which he attempted to shield her from the rain. She suppressed a giggle and had to bite her tongue to keep from pointing out that she was already soaked to the skin. He was trying so hard to be gallant. He took her arm and began to lead her back toward the steps.

It was the umbrella that proved Matt's undoing. He struggled valiantly against a particularly savage gust of wind and stumbled backward just before the big wire-braced hoop turned itself inside out. Jerked off balance, he released the umbrella and windmilled his arms wildly as he plunged backward into the dark, storm-tossed water.

Annie saw his head bob up and his hand reach desperately out of the water as if he expected her to simply reach down and pull him out. "Matt, swim to shore!" she shouted, gesturing. His face turned toward her as he thrashed, eyes wide and full of panic, then he went under again.

"*Jake!*" She'd never screamed so loud in her life. "*Jake!*" She kept her eyes riveted on the place where

Matt had disappeared, till she felt a hand grab her shoulder. "Matt fell in, he can't swim!" Jake, a dark blur beside her, plunged into the icy water. Annie watched him tread water for a few seconds before he disappeared beneath the turbulent surface.

Joe jumped from the boat to the pier and began stripping out of his rubber gear, but before he could get his boots off, two heads bobbed up side by side. Jake had Matt in a lifesaver's hold and was making for shore. Though the distance was only about twenty feet, the going was rough with the waves pushing the two of them repeatedly against the pier.

Annie and Joe ran to meet them, Joe sliding down the slick rocks and wading into the churning water up to his knees. He reached for Matt's arm, and together the two men dragged Matt ashore and deposited him, retching and coughing, on the rocky ledge. Annie rolled him onto his side and crouched over him.

"Matt, can you hear me?" He heaved and gagged up another mouthful of seawater. "You're going to be fine. Keep coughing. We'll get you up to the house and out of these wet clothes."

By the time they reached the farmhouse, Lily had kindled a fire in the stove to warm the kitchen. She held the porch door open as they came inside with a gust of rain and slammed it shut behind them. "B'God," she said, "but don't you look like a bunch of drowned rats."

"Daddy," Amanda said as Jake squelched into the kitchen, supporting one side of the coughing Matt. "Me'n Sally saw you jump in the water. Did you go swimming?"

"Yup," Jake said, helping to lower Matt into a chair.

"Was it cold?"

Jake stepped back and let Annie tend to Matt, turning to his daughter and catching Lily's sharp eye as he did. "Yup."

"Stand over by the stove and strip out of those wet clothes," Lily ordered him. "You girls go on upstairs for a while till we get the menfolk taken care of. Now," she said to Jake. "Off with those wet things."

Jake hesitated, glancing at Annie, but she was focused entirely on Matt, unbuttoning and stripping off his shirt while he coughed and gagged, then doing the same with his undershirt. With a dry towel she began briskly rubbing his almost-blue skin. Lily took Jake firmly by the arm and nodded to the pantry door. "Get shed of those wet clothes, young man, unless you want to get a good case of the grippe."

Jake allowed himself to be herded toward the pantry. "I don't have any spare clothes," he protested as Lily pushed him inside, handed him a towel and shut the door. "And what's the grippe?"

"That's something you don't ever want to get," he heard Lily say. "And don't worry, I'll find you something warm and dry to wear."

By this time Jake realized the futility of arguing with Lily Houghton. He undressed and toweled himself dry. His skin was the same color as Matt's and bristling with goose bumps. Annie was fussing over Matt as if he were on the verge of kicking the bucket. Jake couldn't suppress the surge of jealousy. He wanted Annie to be fussing over him, trying to warm him up. He could think of a few ways she might do that. More than a few.

The tap on the pantry door made him jump. "I have some things for you," Lily said. "I'll pass them through." He opened the door a crack and took the bundle of clothes from her, mumbling his thanks. They must have belonged Lily's husband. The pants were green melton wool, old-fashioned and unlined. Scratchy. Huge around the waist, but she'd provided a belt. There was a thick, soft red-and-black buffalo plaid flannel shirt, also huge. Thick wool socks that had been neatly darned in both heels. He pulled on the dry clothing, tightened the belt to the last notch, and stepped out of the pantry with his armload of wet garments.

Lily had strung a line behind the cookstove and he pegged them onto it. Annie was still hovering over Matt, who was wrapped in a blanket and shivering miserably in front of the open oven door. His coughing and retching had diminished, and when Jake stepped into the room he glanced up and said gruffly, "Thanks. I owe you one."

"I'd tell you it was my pleasure, but I'd be lying," Jake admitted. "That water was just too damned cold."

"That's about as toasty as it ever gets," Joe said.

Annie finished toweling Matt's hair and hung the towel over the line Lily had rigged. She took a deep breath and ran her fingers through her own damp curls. "I think we could all use a cup of hot tea. Lily, you sit down and I'll fix it. Girls?" she called up the back stairs. "It's all right. You can come down now."

ANNIE WAS EXHAUSTED. Just lifting the teakettle was an enormous effort. She filled the mugs. Tea for the adults, hot cocoa for the girls. Outside the kitchen windows the storm howled in strengthening fury, the wind moaned through cracks in the window frames and rain lashed against the glass panes. A loose piece of metal roofing rattled incessantly, and the deep rumbling vibration of waves against the ledge intensified.

It felt like midnight, though it was only 6:00 p.m. Matt had opted to go up to his room. After Annie had distributed the tea and cocoa around the table, she carried a mug up to him and sat for a moment on the edge of his bed. "You're looking much better." She smiled. "I think you'll live."

He reached for her hand and gave it a grateful squeeze. "Thanks, Annie. I'm sorry to have caused so much trouble."

"I'm sure you didn't fall in on purpose. Drink your tea. I'll bring you up a plate of food a little later." She rose to her feet. "Tomorrow, I'd like to get you checked out at the hospital in Ellsworth, just to make sure your lungs are clear."

"You already listened to them and said they were fine."

"I'd like a second opinion."

"Your opinion's the only one that matters to me."

"Tomorrow. Hospital. Ellsworth," she said, then descended the narrow steep stairs into the kitchen. Caught Jake's eyes across the room and felt her cheeks warm. She sank into her chair at the table and pulled her mug of tea toward her. "I'll give you a ride home in a few minutes, Joe," she said, blowing across the surface of the hot tea, studying the steam to keep her eyes in a safe place.

"I'll do it," Jake offered. "We have to be leaving pretty quick if we don't want to be driving in this weather after dark. Besides, you look exhausted."

Annie raised her eyes briefly to his. "I am," she admitted. "Too much excitement for one day. I used to thrive on it, but now I think I'm ready for bed."

"You and me both," he said, and she read something in the clear intensity of his gaze that made her heartbeat quicken as she watched him push out of his chair. "Pinch? You about finished with that cocoa? We have to take Lily and Joe home. People will worry about them if they don't show up pretty soon."

Amanda sighed. She stood and gave the puppy a farewell hug. "I wish we could stay, Nelly," she whispered. "I wish we could."

"I'll call the nursing home and tell them you're going to be a little late," Annie said.

A few minutes later Annie was standing beside Sally on the porch, watching them drive away in Jake's truck. "Jake was so brave," Sally said, crossing her arms in front of her and frowning thoughtfully. "Jumping into the water to save Matt. That was a brave thing to do."

IF THE TREE HAD FALLEN just seconds later, it might very well have crushed Jake's truck and all its occupants. Instead it missed by less than six feet. Amanda cried out as he slammed on the brakes, and in the breathless aftermath of the near-miss Lily's voice calmly said, "Oh, dear. One of my big old pines. What a shame."

They were half a mile from the main road, half a mile from the old farmhouse, and a giant two-hundred-year-old pine lay between them and civilization. "Well," Joe said. "Maybe there's a chain saw back at the farm."

"Maybe," Lily said. "Ruel had all sorts of tools,

and I haven't parted with any. That doesn't mean things haven't disappeared over the years. I don't recall seeing a chain saw in a dog's age, but it could be down in the boathouse..."

"You can turn around now, Daddy," Amanda said. "I bet Dr. Annie will be glad to see you again."

Jake heard Lily's chuckle and could only guess what Joe thought. He turned the truck around. "We'll go back and find us a chain saw."

"It'll have to have a mighty long bar to cut through that pine," Joe said.

"Oh, yes," Lily stated proudly. "Some of the biggest pines in Maine are on this land. There's one in this grove that falls just shy of the state record of an eighteen-foot circumference."

"That's a big tree," Jake agreed.

ANNIE HAD LIT the lamps in the kitchen and the warm light glowed welcomingly through the gathering gloom as they neared the house. The kitchen door swung open and Jake couldn't help grinning like a fool at the sight of her. "We're back."

Annie helped Lily up the porch steps into the kitchen while listening to Amanda's excited account of the big pine falling. She reached for the flashlight and her raincoat. "I'll go see if there's a chain saw down in the boathouse."

Jake was beside her in the space of one heartbeat. "I'll go with you," he said.

Lily made him wear an old oilcloth slicker of Ruel's that snapped and billowed around him at the whim of the wind, but he held Annie's hand to steady her as they climbed down to the stone pier. He was still holding her hand when they stepped inside the boathouse. She panned the flashlight around the interior and he promptly took it out of her hand and switched it off.

"Good God, woman," he growled. "Are you really all that anxious to find a chain saw?"

He couldn't see her face in the darkness but he could picture the sweet curve of her cheek, the damp tangle of her hair, her fine, clear eyes and her white teeth flashing as she smiled. He could hear the smile in her voice as she squeezed his hand.

"What chain saw?" she said.

It was dark in the boathouse, but Jake knew exactly where Annie stood. He placed his lips on hers in a tentative, questing insinuation that rapidly progressed into a passionate hard kiss that left them both breathless and trembling.

"Jake…" Annie gasped, her knees buckling so that he dropped the flashlight and caught her against him, her warm breath fluttering against his neck. "Jake…"

Had he ever felt quite like this before? He didn't think so. Her hands were moving, searching, asking mute questions as her mouth moved beneath his, opening to him, inviting…

Then they were on the floor. She was kneeling above him, unbuckling the leather belt that held up the pair of huge pants. He was stripping off her dripping raincoat, fumbling to undo her blue denim shirt, cursing the buttons even as she cursed the zipper on the wool pants. He was sliding his hands against the silken warmth of her skin while she struggled futilely with Ruel's old-fashioned pants…

"Annie…" he whispered hoarsely over the roar of wind and the rhythmic crash of waves, pulling her down on top of him. Her hands gave up on the stubborn zipper and moved upward, as they kissed, pulling him closer until finally they both came up for air.

"Oh, Jake..." she gasped, moving against him.

"Annie, tell me something before I go crazy. Is there anything between you and Matt?"

Her body went rigid, then she wrenched out of his embrace. "How could you possibly ask me that?"

He caught her arms, pulled her back down against him. "I'm sorry. I can't help it. I have to know."

"Matt and I are good friends," she replied in a rapid pant. "We've worked together for a long time..."

"But were you... I mean, did you ever...?"

"No! I'm not in love with Matt. There's never been that kind of relationship, nothing even close to the way I feel when you..." She uttered a sudden cry that resonated with frustration. "Oh, let go of me! If I have to explain how I feel about you then obviously we're not on the same track." She struggled to free herself.

"I'm crazy about you, Annie," he said, holding her firmly in spite of her plea. "That's the track I'm on, and it's killing me. I can't stand being so close and not being able to touch you, not being able to make love to you..." She ceased struggling and held still for a very long moment. "Kiss me once more, Annie," he pleaded in desperation. "Just one more time. Give me hope."

He felt her soften in his arms. "Oh, Jake," she said in a voice barely heard above the wind and waves. And then she bent over him, melted against him, kissed him tenderly. Traced her thumbs along the edges of his cheekbones. Along the outline of his lower lip. Kissed him again as he ran his hands inside her shirt, unfastened her bra, slid his palms to cup the warmth and weight of her breasts while she moaned into his mouth and moved against him.

"H'lo?" a voice hailed from the darkness beyond the boathouse. Joe was coming to check on the chain saw.

"Ohmigod," Annie gasped, jerking back and away, her fingers frantically buttoning her shirt. Jake lay flat on the floor and stifled a moan of pure agony.

"Annie? Jake? You in here?"

Joe's flashlight bobbed as he approached the boathouse door just as Annie scrambled to her feet, snatching up her discarded raincoat. "We're in here Joe…Jake tripped over something, he fell…lost the flashlight…" she gasped, wrapping the raincoat around herself, "but it's here somewhere… Oh, there it is…" She pounced to retrieve it, switched it on and played the beam wildly on the wall, the roof, and then on Joe as he came into the boathouse.

Joe was carrying his own flashlight and he stood just inside the door, taking in the flushed faces, the disheveled clothing and Jake struggling awkwardly to his feet. "Well," he said deadpan. "I guess you didn't find the chain saw."

CHAPTER ELEVEN

ANNIE WIPED THE STEAM from the bathroom mirror and studied her face in the blurred glass. Her feelings must be written upon it plain as day for Lily to have given her that pleased look and for Matt to have plummeted into a morbid depression. Joe's decision to walk home probably had less to do with Annie's feelings than the fact that the phone lines to the farmhouse were down and he didn't want his family to worry. He'd also promised to call the nursing home to explain Lily's absence.

Annie smiled wryly at her reflection and finger-combed her wet curls. "You shameless wench," she told the woman in the mirror, smiling at herself because she didn't feel the least little bit guilty about any of it. If Joe hadn't come along when he had and put an abrupt end to things down in the boathouse, she still wouldn't have felt guilty. In fact...

She exited the bathroom, padded into the kitchen barefoot, clad only in her nightgown and bathrobe. She hit the switch that killed the diesel generator in the shed and instantly returned the old cape to an earlier time of oil lamps and woodstoves.

It was close to midnight and the storm still raged, the waves still thundered, yet here in the snug kitchen she was warm and safe. Everyone was tucked into bed. The girls, Amanda and Sally, shared the bedroom next to Matt's with two twin beds. Lily was on a cot in the parlor, with Rebel somehow curled at her feet, the both of them happy as clams. Jake was in the bedroom at the head of the living room stairs, as far away from Matt's bedroom as he could be but just one door away from Annie's...

She carried the oil lamp up the front stairs and paused briefly beside Jake's door, listening, but all was quiet. She continued on to the girls' room. Opening the door quietly and peeking inside, holding the lamp high. She saw two young faces in peaceful repose. Closing the door gently, she went to her own room. Placing the lamp on the bedside table, Annie pulled down the coverlet, climbed in and reached for the current copy of *Yankee* magazine. She adjusted the wick of the lamp for reading, then stared at the page for several minutes before turning it automatically. Stared at the next page. Looked at the pictures without seeing them. Read the words without understanding them.

Finally she tossed the magazine aside, blew out the lamp, threw back the coverlet, walked quietly to her door and opened it. She stood in the hallway, surrounded by the muted sounds of the storm yet hearing none of it, heeding only the tumultuous storm pounding in her own heart. Outside his door she listened again, but as before, all was quiet within.

She stood for what seemed like a very long time with her hand on the doorknob before turning it ever so slowly and pushing the door inward. The room was dark. Once inside she moved to the foot of his bed, listening for the sound of his breathing but hearing nothing but the rumble of the surf against the ledges and the moan of the wind through the cracks in the window frame. She could feel the rapid rhythm of her heartbeat, the quick rise and fall of her breasts as she fought to steady her breathing. Such a fool she was to be standing here like this while he lay sleeping, but she wanted him. She needed desperately to be with him, even though she knew that whatever happiness she might find with Jake could only last the summer.

Something touched her arm in the darkness and she jerked back and might have cried out if he hadn't spoken her name soothingly, breathed it into her ear as his warm, strong hands found where they belonged on her body and turned her toward him.

"What took you so long?"

FOUR HOURS PASSED in such a way as four hours had never passed before, bracketed by the night and the savage storm, intensified by the passions that swept them both up and kept them aloft, ending only when utter exhaustion and the first faint light of morning conspired to bring them back to earth.

She was aware only of Jake—the feel of him, the smell of him, the taste of him, the sound of his breathing, the way he moved. She was aware only of the way her body responded to him and the way his responded to her, the exquisitely sensual give-and-take between them that seemed so natural, so perfect.

She became aware gradually, grudgingly, of the coming of the dawn. She closed her eyes against it and held him close. "I have to go," she murmured.

"No, you don't," he responded, his arms tightening around her. "You can stay right here in my arms forever."

"The girls…"

"Would think it was neat," he said.

"Lily, Matt..."

He made a small noise of frustration. "It's still dark."

"Everyone will be waking soon."

In the darkness his fingers traced the curve of her cheek. "What will I do without you?" and while Annie knew that he spoke in terms of daylight coming, she wished with all her heart that she could somehow make this summer last forever.

LILY WAS FULLY DRESSED and in the kitchen when Annie came down the front stairs in blue jeans and a baggy sage-colored cotton sweater, carrying her sneakers. The sharp fragrant smell of coffee permeated the room and Lily wordlessly poured her a cup when she made her appearance.

"Still raining," Annie said, dropping into a chair.

"Yes it is, and don't I love a rainy day." Lily topped off her own cup and sat across from Annie. She pushed the cream and sugar toward her but Annie shook her head. "If I'd had the ambition I'd have made some doughnuts," Lily said, looking supremely contented. "But I didn't." She studied Annie with a frankness that brought heat into the younger woman's cheeks. "Should I start another pot of coffee?"

Annie hesitated. "Wait a bit. We need to talk about some things. Your son has listed the farm with a Boston Realtor. Clients will be coming to view it sometime this week. Jim has all the legal papers and I've asked to see them."

The contented look instantly vanished from Lily's face. "I see," she said quietly. "Jim's in on this, too, then."

"No, at least not the way you think. Jim's the one who alerted me and told me it was wrong of Lester to do this. Lily, we may need to find a very good lawyer."

For a brief moment Lily looked overwhelmed, and then she drew herself up and resolve steeled her expression. "I have a considerable sum set aside in an account my son knows nothing about. Money from selling my artwork. It will be enough to cover any legal fees, if you think a lawyer is necessary."

"It may be." Annie took an even breath. "This could get nasty if Lester tries to sell the farm against your will."

Lily nodded her understanding. "I don't intend to give this place up without a fight." A flicker of uncertainty shadowed her expression. "The reports from that famous physician will help, won't they?"

Annie reached across the table to grip the older woman's hands in her own. "Yes. Elsa Morrow's statement will probably be all we need to overthrow your own doctor's statement, but I think it would be prudent to line up legal representation, as well, just in case."

"Then we shall have it." Lily's chin tipped up at a stubborn angle. "Rebel and I have no intentions of leaving home ever again." She glanced at the dog who curled at her feet. "Do we, old friend?"

AMANDA'S VOICE pried into Jake's subconscious mind and prodded him into an awareness that materialized slowly, gradually. He was lying on his back, bed sheet tangled around his lower body, arms outflung. He propped himself on his elbows, blinking sleep from his eyes. His daughter was sitting at the foot of his bed, injured hand swathed in white bandaging, eyes wide upon his face.

"Pinch," he said on the tail end of a yawn. "You okay?"

"Daddy, you didn't answer when I talked to you. Are you sick? I thought you were all better from being hurt."

"I am, Pinch. Guess I was just tired. How's your hand? Can you move your fingers? C'mon up here and sit beside me."

She wriggled like a pup into his arms and he breathed in the tender sweetness of her. "Daddy, you scared me when you didn't wake up," she said.

"Next time, jump on the bed. Can you wiggle your fingers?"

She wiggled them obligingly.

"Does your hand hurt?"

She shook her head.

"Good. Hungry for breakfast?"

She shook her head again. "Daddy, can we stay here with Dr. Annie?"

"No, Pinch, this isn't our home. Don't you like our cabin?"

She hesitated. "Yes, but I like being here better."

Me, too, Jake thought to himself. "Well, we can't stay, but we had a fun sleep-over, didn't we?"

Amanda nodded. "Maybe we can do it again."

"We'll have to wish for another big storm. Or maybe not. Maybe the big storm hasn't left yet. Hear that wind? Maybe we'll be stuck here for another day."

"Oh, I hope so, Daddy. I know Dr. Annie would like it, too. I wish we could stay here forever."

Jake pulled his daughter into the curve of his arm. "What about your mother, Pinch?"

"I don't want to live with her anymore," Amanda stated.

"Your mother loves you."

"I don't care. I don't want to live with her anymore," she repeated.

To this astonishing revelation, Jake had no reply.

MATT BRINK packed his bag with glum finality. He would leave today, first thing. He would call the airline and get the earliest flight out this morning. Annie would take him to the airport. She'd be happy to be rid of him. Yes, she'd be ecstatic.

Well, maybe not ecstatic, but certainly relieved.

He didn't blame her. How could he? She had found something in that Mel Gibson look-alike cop that clearly outshone this Jay Leno look-alike doctor. Never mind that he and Annie had so much in common—careers, a love of kids, a love of New York City…

Did she love New York City? Or had he only assumed she shared his passion for the center of the universe? He must have misread her completely. How could she be so content to live here, on this remote rocky peninsula in the middle of nowhere? No operas, no plays, no musicals, no eclectic bookstores sporting Starbucks coffee and big-name book-signing authors. No *microwave,* for God's sake. Yet she didn't seem to miss any of it. She could watch the pattern of waves rolling up against that stone pier for hours and think that her life was complete.

Would she ever snap out of this strange contentment or would she metamorphose into some flower child of the new millennium and turn her back on everything she had worked so hard to achieve? Was she going to regret giving up being the chief trauma surgeon at one of the finest hospitals in the world?

Matt zipped up his bag and hefted it calculatingly. Yes, it would still pass for carry-on luggage. The sooner he got back to the city, the better. Annie Crawford had drifted way beyond his reach. His only comfort would be returning to the place he knew as home, taking up the threads of his life and carrying on.

By 10:00 a.m. Joe had arrived at the farm in an old Ford F-250 four-wheel-drive flatbed sporting a chain saw with a thirty-inch bar that must have hailed back from the time of tall trees and tough men. He had sawed through the big pine and used a chain fall to drag the section of trunk off the road.

Matt was relieved.

Jake Macpherson was visibly disappointed.

Joe stood on the porch, holding the enormous chain saw. Sheltered from the driving rain, he eyed both men and the woman who stood between them. "Well, I found a chain saw," he said.

"I guess to hell you did," Jake concurred.

"All of you who want to leave, can," Joe said. "Road's open."

"No planes will be flying in this weather, Matt," Annie said. "Besides, I'd really like to get you checked out after that lungful of water you inhaled yesterday. You know only too well that pneumonia often follows a near drowning. Do it for me, if not for yourself. Please?"

Matt wavered. "Well, if there are no flights…"

Lily chose that moment to come out onto the porch. She still used her cane, but was relying upon it less and less. "Joe, did you get hold of the nursing home last night?"

"Not to worry, Miss Lily, I called 'em soon as I got home," Joe said. "They'd already figured out that you were probably waiting out the storm here. And I fixed your phone line on my way in. That old pine busted it clean in two when it fell."

Lily nodded. "Well then, I guess it's time I got back."

"No," Annie said abruptly. "You're staying right here where you belong. I'll call the nursing home and tell them you're spending the summer at home."

"I don't want you getting into trouble on my behalf," Lily said.

"Look at you, Lily," Annie said. "You got up and got dressed by yourself this morning, you made coffee and had it waiting for me when I came downstairs. You started the woodstove to take the chill off the kitchen. You fed Rebel and filled his water bowl. You're hardly even using that cane of yours to get around, and your mind is as sharp as a tack. This is your home and you belong here. You do want to stay, don't you?"

Lily's hesitation spanned a single heartbeat. "Yes," she said, her voice quavering with emotion.

Annie nodded grimly. "Good. Then it's settled. I'll stop at the nursing home today and pick up some of your things. Jake, I'd appreciate your help if you have the time. I'm sure Sally and Lily wouldn't mind watching Amanda for a few hours."

"There's nothing I'd rather do than help Lily break out of that place," Jake replied, much to Matt's disappointment. It would have been nice to have had

Annie to himself just one more time before their final goodbye.

"Well, we'd best batten down the hatches," Lily said, "because sure shootin', this is going to cause another big storm."

"Bring it on," Annie said.

AS FAR AS Jake was concerned, few things on earth could possibly be any worse than sitting in the back seat of Annie's vehicle, listening to her chat with Matt Brink, the man with whom she had shared a close friendship for several years and who also shared her big-city lifestyle, had a big, fancy medical degree, was smarter than Intel Inside, and made tons of money.

In the long run, Matt had so much more to offer her than Jake ever could, and at summer's end, Annie would return to that life and to the close companionship of her colleague. All Matt had to do was wait, and Annie would walk right back into his world. The thought caused Jake's stomach to curdle.

"Hey?" he said, leaning forward and resting his arms on the back of Annie's seat. He could smell the sweet fragrance of her hair, see the strong column of her neck, the gentle curve of her cheek; had to forcibly quell the urge to reach out a hand to touch her. Still, if he moved his left hand just fractionally, shifted his fingers just so, he could touch her neck beneath that sensual gloss of dark hair and be completely unobserved by Matt Brink...

Her skin was like warm silk. His fingertip traced up behind her ear then gently trailed back down. "Yes?" she said tersely, holding her upper body perfectly still as she drove.

"I know a lawyer, a real diehard. She'd be perfect for Lily's situation."

"Really?" Matt said, giving him a skeptical back-seat glance. "What kind of lawyer?"

"A good one, doesn't back down from anything. A real bull dog…"

"Yes, but what does she *do?*" Matt prompted.

"She wins cases."

"Yes, but what *kind* of cases?"

"Matt's right," Annie said, eyes fixed on the road. "I mean, if your attorney friend is an expert in real estate law, or if she's not licensed to practice in Maine…" She caught her breath as his finger dipped beneath the collar of her shirt.

"I don't think she knows a damn thing about real estate law, but I do know she's licensed just about everywhere, she's in such demand. She hardly ever loses a case." He smiled wryly. "We're always on opposite sides. Cops pick 'em up, she gets 'em off."

"But, Jake," Annie interjected, her voice sounding just a tad breathless. "Do you really think we need a criminal trial lawyer? Lily hasn't done anything wrong, she just wants to live at home."

"A little overkill can't hurt. Lily's son might draw in his horns and give up the fight before it even starts if he thought he might get gored by her," Jake said, stroking Annie's neck. Had a woman's skin ever felt so soft, so smooth, so damn sexy?

"Is she a…ahh-hh!…a friend of yours?" Annie asked, eyes on the road.

"Yeah. Good friend. In spite of our differing opinions in court, she'd do anything for me." Jake gave her left earlobe a gentle tweak and then leaned back in his seat and pointedly ignored Matt's dour look.

"I see," Annie said, flashing him a red-hot glance in the rearview mirror. "Well, maybe you should give her a call...run this by her...see what she thinks..."

"Okay."

"What's her name?"

Jake glanced at the rearview mirror and caught Annie's eye. "Kathryn Yeager," he said with a slow grin.

"Kathryn. And she'd do anything for you?"

"Kate," he amended. "And yes, just about."

"I see." Annie didn't say another word until they reached Ellsworth.

JAKE USED THE HOSPITAL pay phone to call Kate Yeager while they waited for Matt to get checked out. Kate wasn't in her office and he didn't expect her to be, but he left her a brief message outlining the situation and telling her he'd try her again later that evening. He then dialed his ex-wife's number in Paris and waited through a series of clicks and bursts of static. He didn't hear the phone ring but suddenly a man's voice greeted him. He recognized it instantly and was in the act of hanging up when the rough voice with the heavy German accent said, "Jake?"

Jake sucked in a deep breath. Hans Gatt was the director of Linda's movie. They'd met several times before Jake and Linda were even divorced. The animosity between them had been instantaneous. "Jake," Hans said. "You call for Linda, I know, but she is not here. We finished filming two days ago, ya. She flew back to the States yesterday."

"She told me she'd be in Paris all summer," Jake said.

"Oh, no, no. We only filmed part of it here, the

rest will be done in California. But you should know this, Jake. She has this news for you, to tell you. We are getting married sooner, in September.''

"Ah." Jake's hand tightened on the phone. "Well. Congratulations. I hope the two of you'll be happy."

"I am certain that we will."

A sudden thought seared through him. "But—" Jake said, and then stopped speaking because the line had gone dead. "But what about my daughter?" he said as he hung up the phone. "Growing up with Hans as her stepfather? No way in hell."

He wandered back to the waiting room outside emergency and dropped into a seat beside Annie. "Matt okay?" he said.

"They're still checking him out. Did you get hold of your good friend, Kate?"

He shook his head. "She wasn't home. I left a message, then tried to call Linda, to touch base with her about Amanda. We promised we'd speak every day. She wasn't there. Seems she left Paris yesterday, homeward bound. They've finished filming."

"Oh," Annie said, her voice sympathetic. "You think she'll want to take Amanda back right away?"

Jake slumped in the hard plastic chair. "She's getting married to Hans Gatt in September."

"The movie director? Wow."

"Yeah, wow. Annie, he'll be *me*. He'll be Amanda's full-time father."

"He'll never be you, Jake, and he'll never be Amanda's father. Not in a million years." Annie reached for his hand and squeezed it reassuringly.

"Amanda's been so upset about something lately," Jake said. "She doesn't want to talk to her mother. She said she doesn't want to live with her anymore."

"Amanda told you this?"

Jake nodded. "Just this morning."

"When did the two of them talk last?"

"Two days ago. I practically had to drag her to the phone."

"Has Linda said anything to her about getting married?"

"If she has, Amanda's not telling me."

"Poor little girl," Annie said. "Who knows what she's going through? I feel sorry for my own daughter, and guilty that my failed marriage had a negative effect on her. She loves her father, yet she hardly ever sees him."

"I don't want to give Amanda up," Jake said. "And I sure as hell don't want her living with that cold-blooded son of a..." He was silent for a moment. "I suppose I could take Linda to court and fight for custody, but the mother always wins," he continued. "Especially when she's rich and famous." Jake's hand tightened involuntarily on Annie's as he spoke. "This Hans Gatt character is such a loser that he's already been married and divorced four times. *Four times.*"

Annie turned to look at him. "We've both got ex-spouse problems," she said. "I can't help wonder *why* Ryan moved to Maine. Trudy's not from Maine and neither is he. It makes no sense." She shook her head.

"I came here expecting to have a quiet, peaceful summer. I thought Sally would be with her father most of the time and the biggest challenge of my days would be deciding what to cook for dinner and which novel to read. And now both Trudy and the baby are sick, and Ryan is turning to *me* for comfort. Ryan, who was so disinterested in our marriage that I mentioned divorce to him, hoping it would wake him up and make him take more notice of me. Instead he agreed to it. Agreed that getting a divorce would be the best thing for us to do. Can you imagine?''

Matt walked into the waiting room and plopped into the chair on the other side of Annie. ''Just in case you're wondering, I'm going to be fine. My lungs are clear as a bell.''

Annie continued as if he hadn't spoken. ''And then, just months after our divorce, he married Trudy.''

''Ryan's *worse* than a jerk,'' Jake said.

''Poor Sally,'' Annie sighed. ''Trying to make sense of it all.''

''Sally's a strong kid,'' Jake said. ''She'll be fine. It's her mother I'm worried about.''

''Her mother needs some serious R and R, which is why I'm flying out of here tomorrow,'' Matt said. ''I'll stay at the airport hotel tonight.''

''Oh, Matt, that's foolish,'' Annie protested.

Matt gave her hand one final squeeze before pushing wearily to his feet. ''Then I guess I'm a fool.'' He shrugged with defeat. He turned to Jake and extended his hand. ''Thanks for pulling me out of the drink yesterday. The crabs would be eating me for lunch right now if you hadn't.''

''Along with some very large lobsters,'' Jake said, rising to accept the extended hand. ''Leroy, Leonard and Leticia…''

''Don't forget Lorena and Lucy,'' Annie added.

Matt looked between the two of them, eyebrows raised. ''Family pets?''

Annie laughed. ''In a manner of speaking,'' she said. ''I guess you had to be there.''

''Yeah,'' Matt sighed. ''I guess.''

CHAPTER TWELVE

IT WAS PAST LUNCHTIME when Jake pulled into the long winding drive that led to the farm. They had stopped by the nursing home to pick up some of Lily's things and the atmosphere there had been surprisingly cooperative. The administrator had been phoned in advance by Annie that morning and Lester had been notified. Annie had expected resistance, and was surprised that a box of Lily's things had already been prepared. "Good luck," the charge nurse said as she handed it to Annie. "It may not seem like it to you, but we're all rooting for Lily to be able to live at home. It's where she really wants to be."

Jake paused beside the mailbox while Annie rolled down her window to retrieve the stack of bills and letters, sorting through them as they traveled the last mile. She opened the phone bill she'd received and scanned through the calls, instantly frowning. She reached for her cell phone and dialed a number. A girl answered. "May I speak with Tom Ward, please," Annie said. "Yeah, sure, hang on," the girl replied, and Annie ended the call and held the cell phone in a tight grip. "Sally *promised* me she'd have no contact with him, but Tom's number fills up this phone bill!"

"Thirteen years old is a hard place to be," Jake said as he pulled into the yard and parked beside an unfamiliar vehicle. "Looks like you have company," he said, his voice as calm as hers had been furious.

"And Sally just got a last-minute reprieve," Annie seethed.

The wind had abated but the rain had held on. They ran through a solid wall of it to gain the shelter of the porch. Inside, Lily had lit the lamps against the dark afternoon. Amanda and Jim, the Realtor, sat at the table while Lily sautéed onions and salt pork in the deep cast-iron kettle. "I hope you don't mind," Lily said over her shoulder to Annie. "I called Jim and asked him to bring some groceries. Thought you might be too tired to cook, and it's a good day for a fish chowder and some hot biscuits."

"That sounds wonderful," Annie said, lying the stack of mail atop the counter, stuffing the phone bill in her pocket and feeling the tension within her ease. It was hard to remain angry in this warm, wonderful country kitchen with all those savory aromas and all these good people surrounding her. "Where's Sally?"

"In her room, listening to music. She wasn't interested in playing cards with us."

Jake carried Lily's things into the parlor then returned to the kitchen and gave Amanda's bandaged hand a once-over. "You been good, Pinch?"

"She's been great," Lily answered. "She's been advising me how to play my cards and beat Jim."

"What can I do to help?" Annie asked.

"You can finish my hand for me. You can't lose as long as Amanda's sitting beside you."

Annie laughed. "You'd better play your own cards, Lily, and let me peel and cut up the potatoes for the chowder. I don't know a thing about card games. Solitaire's my strong suit."

"Solitaire's a lonely game," Jake said, resting his rump against the edge of the counter and shoving his hands into his jeans' pockets. "Poker. That's a game to rouse the blood. Seven card stud."

"Oh, my, that sounds dangerous, like you'd need a bottle of whiskey and some half-dressed women." Lily wiped her hands on the apron she'd tied over her plain cotton dress and limped over to the table. "Bridge is my real love, but it takes four people, and our club dissolved after Thelma died and Helen got Alzheimer's. Jim's kind enough to play cards with me, though. He's almost as good a whist player as Beatrice Goodwin."

"Almost?" Jim said. He was nattily dressed in a pair of tan chinos and a green-and-black-plaid Filson shirt. His silver hair was combed carefully back. It struck Annie as she washed her hands at the sink that Jim had come both to make amends and to court Lily, and she found herself smiling.

"Penny for your thoughts," Jake murmured as she reached for a clean dish towel.

"I was thinking that we need to set the parlor up like a regular bedroom. Lily should have her own bed, the one upstairs in the room I'm using. Maybe as soon as I get these potatoes finished, we could go look things over."

"I'd be more than happy to examine any bed with you," he said with a grin that caused a strong flutter in the pit of her stomach. "'Course, if you give your own bed away, you'll need to find another one. There could be one out in the barn. There's a lot of stuff stored out there."

"It's a big barn," Annie agreed, working the paring knife around the potato.

"Bet it has a great hayloft," Jake said.

Annie felt her cheeks warm. "No doubt."

"Haylofts can be wonderful places."

"Here," Annie said abruptly, pushing the pile of potatoes toward him. "Wash and cube these into the pot, keep stirring the onions, then ask Lily what to do next. I'd better go see what Sally's up to." She fled the kitchen, cutting through the pantry that led to the ell, which led to the woodshed, which led to the open breezeway, which wasn't the way to Sally's room, but good God, just standing near Jake filled her with such a level of sexual tension that she could scarcely breathe.

She stood in the open breezeway and let the cool, wet air blow over her, hoping to put out the fire in her blood. She was trembling all over. "Oh, Lord, what am I going to do?" she moaned out loud.

At length her blood had cooled to the point that she was ready to face her daughter. She tapped on the door to Sally's room and peeked around it. The girl was sitting cross-legged on her bed, headphones clamped to her head. She took them off grudgingly when Annie closed the door behind her. Without saying anything, Annie held the phone bill out to Sally. For several moments her daughter studied it, the color deepening in her cheeks, then handed it back. "So?"

"So we had a deal," Annie said, trying to control her temper. "You weren't supposed to have any contact with Tom at all, yet you've been calling him on the phone repeatedly. All the calls I thought you were making to your father, you were making to New York."

Sally's expression became stony. "Not all."

"No, only one hundred and forty-six dollars'

worth. No more, Sally. I mean it. And the police meant it, too, or have you forgotten that agreement you signed?''

''Okay.''

''The only calls you'll make on this phone will be to your father. Do you understand?''

''I said *okay*,'' Sally snapped back, before putting her headphones back on, thereby dismissing her mother. Annie seethed for a few moments more, then left the room. She descended the stairs, struggling to understand Sally's defiance, wishing they could return to the closeness they'd once shared. She entered the open breezeway and let the push of the wind calm her. This was just a stage Sally was going through. She was growing up, which was a painful process—especially with the wrong kind of peer pressure.

Annie heard a movement behind her and half turned. Jake stepped out of the woodshed and joined her in the breezeway. ''How's Sally?''

''Predictably sullen and defiant,'' Annie said wryly.

''The potatoes are in the pot with the onions and salt pork and just enough water to cover. Amanda's giving Nelly a hard time about chewing on her sneaker. Lily and Jim are on game number three and paying no attention at all to anything but each other, so I thought I might just as well come out and show you what a hayloft looks like.'' As he spoke he reached out a warm, strong hand to massage her shoulder and at his touch Annie felt her heart rate tremble and her knees grow weak.

''I know what a hayloft looks like,'' she murmured.

''But do you know what *this* one looks like?''

''I can...imagine...'' she said, trembling with a

great, overwhelming need. She turned toward him as
his hands shifted, pulled her close, pulled her up
against the lean, hard strength of him.

"We'll never make it," he said.

"Make it where?" she gasped, her body respond-
ing to his touch with a will of its own.

"To the loft." He bent his head and kissed her,
and she moaned into his mouth and reached her hands
to twine her fingers in his hair. He was so vital, so
alive, so beautifully male, and he knew just where to
touch her to drive her wild...

"Daddy?" Amanda's voice brought a frustrated
groan from Jake. They froze in each other's arms and
broke off their kiss, but before she released him Annie
pulled him fiercely close. "I'm going to go blind,"
she murmured in his ear, causing him to laugh.

"Daddy?"

"Here, Pinch," Jake said as Amanda's light footsteps pattered through the woodshed. She peeked out
into the breezeway. "What is it?" Jake said. "What's
wrong?"

"Miss Lily says to tell you it's almost time to put
the fish in the pot."

"Tell her we're coming." Amanda turned obediently and retraced her steps toward the kitchen and
Jake pulled Annie back into his arms for one more
kiss. "If this keeps up much longer," he said, "we're
going to have to invest in Seeing Eye dogs for both
of us."

JAKE DROVE HOME that night deep in thought,
Amanda sleeping in the passenger seat. Being parted
from Annie created a physical pain deep inside him
that bordered on agony. Already he missed her,

and they'd said goodbye a mere ten minutes ago. The fish chowder and biscuits had been delicious, but he had barely tasted any of it, hadn't been able to concentrate on the lively banter at the supper table, could hardly restrain himself from watching her every move. Sheer torture to share a room with her and not be able to touch her.

"I'm going crazy," he said out loud. "I'll never survive this."

Already he was thinking about summer's end and what would happen next. Where would their relationship be? What would Annie's future hold for her? She had mentioned more than once not returning to the big city so that Sally could see more of her dad, but had she meant it? Would she be happy living in a tiny village like Blue Harbor? Could she find fulfillment working in a small family clinic or covering shifts in the emergency room at the Ellsworth or Bangor hospital? And where did he and Amanda fit into Annie's future if they were in California?

The rural road unwound in front of him, a dark tunnel of trees illuminated in the glow of his headlights as the windshield wipers rhythmically slatted the rain aside. Amanda murmured in her sleep, a small innocent sound that tugged at his heartstrings. Linda was back in the States. She would most certainly come looking for her daughter. Would she allow Amanda to spend the rest of the summer with her father, as they had planned, or would she want Amanda to return to Los Angeles with her? And why was Amanda so upset with her mother? What had transpired between the two of them?

His thoughts were as dark as the rainy night, and by the time he turned down the road that lead to the cabin, he was filled with a kind of churning despair. His despair turned to disbelief as he pulled into the clearing beside the cabin and saw that a tree had fallen onto the roof, obviously blown over in the fierce winds that the storm had brought. ''Damnation.''

He left Amanda sleeping in the car while he checked out the roof. It was worse than he'd feared. The big pine had torn a gaping hole through which a large broken-off branch protruded into the room itself. Rain water dripped steadily and the floor was soaking wet, but the area by the bunk beds was far enough away from the hole to have kept the bedding dry.

He lit the lamps and started a small fire in the woodstove to battle the dampness in the room before carrying Amanda inside and depositing her on her bunk, fully clothed and asleep. He unlaced her sneakers and pulled them off her small feet, bundled her into the sleeping bag and kissed her warm, moist forehead. In the morning she might complain a little about not being at Annie's but she'd be happy to be with him. She trusted him so completely, loved him so blindly. It was a humbling thing to be a father, a frightening responsibility. He would keep Amanda safe for as long as he lived. No matter what happened, he would always be a big part of her life. If that meant moving to California, he'd move to California. And therein lay the dilemma.

What about Annie Crawford?

SUNSHINE.

It seemed such a miracle after that long, wet storm. Relishing the solitude and the early quiet, Annie sat on the porch with her mug of coffee. Lily had been up for hours, going through her old beloved artist's box of oil paints and sorting through her brushes at the kitchen table while Rebel patiently and contentedly held court at her feet, head resting on his paws, loyal eyes fixed upon her face.

Sally would sleep until noon if given the opportunity.

The sun was rising over the Atlantic, long golden fingers of light flickering like tongues of fire over the tops of the white-crested waves beyond the islands, waves made big by the storm, an ocean still wildly aroused, still flexing its enormous muscles. Yet the lobster boats were heading out of the harbor. One after the other, engines chugging, sturdy bows plowing into the rough chop, they departed the safe waters and headed into the unknown. Annie wondered if the lobstermen ever got seasick, those old salts whose livelihoods depended upon the ocean. She felt herself getting a little queasy just watching the stalwart, broad-beamed boats pitch and roll.

The screen door squeaked open on its spring hinge and Lily emerged, coffeepot in hand. "Thought you might be ready for a refill," she said. Lily's rapidly increasing vigor could only be credited to her returning home. Like a displaced captain being returned to the bridge of her ship, she had rediscovered a reason to live. She came onto the porch without using her cane, limping but steady on her feet, and refilled Annie's mug. "It's going to be a beautiful day," she said in reply to Annie's thanks. "We call this a storm-washed morning, clean and clear."

"A storm-washed morning," Annie repeated softly, taking a sip of coffee. "Lily, did Jim show you the papers yesterday?"

Lily nodded. She sat in her rocker and placed the coffeepot on the side table between them. "I read them." She folded her hands in her lap and gazed out across the harbor for a long, quiet moment. "I can't believe that my son would do such a thing without at least talking to me about it first."

"He can't break this lease. He created it and I signed it, and nowhere in it is there a clause that states he has the right to show the property while I'm living here," Annie said. "Simply put, he can't bring any potential buyers here until after I'm gone. Jim seemed somewhat reluctant to call him and warn him off, so I'll do so myself this morning."

"I suppose I should be the one to call," Lily said. "After all, he's my son..."

"No. Let me be the bad guy. I'm good at it, or so I've been told."

Lily laughed. "All independent women have to be good at it. It comes with the territory."

"You, too?"

"Of course, dear. A few years ago I hired a contractor to paint the house. He gave me a high estimate, but it's a big house if you take into account the shed and outbuildings. He and his crew did a terrible job. They didn't scrape the old paint off or prime the bare spots, they just started slapping on the paint. He probably thought I was so old I wouldn't notice. When I pointed these things out to him and told him that he wouldn't get paid the balance due unless he did the job right, he flew off the handle and called me an old bitch."

"My goodness," Annie said. "Did he fix everything?"

Lily smiled slyly. "I held back half the money to

cover just such a contingency. That's the ticket to being a successful old bitch—having a little money and knowing how to use it.''

Annie burst out laughing. ''Lily Houghton, you're wonderful.''

''I've learned a thing or two, living alone. And I've been thinking about what you said, too. About me not being able to stay here all by myself. I've drawn up some plans for the old place and I'd like to show them to you. You wait right here and I'll fetch them.''

She brought them out, unrolled them, and Annie studied them carefully for ten minutes without saying a word. At length she looked up at Lily and smiled.

''So,'' Lily said, resting one hand atop Rebel's head. ''What do you think?''

Annie propped her bare feet up on the porch rail, laid the drawings across her thighs and inhaled a deep breath of salty ocean air spiced with the sweet perfume of the rugosa roses. ''I think your idea is marvelous and these plans are great. My word, Lily, your vision of the future of this farm is the perfect solution.''

Lily's anxious gaze softened with relief at Annie's words. ''I could have a real architect draw up the plans,'' she said.

''If this thing goes to court, that would be important. Maybe you should ask your son to visit so you can speak with him about your ideas and show him your drawings. He and his wife could spend a couple of days here. If he could see firsthand how much better you're doing and how you're planning for your future…''

Lily gave her head a little shake. ''Lester brought his wife here once, right after they were married. She had very long fingernails and broke one of them on the very first day. She acted as if the world was coming to an end. I finally suggested that she simply trim all the others to match the one she broke. It seemed reasonable to me, but I don't think she's ever forgiven me for that. She didn't like my paintings, the remoteness of the farm, the cry of the seagulls or the dampness of the air, and she told me that the flowers I put in her room gave her hay fever. They had planned to spend a week but left the following morning.''

''I see,'' Annie said, her heart sinking. ''Speaking of flowers, I need to do more work in those beds. The rose mallow and the phlox are both pretty cottage flowers but they've completely taken over this front border. I thought I might dig some of them out and transplant them to another spot. What do you think?''

''Good idea. The delphinium's being choked out, and it's such a lovely perennial. Speaking of perennials, is your young man coming to visit today?''

Annie stared at Lily. ''My young man?''

''Jake.'' Lily frowned. ''Do you have more than one?''

''No…'' Annie felt her cheeks warm. ''I just… Well, I mean, I'm not exactly young…''

''Oh, yes, you are,'' Lily informed her. ''And so is he. He's quite a sweetie, too. If I were a little younger, I'd give you a run for your money.''

Annie laughed. ''What about Jim?''

It was Lily's turn to blush. ''Jim's a fine man,'' she said, chin lifting. ''He's been a good friend to me all these years, and I was wrong to turn him away.''

''I think we should count our blessings,'' Annie said.

''Amen,'' Lily agreed with a firm nod. ''Two good men, two great women.''

"PINCH? Time to get up. The sun's shining, breakfast is ready and this time your daddy didn't burn one single thing." Jake bent over his daughter's bunk and peeled her out of her sleeping bag like a little human banana. She was drowsy, sleepy-headed and slow to respond.

"What's for breakfast, Daddy?" she yawned as he fumbled her sneakers back onto her feet.

"Cold cereal and orange juice," he replied.

"But, Daddy, how could you burn that?"

"Couldn't, that's why we're having it. Okay, you're all dressed and ready to roll. That was nice and quick, huh?"

Amanda pushed off the bunk and blinked up at the broken section of pine tree that now inhabited the upper reaches of the cabin. "Wow, Daddy," she said. "A big tree tried to come inside while we slept."

"Yep, and it almost made it. Now come on over to the sink and I'll help you wash up. How's your hand?"

"Good. Are you going to let the tree stay here?"

"No, Pinch. I'll have to find a chain saw and cut it down, get it off the roof, then fix that big hole."

"Maybe Dr. Annie has a chain saw you can borrow," Amanda said. "Maybe after breakfast we should go over there and find out."

"I was thinking you might want to do a little fishing first. We could take the canoe out onto the pond for a while."

"Okay," she agreed. "But after, we should go to Dr. Annie's. We have a lot of work to do, to fix the roof before it rains again. Maybe she can help us. I bet she knows how to use a chain saw."

"Huh?" Amanda's words took him aback. "I doubt it, Pinch."

"Well I'm going to ask anyhow, 'cause I'll bet she does."

An hour later he was tying a muddler minnow onto a leader, wondering if he still remembered how to fly cast. It had been so many years. Just being out on the pond in the old canoe reminded him of his grandfather, a quiet man who'd worn a faded green slouch hat with a felt band for holding his favorite flies. He'd smoked a pipe, stoutly maintained that Old Woodsman Fly Dope was the only concoction that could turn the black flies and condemned hardware and bait fishermen with the true fervor of a devout Isaac Walton.

His grandfather had been an artist with a fly rod and had tried to instill that same love of fishing upon his only grandson, but Jake had been a mediocre student who'd lacked the grace, instinct and desire to outwit the wily brook trout. At the time he'd been far more interested in Jenna Hogan's breasts, a phenomenon that had all the boys summering in camps on that pond endlessly whispering.

Now he wished he'd paid more attention to what his grandfather had been trying to teach, because in the process of trying to pass these traditions on to his own daughter, he realized that he didn't have the foggiest idea where to begin.

"First of all, Pinch, the thing to remember is that fishing should always be fun. Relaxing." Cripes, he'd forgotten how to tie the fly onto the leader. He stared down at the snarl of fine monofilament in his hands and felt a twinge of uneasiness. "It's just you, the fish, the beautiful morning, the mist rising off the water..." How could he have forgotten such a basic knot? It was called a surgeon's knot... Worse case scenario, Annie could refresh his memory.

"Does it hurt the fish when you catch it?" Amanda asked.

"Not hardly a bit. I filed the barb off, so we can take the hook out quickly and easily and turn it loose again."

"The fish won't die?"

"No, the fish won't die. It'll just get a little education." *Like I need right now,* Jake thought, trying another series of convoluted twists and loops. He tightened the knot down and held the fly up, scrutinizing his work. "There. We're ready to begin. Now, the first thing is to find where the fish are. This requires a little bit of knowledge of the pond itself, where the spring holes are, where the inlet is..."

"What's an inlet, Daddy?"

"It's where a brook comes into the pond. The brook carries all sorts of treats for the fish in addition to lots of oxygen in the water, which makes it easy for them to breathe, so they often hang out right in that spot, waiting for their next meal."

"What's a spring hole?"

"It's where an underground spring feeds into the pond. The water is cold there, and in the summer the fish, especially trout, like the cold water. So they hang in those spots."

"Unless they're hungry," Amanda said. "And then they go to the inlet to get fed."

"Right. Unless there's a hatch on. A hatch is when a nymph, which is like a little swimming bug in the water, turns into something that can fly through the air like a butterfly. It comes to the surface, sheds its old skin and lifts off into the air. The trout try to eat these nymphs before they can fly away.''

"Oh," Amanda said, nodding, her brows drawn into a frown of intense concentration. "I'm glad I'm not a nymph."

"Well, you're my little nymph, Pinch. In a few years you'll be all grown up and beautiful, like a butterfly, flying away."

"I'll never fly away from you, Daddy. Never. Only Mommy flies away."

Jake laid down his fly rod, picked up the paddle and tried to think of a response to Amanda's observation. He stroked the canoe through the water, remembering the smooth, easy swing of the paddle and the feathering twist of the blade to steer by. "Your mother flies away because she has to, Pinch. It's her work. It takes her away from you sometimes, but she always comes back. She loves you very much."

Amanda faced forward in the bow, her little back straight and rigid. "No, she doesn't," she said. "She doesn't want me anymore."

Shocked, Jake rested the paddle, the droplets of water silvering onto the still surface of the pond. "That's not true," he said firmly. "She wants you very much, just like I do. You're a very loved little girl, Amanda Macpherson, and don't you ever doubt that."

She turned abruptly, rocking the canoe with the force of her movement. Her eyes were wide and pleading. "Can I stay with you, Daddy? Please?"

The anguish in Amanda's face wrenched his heart. What was going on between her and Linda? "I want that more than anything, Pinch," he said. "But we'll have to talk that over with your mother."

CHAPTER THIRTEEN

JAKE WAS PROUD of how it all came back to him. A few tentative casts and he felt the positive energies start to flow. "See how I move my arm, Pinch? Watch closely. No bends, no wiggles. Just a straight, smooth motion from back here to out in front of me. Watch the line. See how it slowly straightens out and hangs right above the water?

"I could let it settle right now but I want to get a little closer to that spring hole, so I'll retrieve it, like so, and then strip out a little more line while working the fly rod smoothly back and forth, like so, and then I'll cast it right where I want it...like so, and watch it settle...settle...settle... There! Perfect touch-down!"

Jake shot a triumphant glance in Amanda's direction and was dismayed to see that she wasn't even watching his performance. She was sitting in the bow of the canoe and facing straight ahead, her eyes riveted on something moving along the far shore, as attentive as a bird dog on its first autumn hunt.

"A moose, Daddy," she breathed, absolutely and joyously transfixed. "A *moose!*"

"A big moose," Jake concurred, then began to play the line in.

"Let's get closer."

"In a minute, Pinch. Just let me... Hey, I got a

bite!'' Not a big one, by the feel of it, but it would be Amanda's first glimpse of the real-life action of fishing. After witnessing it, she'd definitely be hooked. ''Look at that,'' he enthused, watching the line zing back and forth through the black water. ''It's really fighting. A brook trout always gives a good fight. It'll try to rub the hook off, try to tangle the line... Uh, oh, almost lost her...''

''Daddy, quick, the moose might go away!''

''Hang on, I'm reeling her in.''

''Oooooh, look Daddy, another moose, a baby one!''

Jake glanced up, felt the line go slack and jerked instinctively, snapping the line right out of the water, but he lost the fish. ''Damn,'' he said, still looking for the moose.

''Daddy!'' Amanda let out a heart-stopping shriek.

Jake whipped around and stared for a moment in disbelief. The muddler minnow was embedded in her right cheek, just below her eye. An inch higher up and... ''Don't cry, Pinch, you'll be okay.''

''It hurts,'' she wailed, tears streaming out of her eyes and running down her baby cheeks.

''Just hold on, I'll take it out as soon as we're ashore.'' He fumbled for his paddle and drove it into the still waters, throwing up a plume of spray. The canoe leaped forward, and in no time he was pulling alongside the dock, levering himself out and snubbing a line to the thwart. ''Okay, sweetheart, you're doing fine, just sit still a minute more...''

She sat as still as he fumbled for his pocketknife and opened it. He cut the monofilament line about two inches from her cheek where the tears streamed steadily and her body shook with sobs. "Ow! Ow! Daddy."

"I know it hurts, honey. I'm sorry. I hooked myself in the lip once." He helped her out of the canoe and then scooped her into his arms and headed for the cabin.

Never made it.

A silver BMW was creeping slowly down the rutted tote road. It pulled cautiously into the cabin yard and parked beside his vehicle. Jake stopped just outside the cabin with Amanda cradled in his arms and watched the car door open. Saw a woman ease gracefully out and straighten to her full slender height.

"Jake?" she said.

"Linda." His heart plummeted.

Amanda twisted in his arms, clenched her own arms more tightly around his neck and said, "Don't let her take me away, Daddy!"

"My God," Linda said, raising one hand to her mouth in wide-eyed shock as she stared at her daughter. "Amanda, your hand. Your face. Jake, what's going on here?"

"I'm not hurt," Amanda sobbed, tears streaming, clinging to her father.

"Linda, please, I have to get the fish hook out," Jake said, turning toward the cabin.

"Oh, my God! Do you mean that bristly little thing embedded in her cheek is a *fish hook?*"

He paused. "Actually, it's a fly. But, technically, yes, it has a hook on it, though the barb is filed off so we wouldn't hurt any fish, but while I was casting..."

"Dammit, Jake." Linda's face paled. "Something like that could scar her for life, and what if you'd hooked her in the eye? And why is her hand all bandaged up like that?''

"She cut it," he said. "It's not life-threatening."

Linda stared and Jake felt his toes curl as she focused on the big tree lying atop the cabin roof. "I trusted you to take good care of her," she said. "I thought you would be more responsible."

Jake knew how bad things appeared but he tried to calm her. "Honestly, it's not as bad as it looks. The hook'll come right out, I just need to get a pair of tweezers out of my first-aid kit…"

"No way," Linda objected, "You're not handling this. She needs to be seen by a competent doctor."

"Can we go see Dr. Annie?" Amanda whimpered.

"Dr. Annie?" Linda repeated. Her stare intensified. "Surely you don't mean the *same* Dr. Annie that was in New York?"

"She fixed Daddy, and she'll fix me." Amanda sniffled.

Jake's grip tightened on his daughter and he headed for his truck. "All right then, if you want her to be seen by a doctor, I'll take her to a doctor. You coming?"

Linda hesitated only momentarily. "We can talk on the way," she said, retrieving her leather clutch from the BMW. Once she'd settled herself in the passenger seat with Amanda safely buckled up between them, Jake started the truck and began the drive to Blue Harbor. He hadn't driven more than a mile before Linda fumbled in her purse and pulled out a pack of cigarettes.

"Linda, please don't," he said. "You know how I feel about your smoking, especially around Amanda."

"You're one to talk," she said, her cheeks coloring. "Look at her, her hand all wrapped in bandages and a fish hook stuck in her face."

"It doesn't hurt," Amanda sobbed. "Daddy didn't mean to, he was looking at the mooses."

"It wasn't your fault, Pinch," Jake said. "It was my fault, and I'm sorry."

"Dr. Annie will make me better," Amanda said.

Linda put the cigarettes back in her purse. "Dr. Annie. What a coincidence that she should be summering somewhere close by. A fortunate one, too, considering everything that's happened to Amanda while in your care."

Jake didn't answer.

SALLY ROSE AT NOON, just as Annie had predicted, and padded into the kitchen squelching a huge yawn that culminated in a look of foggy surprise. "But it can't be lunchtime," she said, staring at the kitchen table and the stack of tuna sandwiches Lily had just plunked down.

"I hope you like tuna for breakfast, then," Lily replied.

"Where's Mom?"

"Out in the garden. Why don't you call her in?"

Sally wandered out onto the porch with Nelly chewing on her ankles, yawned again, and looked around. Another long, boring day stared her in the face. Why couldn't she have slept until suppertime? Maine was boring. Nothing ever *happened* here. Well, almost nothing. When Jake Macpherson was around, stuff kinda shook and rattled. He was pretty cool, for a cop.

She shoved her hands into her jeans' pockets and

walked barefoot down the porch steps. Now, if only she could stumble across a *young* Jake Macpherson. As if something that good would ever happen to her.

"Ouch! Nelly, leave my ankles alone."

"Sally?" Her mother's voice came from around the corner in the sheltered flower garden. She was on her knees, one gloved hand clutching a trowel, the other a clump of plants. She was wearing that absolutely ridiculous-looking broad-brimmed straw hat that must have hailed from another century.

"Mom, *where* did you get that hat?"

"Lily lent it to me. I'm glad you're up. Your father called a little while ago. He has the day off and he'd like to spend some time with you."

Sally hesitated long enough for her mother to give her a questioning glance. "What about Trudy?" Sally asked.

Her mother used her wrist to tip the brim of the straw hat back and heaved the kind of sigh that a mother does when she's trying to soften reality.

"Trudy's been readmitted to the hospital, Sally. She's still sick, but it's a kind of illness that's different. She has a severe case of post-partum depression, and Ryan thought she needed help in dealing with it."

"I think so, too," Sally said.

"Well, now she's getting the help she needs, and your dad really needs to see you. I told him to come by. I hope that's all right."

Sally shrugged, shoving her hands deeper into her pockets. How to explain to her mother that things had changed? The baby being born so sick, Trudy going bonkers, her father wallowing in a black depression. All she wanted to do now was to go back to the city and hang with her friends, but of course *that* would be a sin punishable by death in her mother's book. "Yeah, sure." She shrugged again.

"Good. He should be here soon."

"Lily told me to tell you that lunch was ready."

Her mother pushed to her feet, holding the trowel and a clump of plant, and gave her an awkward one-armed hug. "Poor Sally. Hang in there, kiddo. It'll be okay."

Sally dropped her eyes to her bare toes and felt a lump build in her throat. Her mother could read her like a book. She blinked her eyes hard against the stinging burn in them. "Yeah, right," she whispered.

Just after they'd finished lunch she heard the crunch of gravel. She stood on the porch, watching as her father climbed out of his car and straightened. "Hey, Dad."

He stared up at her, his face drawn and fatigued. "Hey, Sally. I thought we could spend some time together today."

Sally glanced down at the puppy. "Yeah, sure." She shrugged.

"I thought maybe we could go for a drive. Up the coast, maybe. Have dinner somewhere. That sound okay with you?"

"That sounds great."

"Is your mother…?"

"She just went inside. I'll get her."

"No. I mean, that's all right, you don't have to…"

Sally gazed at her father. "Dad, come inside. Lily's sketching. She says she'll give me lessons if I want. We just ate lunch and there're some sandwiches left if you're hungry. Tuna salad's your favorite…"

Sally waited while her father fidgeted, trying to decide what to do. She heard footsteps behind her and felt her mother's hand close gently on her shoulder. "Hello, Ryan," her mother said. "Come inside for a bit. You have to see this to believe it."

ANNIE TOOK HER PLACE directly behind Lily, watching her sketch with the charcoal pencil, her gnarled hand making smooth, spare movements of grace and beauty, and creating with seeming effortlessness the most amazing drawing.

She watched as Lily created a girl and a dog on the blank sketch pad. Sally and Nell. Up close, intimate, full of the life they both exuded, bursting with the promise of youth, yet at the same time poignant with the certainties of life; that the girl would mature into womanhood and eventual old age, and that the pup would grow old and die. "It's wonderful," she breathed, reaching out and closing her hand gently on Lily's shoulder. "Absolutely wonderful."

Lily shook her head and snorted. "This is just a quick sketch. I'm rusty."

"You should be sketching and painting every day of your life," Annie said. "Your talent is too good to waste."

Sally glanced up at her father from her place on the kitchen floor with Nell. "Like it, Dad?"

"I do," Ryan said. "Very much." At that moment there was a rap on the kitchen door and Annie turned to answer it, surprised to see Joe standing on the porch.

"Joe," she said, glancing over his shoulder to spy the lobster boat tied to the stone pier. "Is something wrong?"

"Nope," he said. "It's Sunday."

"Sunday?" Annie frowned, puzzled.

"Your sailing lesson."

"My sailing lesson." Annie's expression changed and she raised her hand to her mouth in a gesture of dismay. "I'm so sorry, Joe. I forgot all about it. Lily's inside drawing a sketch of Sally and the puppy, and Sally's father just dropped by for a visit..."

"That's okay. Too rough for sailing, anyhow, I guess," Joe said. "The wind and waves'll be up for a couple more days, probably, after that big storm." He paused, catching a glimpse of Sally in the kitchen and returning Lily's wave. "Does your daughter get seasick?" he asked.

Annie shook her head. "I don't know. We've never had the opportunity to find out. Why?"

Joe rubbed his chin. "Well, my youngest son helps me out on the boat sometimes when I haul traps. I thought maybe Sally might like to give it a try, too, and earn herself a little bit of spending money. Maybe I could take her for a ride to see if she's seaworthy. That is, if you approve and Sally is agreeable."

Annie hesitated. "It's pretty rough out there. I can see the whitecaps from here..."

"Yes, ma'am, it is," Joe said, "but it'll be calmer inside the harbor. We could putter around and take in the sights."

Annie relaxed and nodded. "That sounds like a fine idea. Come inside and ask her. And by the way, how many people does your boat hold?"

Joe was about to answer when a truck pulled into the yard. Her heart leaped with gladness. It was Jake, and— Annie's glad heart plummeted. Linda, his ex-wife, was in the passenger seat with Amanda sandwiched between, and none of them looked the least bit happy.

Jake parked next to Annie's vehicle, climbed out, reached to scoop Amanda, and started up the porch steps without waiting for his ex-wife. "Hi, Dr. Annie," Amanda whimpered through her tears as they came face-to-face with her at the screen door. Annie said nothing, just opened the door and motioned them inside the crowded kitchen.

"Well, well." Lily glanced up from the sketch and stared over the tops of her glasses. "You've been fishing, I see."

"I hooked her," Jake admitted.

Annie patted the countertop. "Put her up here. My goodness, Miss Amanda, you're having yourself quite the adventurous summer, aren't you?"

"It wasn't Daddy's fault," Amanda said. "I 'stracted him."

"You 'stracted him. Hmm…" Annie lifted Amanda's chin and tipped her head gently to one side to better observe the hook.

"There was a moose. A *big* moose, and a baby moose, too."

"Two mooses! Well, I can see where that might be a bit of a 'straction."

Linda's entrance caused a small sensation. "Ohmigosh," Sally cried out, eyes rounding as she jumped out of her chair. "I *know* you. You're that famous actress who played in that movie with Tom Cruise!"

"This is Linda Taylor, Amanda's mother," Jake said. "Linda, this is Sally Crawford, her father Ryan, and Lily Houghton, who owns this farm. You've already met Dr. Crawford."

"Don't let her take me away, Daddy," Amanda said, tears flowing faster.

"Hold still, little one," Annie murmured. "No one's taking you anywhere. Sally, run upstairs and fetch my medical kit. It's on top of the bureau in my room. Amanda, it's all right, honey, I'm not going to hurt you. I'm just going to take this little bit of leader off. I can't do anything until I have a pair of forceps."

"There's no barb on the hook," Jake said. "I filed it off before we went fishing." He watched closely as Annie first brushed the tears from Amanda's cheeks, then touched the head of the muddler minnow. She pulled her hand away from Amanda's face and deposited the fly on the countertop. Sally thundered breathlessly into the kitchen, bearing the medical kit, which Annie took from her, opened and retrieved a sterile alcohol wipe. She tore open the little foil packet and gently swabbed the site of the tiny puncture. "There," she said. "All done."

Amanda blinked solemn eyes at her. "But where are the foresteps?"

"Forceps." Annie pulled them out of the kit and brandished them. "Here. But I didn't need to use them. The hook is out."

"It's out?"

"Feel for yourself. Go ahead, it's all right. Your dad could've easily taken it out himself. Heck, I'm surprised it didn't fall out on its own." Annie smiled. "He may have hooked you, but if you were a fish, you could've gotten away very easily."

Amanda reached her little fingers to her cheek. "The other fish he caught got away, too."

"Hello, Linda," Annie said belatedly, scooping

Amanda off the counter and into her arms. "It's nice to see you again. Did the filming in Paris go well?"

Linda nodded. "Yes, very well. In fact, we finished way ahead of schedule, which is why I'm here."

"And you arrived just in the nick of time. We were just about to leave for a ride on Joe's lobster boat," Annie said.

Amanda's eyes lit up, the fish hook instantly forgotten. "A boat ride?"

"All around the harbor. Maybe we'll even see some seals."

"Ooooo, I love seals! Daddy, can we go, too?"

"Well, that depends on Joe," Jake said. "It's his boat."

"The more, the merrier," Joe said amiably, "but I only have two life preservers on board."

"Oh, there's loads of them hanging in the boathouse," Lily countered with a wave of her hand. "Several are child-size, too. It'll be fun, a ride around the harbor."

"Count me out," Ryan said. "I don't do boat rides."

"Oh, c'mon, Dad. It'll be fun," Sally pleaded, but he was not to be swayed.

"I get seasick pretty easy, and those waves look big even inside the harbor. You go without me," he said, but Sally, though she plainly wanted to, shook her head.

"No, that's all right. We'll go for a ride in the car, like you planned," she said, dropping her eyes and heading out the kitchen door.

"I'll have her back in time for supper," Ryan promised Annie before following his daughter.

"You might want to wait for us here," Jake advised Linda as he lifted Amanda out of Annie's arms and started out the door. "Lobster boats smell kind of fishy. It's the bait they use in the lobster traps."

Linda hesitated, watching him carry Amanda onto the porch. Annie could tell she didn't like the idea of getting on Joe's boat, but at length she started after him. "There are some things we really need to discuss, Jake," she said. "I guess a lobster boat is as good a place as any."

Ten minutes later Joe was ushering them aboard and, when they were settled, firing up the *Glory B*'s engine, untying the mooring lines and backing away from the stone pier. Amanda stayed in the wheelhouse with him, fascinated by all the gauges and instruments and Joe's invitation that she take a turn at the wheel once they were under way.

Jake and Linda stood close together in the stern, already immersed in serious conversation. Lily was seated comfortably on a crate in the lee of the wheelhouse, wrapped in a warm coat and wearing a contented expression as she took it all in. Annie joined her there as Joe throttled the boat gently up and steered her in a wide arc back into the harbor. A flock of gulls wheeled in their wake, their cries mingling with the throb of the engine and the splash of big waves breaking at an angle against the bow, rocking the sturdy little boat rhythmically from side to side.

"What's that thing do?" Annie heard Amanda ask as she pointed to the compass rose. Joe patiently explained. Having raised a large family himself, Joe was at ease around children and seemed to enjoy his role as both teacher and tour guide.

Annie took a deep breath of the cool, salty air and felt herself adjust to the pitch and roll of the boat as the sun swept out from behind a cloud and warmed the cool ocean breeze. "This is glorious," she said.

"Heaven," Lily agreed.

LINDA DIDN'T WAIT LONG to broach the subject she wanted to discuss. "I came here to tell you that I am getting married to Hans Gatt."

"I know," Jake said. "I talked with him yesterday when I tried to reach you. He said you were already back in the States. I expected you'd show up sooner or later."

"I wanted to tell the both of you myself, in person," Linda said. "And, Jake, I really think Amanda should come back home with me."

Jake felt his blood pressure soar. "That wasn't the deal," he said. "You promised I could have her for the summer."

"I know," Linda acknowledged. "But I didn't know I'd be home so soon." She hesitated. "Jake, I know you love Amanda, but you haven't had much parenting experience. I really don't feel as if you're paying enough attention to her. Five-year-olds can get into all kinds of trouble in the blink of an eye."

Jake turned and braced his hands on the stern of the boat, staring at the churning wake and the cloud of seagulls hovering behind them and trying to cool his temper. "Amanda and I have been having a good time together, Linda," he said, his voice barely audible above the throb of the engine. "I'm sorry she cut her hand, and I'm sorry I hooked her in the face. But how is that different from the time she fell off the swing at the playground while you were pushing her and she cut her lip? Accidents happen. All I'm asking is that you let her spend the rest of the summer with me.''

Linda shook her head. ''I'm sorry, Jake, but at this point I don't feel that would be wise. Besides, she needs to adjust to the idea of Hans and I getting married, and she'll do that much better back in her own home.''

''Really? Is that why she wants to go back to California with you so badly?'' Jake heard the sharpness of his words and ducked his head. ''Look, we both love her. It does her no good to see us arguing like this. But why *does* she keep saying she doesn't want you to take her away? What don't I know?''

Linda's eyes flickered and then dropped. She turned so that she, too, was facing the rear of the boat. ''She doesn't like Hans. When she found out we might be getting married, she became very upset.''

''Understandably so,'' Jake said.

Linda flashed him a dark look. ''Hans is a wonderful man.''

''He's a cold-hearted son of a bitch and the idea of him raising my little girl,,,''

''You needn't worry about that,'' Linda interrupted, her cheeks flushing. ''Hans has no intention of taking your place. After our wedding in September, he wants us to spend two months in Paris, honeymooning.''

Jake stared. ''Two months? What about Amanda? She should be starting kindergarten this fall. Are you taking her with you?''

''No, we're not,'' Linda said, ''though undoubtedly the experience would be good for her. I've already enrolled her in a private boarding school not too far from Hans's place in Malibu, one of the finest in the country for young girls. She'll be well cared for and educated with excellence.''

Jake was speechless. When he found his voice, his words were louder than he intended. ''No way on earth are you putting my five-year-old little girl in a Malibu boarding school!''

''She'll be six at the end of October, and for God's sake, lower your voice,'' Linda said. ''Everyone's staring.''

Jake glanced toward the wheelhouse, then ducked his head and ran his fingers through his hair. He counted slowly to ten, focusing on the far shoreline of the harbor and then inhaling a deep breath and exhaling slowly. ''Linda,'' he began quietly. ''Could you please explain why boarding school would be better for Amanda than living with me?''

She glanced up at the seagulls, who hovered ever closer and whose cries grew ever louder. ''She needs stability, Jake, and you can't offer her that. Believe me, I know just how unstable your life is. We haven't been divorced so long that I've forgotten how it felt every time you walked out the door to work a shift. I haven't forgotten the four times you were wounded in the line of duty while we were married. *Four times,* and each time you promised it would never happen again.''

''Linda, you're exaggerating...'' Jake began, but she shook her head fiercely.

''No. Hear me out.'' Linda was speaking so passionately that her eyes filled with tears. ''When this last phone call came and they said you'd been shot and it didn't look good, I almost hoped you'd die, because even though we aren't married anymore, I didn't want to go through that hell ever again. And I don't want Amanda to grow up wondering every day if her father's coming home from work. *That's* why I think boarding school would be better for her than living with you.''

Jake scarcely remembered the rest of the harbor ride. He was too deep in turmoil, trying desperately to think of some way to change Linda's mind. In the end he could think of only one thing, though the solution was so alien that at first he pushed it away, but it came back again and again.

By the time Joe berthed the *Glory B* at the stone pier, Jake realized that to keep Amanda he was going to have to give up his very identity. Struggling with this reality, he helped Lily to her feet and assisted her onto the pier. He took Annie's hand as she jumped the two-foot rise that the ebb tide had worked between the level of the water and the pier. He lifted Amanda into his arms and carried her ashore. Finally, he reached his hand out to Linda and hoisted her up.

Joe said goodbye and backed the *Glory B* away from the pier, turning her in a wide arc and heading for home. ''You'll need to give us a ride back to my car.'' Linda spoke coolly at his elbow and Jake nodded. They started up the steps together and Linda glanced back. ''Amanda? Come on. We're leaving.''

Amanda hung back. ''I want to stay with Daddy.''

Jake paused. ''It's all right, Pinch. I'll give you a piggyback up the hill.'' He reached down and scooped her up, sitting her on his broad shoulders, and then started up the steps. His heart twisted at the thought that if his final plea fell on deaf ears, Linda would take his daughter away from him and he might not see her again for a very long time.

CHAPTER FOURTEEN

HALFWAY BACK to the farmhouse, Jake set Amanda down and told her to go ahead with Annie and Lily. He caught Annie's bright blue glance as she took Amanda's hand and moved slowly up the path, keeping pace with Lily. When they were out of earshot he rubbed the back of his neck and struggled for the words that would make Linda change her mind. "Look, Linda, all I want is for Amanda to be happy. Okay, I'll admit we've had a few unexpected mishaps this summer, but we survived them. That's what we Macphersons are best at. Surviving."

"For how long, Jake?" Linda replied quietly. "I *know* you. Fearless Macpherson, that's what they call you at the precinct, isn't it? Sooner or later, there won't *be* any more you, and then what? I've made up my mind. I'm taking Amanda back with me. Please don't make this any harder than it has to be for her."

Jake's eyes studied the ground at his feet, then he looked across the granite ledges to where thousands of years of waves had smoothed the massive stones. "What if I gave up my job?" he said, shifting his gaze to meet hers. "Would you let me keep her then? We could share custody. Anytime you want to see her, spend time with her, travel with her, you could, but she'd stay with me, go to school like a normal kid, have a home life like a normal kid. You can honeymoon for two months in Paris with Hans. Hell, you could stay there indefinitely and call her on the phone every night if you want.''

Linda shook her head. "I know you, Jake," she repeated. "You'll never give up that gun and badge. You thrive on that stuff. It's a big adrenaline rush for you."

"I'll give it up for Amanda," Jake vowed. "I'll sell vacuum cleaners door to door if that's what it takes. She'd be safe with me, Linda. I promise you that."

Linda's face mirrored her doubt. "How do I know you'll really do it?"

"I'll send you every damn one of my future pay stubs." Jake reached out and grasped her shoulders as he made his desperate plea. "Amanda's my daughter, dammit, and I love her. I guess I didn't realize how much she meant to me until you moved away after the divorce. I've only had her for a couple of weeks but it's been so great that I can't imagine losing her all over again. Don't put her in that boarding school. Let me take care of her. I'm asking you." His hands tightened. "I'm begging you."

Linda's brittle mask crumbled briefly, revealing a glimpse of the girl he'd fallen in love with all those years ago. "I only want what's best for Amanda," she said. "Hans thought that boarding school would be good for her…"

"That's because Hans has no time for kids," Jake stated flatly. "I do. Especially for my own."

"I don't know. I'll need some time to think about it." She faltered. "I mean, it's a lot to think about." She glanced up toward the farmhouse and the group of figures that stood on the porch, waiting for them.

"Amanda can stay with you...for tonight, anyway."
She looked up at him. "A vacuum cleaner salesman?"

"If that's what it takes," he repeated.

She paused for a long moment, studying him with
eyes that filled slowly with tears. "Well," she said in
a voice tinged with bitterness, "you've finally realized what it is to truly love someone. You'd give it
up for Amanda, but I wasn't important enough, was
I?"

IT WAS LINDA'S suggestion that Amanda stay at the
farmhouse with Annie and Lily while Jake drove her
back to the cabin to get her car. Jake thought there
must be more that she wanted to discuss in private,
but she was uncharacteristically quiet after saying
goodbye to her daughter. She sat and gazed out the
window at the passing blur of rural Maine landscape.
Her face was still and her expression melancholy, and
in such vulnerable repose Jake felt an unexpected rush
of sympathy for her.

"Amanda's so angry with me," Linda commented
softly, finally ending her long contemplative silence
as he pulled off the main road and began the long
winding drive to the cabin.

"She'll get over it."

"I talked with her before the two of you went away
for the summer. I told her about the possibility of my
marrying Hans and then I told her about the boarding
school. I thought she'd be excited about that because
she'd already made it clear she didn't want to live
with Hans, and they have horses at the school and she
loves horses, but she got so upset." She turned her
head to look at him. "I wanted her nearby so I could

visit her whenever I wanted to." Her eyes filled with tears again. "I really do love her, Jake."

"I know that."

"But I love Hans, too, and marrying him will help my career..." Her voice trailed into silence, and she looked out the window again, impatiently dabbing her eyes with a Kleenex she pulled from her purse, careful not to smudge her makeup. She took a sharp breath, held it a long moment, and exhaled just as sharply.

"All right, Jake. I won't fight you," she said, tossing her hair back in that familiar, queenly gesture, her voice suddenly brisk and businesslike. "If you keep your promise and give up your job, Amanda can stay with you. It's obvious that's what she wants. You're a good father and—" She stopped abruptly when, voice tightened, continuing only when she'd regained control. "And you were a good husband, too. I'm sorry things turned so bad between us. I hope for Amanda's sake this plan works."

Jake pulled to a stop beside his ex-wife's rented BMW. The sun was setting and through the big pines the surface of the pond glowed like burnished gold. Linda got out of the truck and reached immediately into her purse for a cigarette and silver lighter, fumbling in her haste to light up. She inhaled deeply, tipped her head back and closed her eyes.

"You should quit that habit before it kills you," Jake said.

"We all die in the end, don't we, Jake?" She shrugged, blowing a thin stream of smoke. "You should know that better than anyone." She fumbled again in her purse and withdrew her car keys, deactivating the car alarm and unlocking the driver's door. "Tell Amanda goodbye for me," she said, settling herself gracefully in the leather seat. She paused and tipped her head sideways, gazing up at him with her eyebrows raised. "How can I get in touch with you? You obviously don't have a telephone at this cabin, and when I try your cell phone, all I get is static."

He gave her the number to Lily's farm, and she wrote it in her address book. "I'm flying back to California tomorrow," she said, then paused. "I'd like it if Amanda could be at my wedding in September."

"We can talk about that."

"What about your job?"

Jake braced his hand on the roof of the BMW and leaned over the open door. "I think I'll excel as a vacuum cleaner salesman. Someone once told me that I could sell cow shit to a dairy farmer."

Linda stared at him for a moment and then laughed ruefully. "We were fighting at the time, as I recall."

"Well, if you were right, then my financial future should be secure."

Jake drove slowly back to the farm after Linda departed. He was lost in thought, wondering if there could be life beyond the N.Y.P.D. Wondering if he could bring himself to take a job that had nothing whatsoever to do with law enforcement. Knowing that he had to, if he wanted to keep Amanda. Wondering where they'd live, and whether Annie would be as big a part of their lives as he wanted her to be.

He was still lost in thought when he came to the intersection of Route 1 and turned north toward Blue Harbor. He was almost into the village when he saw a girl with a backpack slung over one shoulder standing on the opposite side of the road, facing away from him, arm extended and thumb out toward the approaching eighteen-wheeler. The sight was unusual enough that it roused him from his reveries. Didn't see many hitchhikers in Maine, especially girls, and this one was young, looked almost like Sally...but it couldn't be. Could it?

The truck, slowing to a stop, blocked his view as he pulled abreast. By the time he'd turned his pickup around in the nearest side road, the rig was pulling back into the traveling lane and the girl had vanished. He fell in behind, trying to remember what Sally had been wearing. Hair was the right length and color. Age was right, backpack looked familiar, and in the split second he'd glimpsed her profile before the truck had blocked her from view...

Jake reached inside the center console and retrieved the magnetized blue light. Even if it wasn't Sally, that girl shouldn't be hitchhiking. He reached out his window and felt the heavy magnet thump onto the roof of the cab. He activated the light at the same time he switched on his siren and pulled out just enough so that the driver of the tractor-trailer could see the flashing blue light in his side mirror. The truck immediately slowed and pulled over. Jake killed the siren, got out and walked up to the driver's side. The man who looked down at him from his perch in the cab was middle-aged, burly, had a big tattoo of a coiled rattlesnake on his upper arm, and was working an impressive wad of tobacco around his left cheek. Jake nodded to him. "We're looking for a young girl, thirteen years old, goes by the name of Sally Crawford. Long dark hair, blue eyes. Pretty. You seen her?"

The man glanced at his passenger, who was out of Jake's sight. "You her?" he grunted.

Jake didn't hear the reply, but he did hear the passenger door open and the soft plop of two feet hitting the ground on the other side of the truck. He walked around the front of the eighteen-wheeler and came face-to-face with Sally. She said nothing, just stared at him with the petulant expression of a rebellious teenager. "Into my truck," he said, and she turned with defiant body language and walked toward his pickup. Jake climbed up on the rig's running board where he could see the driver. "Thanks," he said. "Wouldn't want to see you get in trouble for aiding and abetting a juvenile delinquent."

He shut the passenger door, slapped it once and dropped to the ground, whereupon the truck driver wasted no time departing. Sally was sitting in his truck when he climbed back behind the wheel. He reached out his window, wrenched the magnetized blue light off the roof and stashed it back in the center console. "Handy little thing," he said. She was staring straight ahead, her expression sullen. "I guess you've never heard all those horror stories about what happens to girls who hitchhike."

No reply. They sat side by side in silence as sporadic traffic swished past. "I'm just playing a hunch here," Jake continued, "but my guess is you weren't thumbing to your father's house, since you just spent the afternoon with him. My guess is you were heading farther south. New York, maybe. Manhattan. My guess is you miss your friends. Tom Ward, in particular."

This got a rise out of her. She turned her head to look at him. "My mother just doesn't get it," she blurted. "Tom's really nice, but just because he's older than me, she thinks he's bad."

"She thinks he's bad because he's a bad influence on you," Jake corrected, "or have you forgotten the trouble he got you into not long ago? Something to do with an illegal substance, wasn't it? Not to mention his long police record."

Sally flushed and turned her eyes to the front. "There's nothing to do around here. Dad's too freaked out about Trudy and the baby to pay any attention to me. He spent the whole afternoon talking about them and never asked one question about what I was doing. It's like I don't even matter. And Mom thinks staying at that old farm should be enough to make anyone happy. She sits there for hours staring out at the ocean like a zombie and thinks life is great. Well, it's not. It's boring. Maine's boring. I hate it here and I want to go back home."

A long silence passed, both staring out the windshield at the road ahead of them. "I'm guessing your mother doesn't even know you're missing yet," Jake said at length. "And I'm also guessing when she finds out, she's going to be just a little bit upset." No reply. "Okay, Sally, here's the deal," he continued in the same mild, patient voice. "You don't run off, ever again, and you don't hitchhike, ever again. Understood?"

"You're not my father!" Sally stated defiantly.

"No, I'm not, but that doesn't mean I don't care about you or that I can't enforce some laws. That's the deal, and you can take it or I can report all the phone calls you've made to Tom after you signed a specific agreement at the police station to have no contact with him. Trust me, you'll have your day in court." Jake started the pickup and glanced across at Sally. "You ever spent any time in juvenile hall?"

She stared stonily out the windshield, ignoring him. "I thought not," he said, putting the truck into gear. "Well, let me tell you what an average day in juvey lockup is like," he began as they headed for Blue Harbor.

ALMOST 9:00 P.M., nearly full dark, and still no Jake. After Ryan had dropped Sally off, Annie and Lily had fed the girls a simple supper of potato salad, deviled eggs and cold sliced ham. Now Lily was reading one of Robert McKloskey's books to Amanda at the kitchen table, and Sally, who had been untalkative and borderline sullen following her afternoon outing with Ryan, had long since gone to her room to listen to CDs. The farmhouse was quiet and Annie was going quietly crazy waiting for Jake to return.

Oh, such agony it had been, watching him drive away with his ex-wife.

Annie stood on the farmhouse porch, arms crossed beneath her breasts, a pandemonium of emotions churning within. Jake and Linda had once loved each other, and from what she'd seen today there was still lots of emotion churning between the two of them. Some of those feelings they'd once felt for one another were still very much alive. Annie had seen how Linda had looked at Jake in the height of their argument, and she'd seen the answering response in Jake's body language.

Observing it had been painful, but could she condemn him for it? She and Ryan were divorced, as well, and yet they shared an incredible legacy in their daughter. Sally was the glue that would always bond them to each other, no matter what. It was the same with Jake and Linda. They may have grown as far apart as two people ever could, but they still shared Amanda, that precious little girl.

What could be taking him so long? All he'd had to do was to drive Linda back to her car and then return here to pick up Amanda. He should have been gone two hours at the most, yet nearly three had passed. Maybe they'd had an accident. Should she drive over there? A feeling unlike any she'd ever had swept over her at the thought of the two of them alone at that remote cabin. Perhaps he'd given her dinner, and then maybe they'd walked down to the dock and gone for a paddle in the canoe. Perhaps at this very moment they were…

Annie shook herself and paced the length of the porch, gazing through the violet dusk toward the distant twinkle of lights that edged the harbor. There had to be a perfectly reasonable explanation why Jake hadn't yet returned for his daughter. Probably they were still discussing or arguing about Amanda's future and… She heard the phone ring and raced inside to answer it, fearing the worst, but it was Ryan relaying some good news. "I thought Sally might want to know that her baby brother's doing a little better. His blood oxygen levels are up and he's gained two whole ounces."

"That's great, Ryan," Annie said. "I'll tell her."

She went up the stairs to Sally's room and tapped on the door. "Sally?" There was no answer. She pushed it open. The bed was neatly made, which was unlike Sally, and she noticed immediately that Sally's backpack was gone. Resting on the pillow was a sheet of paper filled with Sally's unruly scrawl.

"Sorry, Mom," it read, "but I couldn't stand it

here another moment. Don't worry about me, I'll be fine. Sally.''

Annie whirled and raced down the stairs, clutching the note. "Lily! Lily, did you see Sally go out for a walk?"

Lily frowned. "No. I thought she'd gone up to her room."

Amanda glanced up from the book. "She said she was going for a walk, and not to let Nelly out."

"How long ago?"

Amanda's brow puckered. "A long time," she replied.

Annie frantically searched the huge barn, calling for Sally, but knowing she'd hear no answering reply. Her sense of panic swelled as she ran back into the kitchen and grabbed her purse and car keys. Time was critical. Every moment that passed Sally was getting farther away from where she belonged, and it would soon be full dark. "Lily, Sally's run away and I have to go look for her. Could you keep an eye on Amanda?" Without waiting for a reply she dashed out the door.

Her heart skipped as she heard the sound of a vehicle coming down the gravel road. She spotted approaching headlights and waited at the top of the porch steps with bated breath. It was Jake. She flew down the steps and was beside the truck as it rolled to a stop, speaking through his open window, her words tumbling over each other in a frantic rush. "Jake, Sally's gone, she's run away, she left a note on her bed saying—" It was then that she spotted the passenger sitting beside him on the front seat. "Sally!" she cried, relief and anger blending in her voice. "What on earth were you thinking? Are you all right? How could you have run off that way?"

"She's fine," Jake said. "Couldn't wait to get back here. Isn't that right, Sally?"

Annie caught Jake's subtle head shake as her daughter climbed out of the truck, dragging her backpack behind her. She bit back a barrage of questions and watched mutely as Sally slowly ascended the porch steps, looking over her shoulder when she reached the top. "I'm sorry, Mom. It won't happen again," she said, then went into the kitchen.

Jake closed the truck door behind him and waited until Sally was inside before explaining. "She was hitchhiking. I happened to be driving by so I picked her up and brought her back."

Annie raised her hands to her temples. *"Hitchhiking?"*

Jake reached out and squeezed her shoulder gently. "She's okay," he repeated. "She didn't get very far. Don't be too hard on her. It's not easy being a city girl in the country."

"Oh, Jake," she said, melting at his touch and stepping into his embrace. "Thank you so much for bringing her home." She forgot all her imagined suspicions about him and Linda as he wrapped his arms around her and held her close. She closed her eyes, relishing the safe, protected feeling Jake's presence always instilled in her. The screen door banged and she heard Amanda's voice.

"Daddy?"

"Right here, Pinch." Jake spoke over Annie's shoulder. "Looks like you and me are in business for the rest of the summer, maybe longer. Your mother's going back to California to get ready for the wedding and she's leaving you with me. Think you can stand my company that long?''

"Daddy!" Amanda's voice told all within earshot just how glad she was.

"Okay, you two," Annie said, reluctantly disengaging from Jake's embrace and smoothing her hair back from her face. "You're staying here tonight. Miss Amanda, you're going to bed at a reasonable hour in spite of the nap you had this afternoon. Jake, you must be hungry."

"Starved," he admitted.

Annie led him into the farmhouse, pulled out a chair at the kitchen table and prepared a plate of food for him. She longed to reach out to touch him, but forced herself to be patient. It was 10:00 p.m. when Jake tucked Amanda into bed and shortly thereafter that Annie peeked in on Sally, who was sitting cross-legged on her bed, listening to music. Annie sat on the edge of the bed and waited until Sally reluctantly removed the earphones and heaved an exaggerated sigh. "Go ahead and yell," she said.

"I just wanted to say good-night and to tell you that I love you," Annie said.

Sally stared at her for a moment, then dropped her eyes. "I didn't mean to worry you," she mumbled.

"Well, if you plan to run off again, please let me know ahead of time so I can properly sedate myself, because believe it or not, sweet little best friend of mine, I was worried sick. That comes with being a mother." Annie stood, kissed her daughter on the forehead and left the room.

At eleven, Lily and Rebel repaired to their makeshift bedroom in the parlor, and almost as soon as the door had closed behind them, Jake pulled Annie into his lap with an impatient growl. She twined her fingers through his hair as his kiss ignited the most intimate of fires, and lost herself in the wave of heat that left her breathless and dizzy when they broke apart. Her whole body thrummed with sexual tension. "Blindness is definitely imminent," she gasped.

"Whatever shall we do about that?" he murmured into her ear, toying with the buttons on her sleeveless denim shirt.

"I can think of a treatment that might prevent it," she replied, and by eleven-fifteen, Annie and Jake were half running down the path to the boathouse, Jake carrying the blankets, Annie carrying the flashlight, both of them burning with anticipation.

"DO YOU SUPPOSE," Annie murmured on the edge of sleep, cheek nestled into the warm, solid curve of his shoulder, "that any moment from now on in our lives will ever be as perfect as this one?"

Jake shifted on the blanket, tugging her closer. "I suppose that every moment I spend with you will be..." He paused. "Damn, what's the word I want to use here?" He pondered in the darkness. "Sublime. That's the word that describes it for me."

"Sensational," Annie murmured, marveling at the strong, steady beat of his heart.

"Miraculous," Jake countered, his fingers smoothing the tumble of curls away from her face.

"Miraculous," she agreed. "Totally and completely miraculous. The whole thing. How we met, how we came to be living within a stone's throw of each other this summer, how we came to be in this boathouse tonight, together..."

"Kinda makes you wonder who's steering the boat, doesn't it?"

"Kinda," Annie said. "Jake?"

"Yeah."

"Are you giving it up, really? Being a cop?"

He sucked in a deep breath, ran his fingers along her brow, down her cheek. "Yeah. I am."

Annie nestled into him, pressed against the warm, solid strength of him. "I know it's selfish, but I'm glad."

He lay in silence for a long while, fingers gently stroking. "What about you, Doc?" he said at length. "Which direction are you heading in, come September?"

She sighed. "Oh, Jake, I'm so confused. When I saw you and Linda arguing over Amanda it made me think about Sally. Sally's father lives up here, we live in New York. Ryan does his thing, I do mine, and to hell with what Sally wants and needs. It's the same problem you and Linda are wrestling with. Careers and parenting, except that Ryan isn't fighting for Sally. He moved away from her when he married Trudy, but now I think he realizes how important she is in his life."

"So where does that leave you?"

"I don't know," she said pensively. "But I *do* know I don't want Sally anywhere near that Tom Ward."

Jake's hand leisurely explored the curve of her waist, his warm palm sliding over her hip and along her thigh. "Maybe tomorrow we should get a local paper and check the Help Wanted ads. There are always employment opportunities for people who can assemble things in their own homes and make incredible sums of money doing it.''

"I saw an ad once where you could get paid for reading books," Annie said.

"No kidding? Sounds better than getting shot at."

"Sounds better than patching up people who've been shot."

"Reading books. Wonder what kind," Jake said, tracing his fingers up and down until Annie moaned and moved against him, and just as they were on the verge of discovering another level of intimacy, Annie felt his body tense. "Hear that?"

"No, what?"

"Boat engine. Listen." Sure enough, after a few moments she could make out the low throbbing vibration of an engine as a boat approached the stone pier in the darkness.

"Who'd be boating this time of night?" Annie sat up and pulled the blanket around her.

"A couple of love-crossed teenagers with the same idea we had, maybe?"

Annie smothered a laugh, hastily fumbling for her discarded clothing. "Just as long as one of them isn't Sally."

Jake rose to his feet and pulled on his jeans. "I'll go tell them there's no vacancy. You stay here and keep the blankets warm."

JAKE WAS BAREFOOT, wearing only his jeans as he eased out the boathouse door and stood for a moment in the darkness, sorting through the sounds of the waves breaking against the rocky shoreline and rolling up against the pier. He could hear the boat motor more clearly now, and though there was no moon, starlight gave him a murky view of a low, sleek boat making a cautious approach. No running lights, no voices. The quiet, furtive approach struck him as odd and put him instantly on the alert.

He remained against the boathouse until the boat was nearly to the pier, and then, when he heard the engine slip into Reverse, he walked catlike through the darkness, noting that the tide was high and the deck of the boat nearly level with the top of the pier. There were two men aboard. One remained in the cockpit while the other jumped onto the pier, landing with a stumble and a soft curse, recovering his balance with a forward lurch and spotting Jake for the first time as he did.

"Can I help you gentlemen?" Jake spoke softly but his words unleashed instant action. Jake recognized the swift movement of a weapon being drawn and, without thinking, dove forward. There was a deadly spat of sound as he tackled the intruder and the clatter of metal on stone as they fell in a heap. Luck was with him, for the man struck his head hard on the granite block and was momentarily stunned. With one swift heave, Jake rolled him off the edge of the pier.

Jake's adrenaline surged as he lunged to his feet and took three running steps that landed him on the deck of the boat where the second man was fumbling desperately for something in the darkness of the cockpit. Jake was upon him instantly, knocking him off balance. As he rammed him up against the cockpit wall, he heard the report. There was no silencer on this weapon and the sound was deafening, but the bullet went wild. There was a second gunshot as they fought, and then a third before the pistol dropped to the deck along with the two men.

It was a silent, desperate, savage struggle, and there were moments when Jake felt as though he was losing. His opponent was enormously powerful and quick, his body a writhing contortion of fury, and in the darkness the only sounds were harsh, gasping breaths, blows struck against flesh, the frantic scrabbling for position. The man's hands were strong, so strong, fingers closing around Jake's throat, bearing him down. He chopped his own hands violently against the sides of his opponent's head and the fingers around his neck weakened. Gasping for air, he knifed his body upward, throwing the other man off balance. As he pushed up off the deck, his hand encountered something cold and metallic. His fingers clutched the pistol and in one swift, savage movement he struck out blindly, feeling the heavy weapon connect, hearing the hollow sound of metal against skull.

The man fell back moaning as Jake scrambled to his feet, chest heaving as he struggled for air. He flipped the pistol until the grip was in his palm and extended his arm. "Move and you're dead, you son of a bitch," he gasped.

"Jake!" Annie cried from the boathouse doorway, her voice edged with hysteria.

"Get up to the house," he ordered her tersely. "Call the police."

"Are you okay?"

"Annie, go. Go now, *Run, dammit,* there's more than one man." She stepped out onto the pier, edging gingerly toward the steps. "Go, go, *go!*" he shouted.

As Annie turned to flee, there was a strange noise from beyond the pier. Suddenly the night was lit in a

brilliant flash as multiple beams of powerful searchlights illuminated the boat at the pier and a deep
voice, made hugely surreal by virtue of a loudspeaker,
boomed, *"This is the U.S. Coast Guard. Put down
your weapons immediately!"*

Annie whirled back and raised her arm to shield
her eyes from the brilliant glare. Why hadn't she
heard the boat approach? Jake had raised his arms and
was standing in the searchlight's beam, still holding
the pistol.

"Put down the gun!" the loudspeaker blared.

Jake lowered the weapon very carefully to the deck
of the boat and straightened as the big Coast Guard
cutter moved toward the pier. *"Keep your hands in
the air!"* the amplified voice boomed. He lifted his
hands again slowly.

Annie caught a movement in the wheelhouse.
"Jake, behind you!"

Jake whirled, then dove to the deck as the night
was rent with more gunfire, the shots blurring together
in one long burst of sound. She stood helplessly as
the cutter charged forward and an uncountable number of men wearing dark bulletproof vests leaped onto
the smaller boat's deck, gripping assault rifles as
though they knew how to use them.

"Don't hurt Jake," Annie cried. "He's a cop.
Don't hurt him!"

There were several short spats of gunfire and Annie
collapsed, her knees giving out on her as she raised
her hands to her ears. She had no comprehension of
anything else but that with all that gunfire Jake would
be killed, and that this couldn't be happening,
couldn't be…!

A man's hand closed firmly on her arm. "On your feet," he ordered tersely. "Hold your arms up and out, please. We have to search you."

"There's another man, there were two of them in the boat," she said, teeth chattering with fear, ignoring their instructions. "Don't hurt Jake, he's a cop and I live here, *we* live here, there were two men on that boat but Jake threw one of them into the water and..."

"Lady, raise your arms, please."

"Leave her alone," Jake's voice commanded. Annie turned to see Jake flanked by armed coastguardsmen, hands cuffed behind his back, several guns trained on him. "She lives here, she has nothing to do with this. Annie, are you all right?"

Annie tried to wrench free from the hand that gripped her arm. When she couldn't, she rounded on its owner furiously. "There are two little girls and an old woman up in that farmhouse and they're defenseless. Let go of me, for God's sake, and find that other man before he..."

"We have him, Captain Coffin," a man shouted. "He was crawling out of the water on the portside of the pier."

Annie felt her knees weaken again. "Oh, thank God," she breathed. "Please, let Jake go. He's not involved. We were in the boathouse when those men came. He's a cop, not a criminal. Check his ID and you'll see I'm telling the truth. And if you won't let me go, please send someone up to the house. They're sure to have heard the shooting, and they'll be scared."

One of the Coastguardsmen had already retrieved Jake's wallet. He raised it in his hand, and in the brilliant searchlights Annie saw the flash of the gold badge. "'Lieutenant Jake Macpherson, N.Y.P.D.,'" the coastguardsman read from the photo ID. "'Detective, narcotics division.'" He lowered the wallet and stared at Jake. "What are you doing in Maine, Lieutenant?"

"Vacationing," Jake said.

"You had no idea this bust was going down?"

"None."

"Hey, wait a minute," the captain of the vessel spoke up. "By any remote chance are you *the* Jake Macpherson who used to spend summers at his grandparents' camp on Tunk Pond?"

Jake squinted into the glare of the searchlight. "And might you be Kyle Coffin who thought Jenna Hogan was stacked higher than Raquel Welch?"

"I'll be damned," the captain said. "I know this guy. Uncuff him."

"Captain," one of the men interrupted, "we've got two men in custody and one of them was wounded in that last exchange. I've radioed for an ambulance to meet us at the dock, but the nearest hospital's in Ellsworth. Looks like he's in pretty bad shape."

"Get both of them onto the cutter," Coffin ordered. "Grady, pick three men to stay behind and secure this boat. If it's holding what we think it is, we'll need to get some help handling the cargo. Macpherson, you'll need to be available for questioning, you and your friend both. Thanks for the help with the bust, and sorry about the confusion."

"Annie's a trauma surgeon, one of the best there is," Jake said, rubbing his freed wrists. "If you need to keep that bastard alive long enough to see he stands trial, she can probably do it."

Coffin nodded curtly to Annie. "Can you help?"

Annie hesitated. She had no burning desire to save the life of a criminal who had just tried to kill the man she loved, but she was a doctor and bound by the code. She nodded reluctantly.

"Climb aboard," Captain Coffin said.

"Jake…?" She cast an anxious glance over her shoulder as an officer helped her onto the deck of the cutter.

"Don't worry about anything here," he said, reading her thoughts. "I'll bring Lily and the girls with me to the hospital to pick you up."

CHAPTER FIFTEEN

IN HER DREAMS the sun was warm, the wind was mild, and the damp sand beneath her bare feet was beaten hard by the timeless, rhythmic wash of the waves. A man walked beside her, tall and broad of shoulder, a quiet and solid presence. His head was ducked as he walked along, the wind tousling his tawny hair. In her dreams she felt such a sense of peace and safety in his presence, and such an overwhelming surge of love and gratitude that he was there with her, holding her hand.

In her dreams the whole of her life could be spent just this way, walking hand in hand with this extraordinary man, but the pleasant reverie was brought up short by the touch of an unfamiliar hand on her shoulder and an equally unfamiliar voice saying apologetically, "Dr. Crawford?"

Annie lifted her head out of the cradle of her arms and sat up at the nurses' station desk. "Yes?" She tried to sound professional and awake, but she was fully aware of her groggy voice and appearance. Not her fault, of course. Four hours of emergency surgery in a strange hospital at 4:00 a.m. had taken its toll on her already weary body. She ran her fingers through her hair, smoothing it away from her face.

"Dr. Danforth wanted me to tell you that the patient has regained consciousness. A Medevac chopper is going to fly him to Bangor shortly," the ER nurse said.

"Good." Annie yawned behind a hand. "They can have him."

"There's a man asking for you. A Jake Macpherson."

Annie pushed to her feet and smiled. "Thank you, Christine."

"No, thank *you,* Dr. Crawford. It was an honor."

"I couldn't have done any of it without your and Dr. Danforth's assistance."

The nurse shook her head. "I've never seen surgery like that before. That man should have died."

Annie stumbled through a fog of exhaustion as she walked out of the ER admitting area. She felt a warm remnant of that wonderful dream surge back when she spotted Jake standing outside the automatic doors. She walked right into the solid embrace of his waiting arms and let him hold her for a long and cherished moment. "The girls?" she murmured into the strong curve of his shoulder.

"With Lily, having breakfast in the cafeteria."

"Oh, Jake. That man on the boat had a machine gun..."

"He didn't hit anything with it."

"That's only because you knocked him down."

"You must be exhausted."

"I want you to hold me just like this for the rest of my life."

"Nothing would make me any happier."

She felt tears flood her eyes and pressed more tightly against him. "I was so afraid. I've never been so afraid."

"That's natural when bullets are flying through the

air,'' he soothed. ''You'd be crazy not to be scared at a time like that.''

She shook her head fiercely. ''I wasn't afraid for myself,'' she said, lifting tear filled eyes to his. ''Jake, you could easily have been killed.''

He gazed down at her in silent contemplation and then rested his chin atop her head and remained quiet for a long moment. ''But I wasn't,'' he said at length. ''We're all safe, and everything's okay.''

She took a shaky breath. ''It won't be okay till you actually resign from the force. Maybe you should try being a vacuum cleaner salesman for a year or so, just to see what happens.''

THE DRIVE back to the farm was quiet. The girls shared the back seat of Annie's car with Lily, all three having run out of adrenaline and rapid-fire conversation back at the hospital. Annie sat up front with Jake, dozing with her head on his shoulder as he drove. It was nearly noon by the time they turned onto the road that led down the peninsula. ''Well, well,'' Lily said from the back seat. ''There's no rest for the wicked.''

Annie opened her eyes and moaned. The farmhouse yard was choked with police cruisers and unmarked vehicles. ''I can't stand any more,'' she said. ''I need a hot bath and a long nap.''

''I believe all this fuss has something to do with that boat,'' Lily said, peering down at the stone pier as Jake found a parking spot out by the barn. ''They're swarming all over it.''

Jake identified a bomb squad unit among the vehicles that crowded the yard and glanced in the back seat. ''You girls stay inside the house, you hear me?

No wandering around down by the pier. This is serious stuff." He cut the ignition and for a moment they all sat and stared at the beehive of activity. A uniformed officer approached. State police.

"Sir," he said to Jake, "I'm afraid I'm going to have to ask you to leave. This area is off limits."

"Sir," Lily Houghton rejoined with a healthy dose of starch from the back seat. "This is my house, and I'm not leaving."

The officer peered in the window at the occupants then narrowed his eyes on Jake. "Are you Lieutenant Macpherson?" He straightened. "Sorry, sir. Go ahead with your business. And if you're Lily Houghton, ma'am, your son's waiting for you inside. He arrived about twenty minutes ago. He showed us his ID and we..."

"Yes, yes. Lester." Lily squared her shoulders. "My, oh my. This is turning out to be quite a day."

"Yes, it is." Annie yawned again in spite of herself. "Following quite a night."

Jake opened his door and levered his tall frame out. "Ladies," he said, walking around the vehicle and opening doors. "Shall we?"

Lily's son met them on the porch. He was short, much shorter than Jake had expected. There was nothing of Lily in him.

"I'm Jake Macpherson," he said, climbing the porch steps and thrusting out his hand.

Lester Houghton's features were carefully neutral, his dark hair expertly coiffed, his nails manicured, his suit custom-tailored and of the highest quality. He shook Jake's hand with professional briskness. "Lester Houghton." His glance shifted beyond Jake. "Hello, Mother. I wasn't expecting to find the place overrun with police." He looked to Lily's right. "You must be Dr. Crawford. I should inform you that I've filed charges of endangerment against you," he said.

"Oh, for heaven's sake, Lester," Lily said. "Do I look endangered?"

"You had no right to take my mother out of the convalescent home without my knowledge or consent," he said to Annie.

Rebel came out onto the porch, and Lily reached down to stroke his head. "And you had no right to put Rebel in a shelter without informing me, Lester, or to sell my car," she said. "But you did."

"That was different. You were in no shape to be taking care of a dog or driving a car."

"Lester," Lily said, her steel easily matching that of her son's, "let's go inside and talk about this in private."

"Mother, look around you. Doesn't all this strike you as being slightly out of the ordinary?"

"The police? Yes, of course, but what happened last night *was* slightly out of the ordinary."

"That's what I mean. Do you honestly think you can handle that sort of thing by yourself? Burglars, drug runners, whoever those criminals were? Do you think you could live here alone and be safe?"

"Lester, in all my years living here this sort of thing has never happened, and in any event, I wasn't the least little bit alone." She gave Annie an apologetic smile. "Please, let's all go into the kitchen. I could use a tall glass of iced tea, and I want to show you some plans I've drawn up for the place—plans for my future here."

"Mother, please," Lester said, obviously frustrated

with how the conversation was proceeding. "We've found a very nice place for you, an assisted-living center. You'll have your own private apartment and you'll be close by so we can visit you often. It's a beautiful place, very high-end. They have flower and vegetable gardens, and lots of group activities…"

"I'm staying here, Lester. Right here with Rebel." Lily tapped the porch boards with her cane for emphasis. "Look around you. What do you see in your high-end assisted-living center that could possibly compare to this?"

"You *can't* live here alone," Lester said.

"In case you haven't noticed, she's *not* alone," Annie interjected.

"She will be, once you're gone," Lester shot back. He turned to his mother, his features stern. "I won't let you stay here and risk getting hurt again. The next time you may not be so lucky. You might lie here for days and die from exposure before anyone finds you. I know that once you see this place, you'll change your mind."

"Lester," Lily said wearily. "This is my home and I'm not leaving here. I've drawn up some plans for the place which I'd be happy to show you…"

"Mother, please listen to me. I'm doing this for your own protection. You don't seem to understand that you have no choice in the matter."

Annie put her arm protectively around Lily's shoulders. "I believe she does," she said. "And hopefully, Lester, when you get to be your mother's age, you'll have choices, too. Oh, and as far as showing the farm to prospective buyers, just so you know, that's not happening. Not as long as I'm renting the place."

Lester's eyes lasered into her, and Annie felt a chill

run up her spine. "It's a big mistake for you to meddle in my mother's affairs," he said.

"Perhaps you should listen to what she's saying," Annie replied.

"I only want what's best for her. I want her to be safe, something that apparently neither of you understand."

"If you looked at plans she's made for this farm…"

"I'm sorry but she's my mother and I'm responsible for her," Lester said, his face darkening. "This place is going to be sold, and as for you, I suggest you find yourself a lawyer."

"Oh, we already have one," Jake said easily, leaning against the porch post and looking as mild as the midsummer day. "Kathryn Yeager. Maybe you've heard of her. But if you haven't, maybe you've heard of her father, William Paul Yeager, the supreme court justice."

Jake's words broke through the careful veneer of Lester Houghton's impassive face. It was obvious that he knew very well who both Kathryn Yeager and her father were. For a few moments he stood frozen in place, and then he abruptly descended the steps, walking past them without a glance. Lily's tentative, "Lester?" did nothing to stop his rapid departure. He gained his dark Mercedes sedan and departed the farm with an angry spurt of gravel. Lily watched him drive out of sight and sighed. "Oh, dear. I don't understand why he's being so difficult. Why didn't he want to look at my plans?" she said in a hurt voice.

"Because he doesn't believe they'll ever come to fruition," Annie said grimly.

LATER THAT AFTERNOON, while Annie soaked in a hot bath and Lily sipped iced tea out on the porch, keeping a watchful eye on the girls, Jake walked down to the pier. He could see that the Coast Guard cutter had returned and was docked behind the confiscated boat. Kyle Coffin. Who would've thought he'd end up as a captain in the Coast Guard? Jake's grandparents had tried to discourage the friendship the two boys had forged all those long summers ago. They thought Kyle Coffin was too much of a rogue and would be a bad influence on their grandson.

Jake was grinning to himself as he descended the steep steps to the wharf. Overseeing the activities, when Kyle spotted Jake, he broke off a conversation with one of his ensigns and approached, thrusting out his hand. "Hey," he said.

"Hey, yourself," Jake replied, shaking the offered hand.

"You okay? We treated you pretty roughly last night and damn near got you killed. I'm sorry about that."

"No need to apologize," Jake said. "I know better than most that you were just doing your job."

"Speaking of jobs, does being a big-city cop mandate getting shot full of holes? You look like you've stopped more than your share."

Jake shook his head. "I'm done with all that. I'm here for the summer, and then I don't know. Maybe I'll try selling vacuum cleaners."

"Can't blame you there. Did you ever get your degree, or did that pretty little lady from New York City addle your head all those years ago?"

"I married that pretty little lady and got my degree, too," Jake replied. "We're divorced now. Linda's out in California, making movies. We have a five-year-old daughter, Amanda.''

''Ah,'' Kyle said. ''And the lady doc?''

''Annie Crawford.'' Jake watched the men in the bomb squad lift something out of the confiscated boat and place it carefully in a special container. ''She's a very special lady.''

''I can vouch for that,'' Kyle said. ''She kept that guy alive, and that was beyond the realm of possibility as far as I'm concerned.''

''Not beyond her realm.'' Jake glanced around at the flurry of activity. ''Obviously this wasn't your average drug bust. What was that boat ferrying, anyhow?''

Kyle hesitated. ''You're no doubt aware that there's a lot of drug activity along the Maine coast. All the outer islands make ideal hiding places. Heroin's still the big game—''

''Since when did heroin require a bomb squad for removal and transportation?'' Jake interrupted. ''Look at that swarm of badges. You've got the Feds, half a dozen DEA suits, and what looks like some mighty big guns from an agency I don't even recognize...''

''Okay,'' Kyle said, lowering his voice. ''But this stays under your hat. That boat was carrying explosives in addition to drugs.''

Jake stared. ''The hell you say.''

''We busted the ring by decoding radio transmissions for the past three months. We caught the other half of the operation ten miles out at sea, then snuck in here and picked this boat up.''

Jake shook his head, perplexed. ''What are you

saying? That this is some kind of terrorist organization?''

"I'm saying that boat was carrying enough explosives to blow up the entire town of Blue Harbor.''

Jake swore under his breath. "And they were planning to rendezvous *here?*''

Kyle shook his head. "Doubtful. I think they were onto us and they wanted to off-load their cargo someplace where they could retrieve it later. They picked the first good place, and it just happened to be here, that's all. I don't think you have to worry about a recurring theme.''

"What kind of explosives? What kind of an operation are we talking about here?''

Kyle shook his head. "That's classified, Jake. Sorry.''

Jake glanced back at the confiscated boat, and then up the slope to the old cape. "Of all the places for something like this to go down,'' he said softly.

"Yeah. Not exactly the way life should be,'' Kyle said, then straightened. "Uh, oh. Brace yourself, old friend. Here come the reporters. They've been waiting all morning for you to show up.'' Coffin cuffed his shoulder with a devilish grin. "Ever see that movie *Die Hard,* where Bruce Willis takes on an entire terrorist group single-handedly? Well, guess what? You're their Bruce, and they want a story.''

Two hours later Jake stood beside Lily on the farmhouse porch and watched the last of the police cruisers and unmarked vehicles depart. "Jake,'' she said thoughtfully after the dust had settled, "perhaps now would be a good time to lock the gate.''

"They aren't the bad guys, Lily,'' he said. "And, anyway, they're done. They've taken all the evidence and driven the confiscated boat away. They won't be back. No need to lock the gate, unless you want to keep Jim out.''

She snorted. ''Jim wouldn't be kept out by locking that gate.''

''Wouldn't be much a man if he was,'' Jake admitted.

''There must have been a lot of drugs in that boat. Millions of dollars' worth, to create that much commotion.'' She shook her head with a weary sigh. ''What's this world coming to?'' Before he could reply, she turned to him and said, ''You must be hungry. How about a tuna melt?''

Lily led him into the kitchen where he sat at the table, watching Amanda sketch out a charcoal drawing using Lily's art supplies. ''I'm making this for you, Daddy,'' she said somberly. ''So you can see what we saw.''

''It was dark, Pinch. What could you see?''

''We saw all the lights.'' Amanda's gaze was almost reproachful. ''We saw you in the lights and we heard all the guns. And then we didn't see you.'' Her eyes suddenly flooded with tears and she bent her head back over the sketch to hide them from him.

Jake pushed out of his chair and knelt beside her to study the picture, which he could make no sense of. ''I'm sorry, Pinch. I didn't mean to scare you.'' His fingers brushed a stray lock of hair back behind her ear.

''But you did,'' she said, her lower lip quivering. And then she dropped the charcoal pencil, threw her arms around her father's neck and burst into sobs. Jake lifted her in his arms and carried her out onto the porch.

"Shh-hh," he soothed. "It's okay."

"If you die, Mommy'll make me go to boarding school."

"That's not going to happen. I promise."

He held her until she quieted, patting her back, murmuring soothing words. "I love you, Daddy." She hiccuped.

"I love you, too, Pinch," he said, his eyes stinging. "I'm going to get a job that's so safe and boring that you'll fall asleep when I tell you about it."

She blinked her eyes, thick lashes sparkling with tears. "Promise?"

"Promise."

ANNIE FELL ASLEEP in the bathtub and it was the temperature of the cooling water that finally woke her. She opened her eyes and blinked at the bathroom wall, at the wallpaper patterned in tiny rows of pink and blue flowers intertwined by green-leafed vines, and shifted her body. She sighed wearily and sat up straight, arching her back and rotating her shoulders. Water splashed onto the floor as she stood and reached for a towel. She must be getting old. A hot bath didn't quite work the same miracles it used to.

Nonetheless, she felt better. The cramping aches and muscle kinks that always accompanied a long and complicated surgery were somewhat eased. She wrapped herself in a thick terry-cloth towel and stepped out of the tub. Stood dripping on the bathroom floor, thinking about Jake. Felt a surge of warmth flood through her, followed by a chill of fear. A few short hours ago he had come perilously close to being killed.

Annie walked into the kitchen barefoot, wearing a

baggy gray sweatshirt and faded jeans, her hair still damp from the bath. Lily was just putting the food onto the table. "Come and get it," she announced.

"Where's the rest of the gang?" Annie said.

"Jake's on the porch with Amanda and Sally's in her room writing a letter to a friend. An exciting letter, no doubt."

Annie nodded. "No doubt." She pushed open the screen door and let it bang behind her, shoving her hands into her jeans' pockets and dropping into the chair beside Jake. She leaned back, stretching her legs out and crossing her ankles. "Soup's on," she relayed.

Amanda was leaning against her father's chest, thumb in her mouth, cheeks tear-stained. Annie reached out her hand to smooth the young girl's tousled hair. "Poor girl," she said. "After we eat, I'll change the dressing on your hand, but your face looks just fine. Can't even tell where your dad hooked you." Amanda sniffed and blinked somberly at her and Annie sighed. "I don't blame you," she said. "I feel the same way."

"How's that?" Jake said, glancing at her.

"How do you *think* I feel after everything that's happened?" She heard the sharpness in her words and felt a twinge of guilt. "Let's eat, Jake," she said, her voice gentling. "Lily's fixed a nice meal." But she wasn't ready to move. She felt her body melting into the chair as she gazed out across the sparkling waters, marvelling at the beauty and peace of the place after all the violence it had just witnessed. "God, I hate guns," she said with quiet vehemence.

Amanda took her thumb out of her mouth. "Me, too," she said.

THE PHONE RANG while they were eating their tuna melts and Annie answered it. It was Elsa Morrow, the geriatric specialist from New York who had done the evaluation on Lily. "I've compiled my test results and faxed a copy both to Lily's doctor and to her son, Lester," she said. "My reports gave Lily high marks. She's as sharp as a tack. And she's well on her way to full recovery from her hip surgery. But you were right about Lily's son. He's going to fight this. He called me yesterday and informed me that he had filed charges of endangerment against you, and that he has a place all picked out for her in Boston, an assisted-living center. He said that he refuses to allow her to live in an isolated situation where her health and safety could be jeopardized, and he insists that because he has her power of attorney, he can make this happen regardless of my reports."

"And Lily's doctor? Did you speak with him?"

"I did. He's obviously intimidated by Lester but he said that he respected my opinion and that he could see from my reports that Lily's condition had improved dramatically since the last time he'd examined her."

"So what's next?"

"Well, all the legal paperwork ties things up and keeps Lily in limbo. Annie, as long as Lester has power of attorney, he can sell her land out from under her. I hope I'm wrong, but Lester may be interested in the money. That peninsula Lily wants to live on until she dies is probably worth well over ten million dollars in development potential. You should think about engaging the best lawyer you can find to protect her interests."

"We've already discussed it. Jake knows someone

he thinks can help. He dropped the name when Lester paid his mother a visit yesterday. I must say, it had the proper effect.''

"Good," Elsa said. ''And good luck. Lily's a great lady.''

Annie hung up the phone and relayed the information to Lily, who was searching through her recipe box looking for her grandmother's gingersnap cookie recipe. She listened and nodded. "All right," she said with a firm nod. "Let's get that lawyer. I guess it's time to show Lester we mean business." Lily found the recipe card and gazed tenderly at the graceful, sepia writing that listed the ingredients. "This recipe is over a hundred years old and still going strong."

"Just like you will be," Jake said.

"We'll see," Lily said. "Well, young lady," she addressed Amanda, "you promised you'd help if I found the recipe. Do you still want to?"

"Can I mix it up in the bowl?"

"You can make it, mix it and bake it."

Amanda's face brightened. "Okay. I'll help."

"Good," Lily nodded. She looked at Annie and Jake. "The two of you should get some rest. Go on, I'll watch the girls."

Annie smiled gratefully. "I think I'll take a walk first. I need the fresh air."

"Me, too," Jake said, pushing to his feet. "That is," he added, giving her an uncertain look, "unless you'd rather be alone."

"Dr. Annie shouldn't be alone, Daddy," Amanda said. "Those bad men could come back."

"They're not coming back, Pinch," Jake said. "You don't have to worry about that."

Annie picked a careful path down the slope behind

the house, heading for the ledges on the opposite side of the peninsula from the boathouse. She heard Jake's footsteps but he remained behind, letting her lead the way. The ledges were smooth and still warm underfoot from the afternoon sun. She crept carefully to just above the waterline, where barnacles crusted the rocks and great beards of seaweed moved in the dark water. For a long time she stood there, facing into the breeze and staring out at the Gulf of Maine while Jake stood beside, waiting. She took a deep breath and shoved her hands deeper into her pockets, rounding her shoulders. The late-afternoon sunlight cast her shadow on the water and she studied the tall shadow that stood next to hers, rippling with the movement of the water, and let her breath out slowly.

"I'm so tired," she said at length, "but I'm afraid if I close my eyes, it will all come back. Those men, the guns, the shooting. I still can't believe any of it really happened, but it did, didn't it? Last night really happened."

She pulled her hands out of her pockets and crossed her arms in front of her, protectively. "And how you reacted to that awful violence made me realize that you're an expert at handling that kind of stuff. Criminals, guns and shooting. That's your world, Jake. My God, that's the world you've lived in for as long as I've been living in mine, which is why you and I are both so good at what we do, but it scares me so much because if you don't quit, I'm afraid that's the world you're going to die in."

He made no response but after a long moment he reached out a hand and gently squeezed her shoulder. At his touch she turned into the solid warmth of his embrace and began to cry.

CHAPTER SIXTEEN

ANNIE WOKE to the muted sound of the whistle buoy, bespeaking an early morning fog. She woke without Jake beside her and felt a deep sense of emptiness. It had only been two hours, but it felt as though they'd been parted for days, months, years.

She'd gone to his room in the silence of the night, holding her breath and hearing the beat of her heart, moving to his bed and shivering when he reached out and touched her, trembling as he pulled her night-gown over her head and let it drop with a silken hiss to the floor, aching deep inside as he pulled her down beside him, naked and flushed with the heat of desire.

Hours later they parted reluctantly, wondering what the future held for them. The uncertainties had lent a poignancy to their lovemaking, and Annie knew that her feelings for Jake had grown to the point where she couldn't imagine a life without him in it. Somehow she had to rearrange her world around their relationship and make everything work for both of them, as well as for Amanda and Sally.

Lily was in the kitchen, working on the sketch of Sally and Nell, and she glanced up as Annie made her way toward the coffeepot. "Jake and Amanda are already gone," she said. "They left at the crack of dawn."

Annie froze in the act of pouring herself a mug of strong black brew. "Why?"

"He mentioned something about a tree that had blown down on the roof of the cabin, said he needed to hire someone to cut it down and fix the roof. I gave him the names of a couple of carpenters in Blue Harbor who might help out. He called them bright and early, and they were going to meet him there."

"Oh." Annie dropped into the nearest chair. She pulled her mug closer and stared down at the whorl of steam that rose from its surface.

"Oh, don't worry," Lily said, making a few more Spartan strokes with the charcoal pencil. "They'll be back in time for supper. I told him I wouldn't hear of Amanda sleeping in a cabin that had a hole in the roof, and that they'd both have to stay here until it was properly fixed."

Annie looked up hopefully. "How long will the job take, do you think?"

"Well," Lily said, narrowing her eyes critically on the sketch, "the names I gave him were probably two of the best but slowest carpenters in Blue Harbor. They're notorious for taking long lunch breaks just to go fishing, and that cabin of Jake's is on a mighty fine fishing pond."

Annie jumped from her chair, threw her arms around the older woman and gave her a kiss on the cheek. "Thank you, Lily Houghton. You're a dear."

"DADDY, why is that man looking at you that way?" Amanda whispered, frowning at the lumber store clerk who was figuring out how much roofing material would be needed to repair the cabin roof. He was scowling and glancing at Jake regularly. Jake looked down at his T-shirt to make sure he wasn't wearing anything too bawdy, but it was a plain dark green, no words, no logos and no breakfast food spilled on it.

"Dunno, Pinch. Maybe he thinks he knows me. I used to spend summers around here, back when I was a kid. Should I ask him?"

Amanda grinned and nodded.

The older man looked up. "Ten squares of asphalt shingles, five gallons of roofing cement, sixty feet of drip edge, galvanized, sixteen sheets of exterior grade plywood, five pounds of roofing shingles..." He paused, stared fiercely, and then something clicked and his face brightened. "You were on the news last night," he said. "You're the New York City cop who busted that terrorist group."

"You must be mistaken," Jake said, embarrassed.

"No, he's not, Daddy," Amanda said. "I saw you do it."

"Amanda, why don't you..."

"Well now, son, I want to shake your hand," the older man said, reaching across the counter. "Facing up to terrorists with machine guns, and you empty-handed. By God, I want to tell you, that took grit," he said, pumping Jake's hand vigorously. "You'll always be welcome here, even if you are a flatlander."

Jake's face was still burning ten minutes later, driving out to the cabin to meet the carpenters he'd hired. What bothered him even more than the public display in the lumber store was the fact that probably a lot of people had seen the very same blurb on the news. What if his ex-wife got wind of it? What then? Would she demand that Amanda be returned immediately for breach of contract? "I can't win," he muttered to himself. "It wasn't my fault that boat landed at Lily's pier, and if I'd known they had guns, I'd have run the other way.''

Amanda's gaze was admonishing. ''No, you wouldn't, Daddy.''

''Well, any half-intelligent person would have, and that doesn't say much for me, does it?'' He pulled up in the cabin yard and cut the engine. The carpenters' truck was already there, but they weren't looking over the roofing job. They were standing down on the dock, gazing out at the pond.

Jake walked through the grove of big pines lining the shore, Amanda tagging at his heels. ''There's a hatch on,'' one of the men said excitedly as he approached. ''Look at them trout rising out there. I bet there's pretty good fishin' in this pond right about now, even though it's past prime. Jeez'm crow, you see that one, Walter? Bet that brookie ran two pounds, easy.''

It was hard to wrangle the men away from the water's edge, but at last they were wandering around outside and inside the cabin, rubbing their jaws, canting their heads, staring at this and that, pondering and puzzling out the job. ''Well,'' George concluded. ''Me'n Walter'll have a go at it, I guess. You say the lumber store's delivering the stuff this afternoon? Fair enough. We'll make a fresh start first thing tomorrow morning.''

''You could take the tree down now,'' Jake suggested. ''One less thing to do tomorrow, and that's a big job in itself. That's a huge old pine.''

''Yuh, 'tis.'' Walter nodded. ''But it's nearly dinner time, and by the time we ran down a chain saw big enough to handle that tree, it'd be suppertime. No, we'll get our gear together and be ready at sunup tomorrow.''

''How long do you figure this job'll take you?''

George and Walter rubbed their chins in unison. ''Hard to say,'' George said.

Walter shook his head in agreement. ''Hard to tell, awful hard. That's a big tree. Big hole in that roof. No tellin' how much damage it did to the structural integrity of the cabin itself…''

''What do you suppose that hatch is, anyhow?'' George asked Walter. They both turned and looked down at the pond, eyes narrowing.

''Dunno,'' Walter said, rubbing the back of his neck and silently speculating.

''Bet a muddler minnow'd work,'' George said. ''Number sixteen.''

''You and your muddlers,'' Walter muttered.

''My daddy hooked me with one of them yesterday morning,'' Amanda offered.

Both men stared down at her in surprise. ''You don't say,'' George commented.

''Right here,'' she said, touching her cheek. ''It stuck in.''

''Lordy,'' Walter said. ''Bet that smarted.''

''Say,'' George said as if he'd just thought of something important. ''Ain't you the flatlander that was on the news last night? The one what took them terrorists on single-handedly?''

''No,'' Jake said. ''Must be a look-alike.''

''Daddy,'' Amanda protested. ''That *was* you.''

Walter and George studied him the way they had studied the pond when the fish were rising. ''That was really somethin', happenin' out to Lily Houghton's place like it did. Good thing you were there. You know Lily?"

Jake could see that George and Walter were warming to the subject and he turned to Amanda. "We know Lily, and she's quite a lady. In fact, we'd better get going. We promised Lily we'd bring her back some groceries, didn't we?"

"We did?" Amanda said.

"Yeah, me'n George best skedaddle, too," Walter said, glancing over Jake's shoulder. "Looks like you got company comin'. Fancy rig, that. Too fancy to be on these logging roads. She'll rip the bottom out if she ain't careful."

Jake turned and his heart plummeted. It was Linda's BMW. He felt Amanda's little hand tug at his own when she recognized her mother's rental car. "Daddy, don't let her take me."

Linda parked as George and Walter reached their rickety truck and departed. She sat for a moment in the car and then Jake saw her reach forward to stub out the cigarette she'd been smoking. She got out, closed the door and stood looking at both of them. "Hello, Amanda. Jake," she said in a voice too neutral to fathom.

Jake felt Amanda press against him, hiding behind his legs. "Linda," he said. "The men who just left are the carpenters who're going to fix this place up for us," he said. "They said they could do it in jig time. A day or two."

Linda looked at the enormous tree lying on top of the cabin and made no comment. She looked pale and there were circles beneath her eyes. "I didn't fly out yesterday."

"No, I can see you didn't," Jake said.

"I was at the airport waiting for my flight when I saw the early morning news about the drug bust, and the explosives, and I knew you'd been involved when they described where it all took place. I tried to call Blue Harbor, to make sure you and Amanda were okay, but there was no answer at the number you gave me. So I canceled my flight and went back to the hotel to watch the midday news. I saw a live broadcast yesterday afternoon that included an interview with you."

Jake felt himself bracing for the worst. He watched her carefully, trying to read her but failing. She seemed off balance, as if she wasn't quite sure what she'd come to say, and she didn't seem to expect anything from him. She looked toward the pond and then back at them and smiled a trembling little smile. Her shrug was borderline awkward.

"I just came to say that I was proud of you, Jake, and that no matter what, I'll always be proud of you. You'll always fly through life like a superhero, doing what's good and what's right, regardless of the risk to yourself. That's just how you are. You're a better man than I ever deserved, and the best father Amanda could ever hope to have."

While Jake struggled in astonished silence for some response, Linda focused on her daughter. "And you, Amanda. So patient with the mother who wanted above all things to be a great actress. So patient with the mother who never realized that the most precious gift she'd ever be given was you, and the most important job in life would be mothering you. I'm sorry I let you down. I'm sorry I even mentioned boarding school to you. That was wrong in so many ways that I didn't sleep at all last night. I love you, Amanda, and I never meant to hurt you. I want you to be happy, and if you want to live with your father, then I'll accept that. But I'd like us to be friends, too. Do you think we can be friends?''

Jake felt Amanda shift behind him. Felt her hands tighten convulsively on his pant leg. ''Yes,'' she said in a tentative voice.

''Amanda, I know you don't like Hans, but will you come to my wedding?'' Linda asked. ''It would mean so much to me to have you there.''

''Yes,'' Jake heard her say in the same small voice.

Linda smiled another wan, trembling smile. ''Good. Can you give me a kiss goodbye?''

Jake glanced down. Amanda was regarding her mother with a turbulent mixture of desperate love and wary caution. ''Go on,'' he murmured, and she obediently walked into her mother's embrace and returned it with a fierce, childlike hope that made Jake turn his eyes away.

SALLY WAS WANDERING down to the boathouse just before lunch to check for souvenirs from the big gunfight, wondering how the scheduled surgery was going on her half-brother Adam, wondering how she would ever survive another day so far away from Tom and the city, when she heard the approaching chug of a boat engine. She felt a momentary lurch of fear, then just as suddenly relaxed as the familiar old lobster boat nosed around the point and headed toward her. ''C'mere, Nelly.'' Sally scooped the pup into her arms, holding her while the *Glory B* pulled up alongside the pier.

Joe was in the wheelhouse, but another person jumped out to tie the boat to the piling. A boy. Sally stared as he expertly dallied the rope in a series of half hitches and then straightened. He was tall and tow-headed, his smooth complexion browned by the sun, his eyes the color of an October sky. Sally felt a peculiar thump within her chest and suddenly felt extremely shy.

"Hello," she said, ducking her head and gazing warily up at him through her eyelashes. "Who're you?"

Before he could answer, Joe jumped onto the pier. "Cal, this is Sally Crawford. Sally, my youngest son, Calvin. He helps me haul traps in summer. Your mother to home?"

"Yes," Sally replied, stumbling over the word. "She and Lily are working in the garden."

"I thought she might let you come out with us for the afternoon run. We'll be hauling and baiting about twenty more traps, the ones closest in. Would you like to go along?"

Sally studied her bare toes for a moment before casting a quick glance in Cal's direction. She shrugged. "Sure, I guess."

"Should I ask your mother?"

"I guess."

"Do you *want* me to ask your mother?" Joe said.

Sally glanced up at him, then snuck another peek at Cal and felt that peculiar thump again. "Yes, please," she said.

"Well, let's walk on up, then."

ANNIE WAS ON HER KNEES in the flower bed that ran along the south side of the old cape. She was wearing gardening gloves and Lily's big straw hat. Lily was sitting on the garden bench, leafing through a landscaping book while Rebel dozed in the shade of an old lilac. All three glanced up at the sound of approaching feet.

"Hello, Joe." Annie sat back on her heels and pushed the straw hat back with her wrist. "Good to see you."

Joe smiled, then nodded at the young man standing beside him. "This is my youngest son, Calvin. I thought maybe Sally'd like to come with us for a little while this afternoon to haul traps. That is, if she isn't busy."

Annie glanced at her daughter and Joe's son. She hid her smile at the two of them trying to appear totally disinterested in each other and yet sneak an eyeful at the same time. "I think that's a fine idea, Joe. The life preservers are hanging in the boathouse."

"I brought along an extra, just in case," Joe said.

"Sally, you get some sneakers on and take your jacket," Annie said. "You know how cold that ocean breeze can get. And take something to snack on. You haven't had lunch yet."

Sally started inside and then glanced back, her expression changing. "Telephone," she said. "Maybe it's Dad!" She dashed inside to answer it and after a brief silence Annie heard her high, excited voice drift through the open windows. "Dad? Dad, slow down, I can't understand a word you're saying." Then, a few moments later, "That's *great,* Dad. That's *great.*" A longer silence followed and then, "That's really, really great." A final short pause and then, "Love you, too, Dad. I'll tell Mom."

Sally burst out onto the porch, screen door banging shut behind her. "That was Dad," she announced with a huge grin. "The surgery on Adam went fine and he's going to be okay. Dad said he'd call tomorrow to talk to you. He's still at the hospital in Boston. Mom, Adam's going to be okay!"

Annie's relief was heartfelt. "Oh, Sally. That's wonderful news."

"Yeah." Sally's face was a pandemonium of emotions. "Can I still go out on the lobster boat?"

"Of course you can. You won't be able to see Adam for a while yet," Annie said. "Wear your life jacket at all times, and Nelly stays here with us. Put her inside so she won't follow you to the boat."

Sally raced inside for her sneakers and thundered back out, carrying her jacket. She gave Annie a quick and much appreciated hug. "Love you, Mom."

"There's plenty to eat on the boat, and we'll have her home by suppertime," Joe promised as the three of them departed for the *Glory B.*

The lobster boat was just backing away from the pier and motoring into the harbor when two vehicles came down the long drive and pulled into the yard. The vehicles were packed with people and the driver of the first one got out, hitched up his pants and looked around with bland curiosity. When he spotted Annie and Lily, he started toward them.

"This the place where the terrorists landed?" he asked.

Both Annie and Lily stared for a moment, taken aback, then Annie pushed to her feet, still holding the trowel. "This is a private residence. Do we know you?"

The man was staring down toward the pier. He looked back at the two vehicles and gestured with one arm. "This is it, this is the place," he bellowed so they'd be sure to hear. "That's the same boathouse we saw on the news!"

The car doors immediately opened and people spilled forth—little kids, women, men, big kids. Without so much as a glance at Annie and Lily, they all started toward the path that led to the boathouse.

"Excuse me," Annie said, moving to intercept. "This is private property, and I'm going to have to ask you to leave."

One of the younger women holding a small baby paused. "But we just want to see where it happened," she said.

"I'm sorry, but I can't allow that. The police don't want anyone down there and they said to call if there were trespassers," Annie ad-libbed.

The frown deepened. "Lolly?" the woman called. "Lolly, the lady says she's gonna call the cops. She says we ain't s'pose to go down there."

The entire group paused and looked back. Annie heard another vehicle approaching and felt a surge of relief when she recognized Jake's truck. "What's up?" he asked, and Annie gestured to the small crowd as she explained the uninvited guests.

Jake listened and nodded. He reached into his hip pocket, withdrew his wallet, and walked toward the group with the authoritative swagger of someone who was used to being obeyed. "Lieutenant Macpherson," he announced, flashing his badge. "You people are in violation of a police barricade, and if you don't leave now, you'll be arrested on charges of criminal trespass. That includes babies and little children. This is a matter of national security."

The group exchanged nervous glances and almost immediately began retreating toward their vehicles.

Within minutes they were gone, two thick rooster tails of dust marking their rapid departure.

"Thank you, Lieutenant Macpherson," Annie said. "Who knows what might have happened if you hadn't arrived when you did. But really, threatening to arrest babies and little children?"

"Think I was being too harsh?" he said with an air of innocence. "Hell, I vote we put up a toll gate and charge admission." He slid his wallet back into his hip pocket, returned to his truck to fetch a box of groceries out of the back and followed Amanda up the porch steps. He paused at the top and nodded to Lily. "At least they weren't packing guns."

Lily was leaning forward in her chair, watching the dust settle in the driveway. "Honestly, the nerve of some people," she said. "Driving in here just like they owned the place."

"Well, I doubt they'll be back," Annie soothed. "Lieutenant Macpherson was most intimidating."

Jake went into the kitchen to deposit the box of groceries on the counter and came back out onto the porch wearing a faint grin. "Ladies, if you don't mind, I think I'm going to lock the gate behind them, just in case there are any others."

"You have my blessing," Lily said. "I'm more than ready for a little peace and quiet."

Jake caught Annie's eye. "You up for a two-mile, round-trip walk and talk?"

Before Annie could respond, Lily said, "You two go on. Amanda and I'll get lunch started. Take the blueberry pail along if you want a pie for supper. If you follow the footpath back along the shore you'll pass by the barrens just before you reach the ledges. We used to lease them out to blueberry growers, but

Ruel revoked the lease the year the growers burned
the field and nearly burned the farm down, too.''

Annie carried the tin pail in her right hand and held
Jake's hand with her left. The sun was high, the sky
cloudless, and the only thing that kept the afternoon
from being too hot was the steady ocean breeze. They
walked without speaking along the winding drive,
through the meadow, across the orchard and finally
into the deep shade of the pine woods. The silence
between them was comfortable. They were content
simply to be in each other's company, side by side,
hand-in-hand. When they reached the gate Jake
swung it closed with a clang and fed the padlock
through the hasp, snapping it shut.

"There," Annie said softly. "The rest of the world
is now officially shut out."

They stood for a moment longer in the deep shade
of the centuries' old pines, listening to the lonesome
sough of the wind through the high crowns. Jake took
a deep breath and said, "I stopped in Danfield on my
way here to make a phone call. I talked to the captain
at my precinct and gave my notice. I'm not going
back, Annie. I quit the force."

Annie tried to keep the joy from her face because
she could read quite clearly the regret on his. She
tipped her head to one side, studying him. "And how
do you feel about that?"

"Scared," he admitted. "I've been a cop for so
long that I can't imagine doing anything else."

Annie reached for his hand. "Something will turn
up, and whatever it is, you'll be great at it. The important thing to remember is you have your daughter."

Jake pulled her close and wrapped his arms around

her with a kind of desperation. "Somehow that scares me even more. I have to provide for her."

"You will. Now come on. Let's go pick some blueberries."

They followed the shore path back and found the barrens Lily had spoken of. The blueberries were coming ripe and they were abundant, the vast field a vivid sweep of blue. They picked until their pail was full, and then they found something else, a sheltered grove of trees that hid a small, enchanting pond. The water was deep, clear and cold, and the lure of a swim in the heat of the afternoon impossible to resist. Afterward they discovered a patch of soft grass just big enough for them to lie down on and, cradled in the cool, green privacy of this little sanctuary, they made love and dozed until the afternoon shadows grew long.

Annie felt Jake's fingers brushing the hair back from her forehead and her eyes fluttered open. She smiled, reaching for his hand to pull him closer, but his expression was so somber that she stilled, her own smile fading as he leaned over her and twined his fingers with hers. "Do you think you could ever fall in love with an ex-cop who might end up selling vacuum cleaners or used cars for a living?" he asked.

His gaze was so earnest that Annie felt a pang in her heart. "Oh, Jake," she said. "Of course I could. I already have."

CHAPTER SEVENTEEN

THE PHONE CALL came early the following morning. It was a woman, with a clipped, professional, well-modulated voice, asking to speak with Lieutenant Macpherson.

"May I tell him who's calling?" Annie asked.

"Kathryn Yeager," she replied. "I'm returning his message."

Jake was out in the barn working on Ruel's old tractor, the parts laid out on a clean rag, hands covered with grease and a frown furrowing his brow. "You have a phone call," Annie said. "Kathryn Yeager."

The frown was replaced by a broad grin. "She's the lawyer we need to get Lily out of this mess if Lester doesn't back down," he said, wiping his hands.

"Yes, I recognized the name," Annie said. She trailed after him into the kitchen to finish the breakfast dishes. After he had hung up he walked up behind her and embraced her from behind, kissing her on the neck. "She's coming," he announced victoriously. "One of the finest defense attorneys working the New York City courts is coming to Blue Harbor, Maine. What do you think about that?"

"Either she owes you a pretty big favor," Annie said, "or else she likes you an awful lot."

"Both, as a matter of fact," Jake said. "She's flying in this coming Sunday. Wants to talk to Lily before reading the riot act to Lester.'' Jake's strong hands turned her around to face him. "Bottom line, Annie, there's no way Lester's going to boot his mother out of here, not with Kate on our side.''

Annie held a plate in her soapy hands, water dripping on the floor. She tried to feel the same rush of victory that Jake was feeling, but all she could see was the excitement in his eyes at the thought of Kate Yeager coming to Blue Harbor right on the heels of his ex-wife's departure, and she couldn't help but feel a twinge of anxiety.

IT WAS A QUIET WEEK, almost pastoral in its serenity. Each morning Jake and Amanda would depart for the cabin to monitor the progress of the two carpenters repairing the roof. Each morning Joe would dock the *Glory B* at the pier just long enough for Sally to jump aboard with a bounteous lunch for all three that Lily had fixed. Sally's days, with the advent of Cal and her job as official trap baiter on Joe Storey's lobster boat, had turned golden with promise. She seemed to have forgotten all about Tom and the big city.

Each morning Annie would go for a long walk along the rocky coastline of Lily's peninsula before the fog burned off and the sun showed its hot August face. She'd work in the garden, bring more of Lily's unfinished paintings up from the boathouse for her to assess and arrange on the walls, eat a light lunch, do a minimal amount of housework, read a book in the shade of the porch. By late afternoon everyone returned to the farm. Jake usually tinkered on the tractor or mowed the lawn or did household repairs while Lily and Annie prepared the evening meal.

It was such an idyllic existence that Annie had to shake herself from time to time to make sure it was all real, but their time in paradise was running out. One more month in this precious place, and then what? She was no closer to finding the answers than she had been on the day she'd handed in her resignation back in June. She and Jake tiptoed around the subject of September, pretending that the summer was endless, the way the summers of childhood had been. Pretending that there were no huge decisions to make.

Pretending.

Yet there were stark reminders. A phone call from her housekeeper, Ana Lise, who, having returned from visiting her sister in Copenhagen, was wondering when Annie was coming home. Another from Matt, wondering the same thing. Then the hospital administrator called, offering her the sun, the moon and the stars if she would only return to her old job. And could she give him an *exact* date when she might be coming back?

She had felt no pangs of homesickness thus far. No burning desire to return to the emergency room of a big city hospital, to the chaos and noise of New York or to the comfortable apartment in Manhattan. She loved it here. She felt as if this was where she truly belonged. But this was Lily's home, not hers, and in less than a month her lease would be up and the summer would be over. Sally would have to return to school, and Annie would have to decide what direction her own life would take. As for Jake, a part of her knew that every decision she made would depend upon him. It was high time for them to finish the conversation they'd started in the blueberry barrens.

It was time for them to talk about September.

"IT'S HOPELESS," Jake lamented that evening before supper, sitting out on the porch with Annie and Lily, drinking a cold beer and watching Amanda play with the puppy on the lawn he'd just mowed. The smell of fresh-cut grass mingled with the sweet-spicy perfume of the pasture roses in the warm air and he took a deep, appreciative breath. "Walter and George are nice enough guys and I'm sure they really know their stuff, but, Lily, I've never seen two carpenters work so slow or talk as much."

Lily rocked back and forth gently in her chair, Rebel lying at her feet, her gnarled fingers fixing a bag of green beans that Annie had bought at a local farm stand. "George and Walter like to do things just so." She nodded. "They're real craftsmen. They don't rush through a job, that's a fact."

"Did you ever have them do any work for you here?"

"No, but I'm a lot older than you."

"What's that got to do with it?" Jake asked.

"Quite a bit," she said. "I like to think if I hire out a job, I'd live long enough to see it finished."

Annie laughed out loud in the silence that followed and Jake glanced skeptically at the two women. "They'll do a fine job, Jake," Lily reassured him. "That cabin will stand for another century when they're done with it, and in the meantime, you can mow my lawn, get that old tractor running, keep the house in one piece, and keep Amanda here where I can enjoy her company. Besides, I feel a lot safer having you around after what happened the other night."

"Your lawyer friend's coming tomorrow, isn't she?" Annie said, changing the subject.

Jake nodded. "I'm picking Kate up at the Bangor airport. Her flight arrives at noon. I thought I'd bring her here, and maybe she could stay for supper. She has reservations at a place in Danfield but if she could just spend some time with you, Lily, I think she'd understand your situation a lot better."

Lily looked up at Jake. "Why, don't be ridiculous. She'll stay right here with us, of course. There's an extra bedroom. Annie, can you make sure it's ready for company?"

"Certainly," Annie said, her cheeks a most becoming shade of pink. She retrieved another handful of beans from the paper sack and snapped the ends off before adding them to the pot in Lily's lap.

"String beans for supper, I'm guessing," Jake said.

"String beans, baby potatoes, garden salad and poached salmon." Lily nodded. "And a nice strawberry shortcake for dessert. I've asked Jim to supper."

"Maybe we could play a few hands of poker afterward." Jake glanced around. "Where's Sally? Isn't she usually home by now?"

"That girl comes home a little later every day," Lily snorted. "She's smitten with Joe's youngest boy, and my guess is Cal's so befuddled by her that he's more of a hindrance than a help to his father, so it's probably taking Joe longer and longer to haul his traps."

"Cal's older than Sally, isn't he?" Annie said.

"By about three years," Lily admitted. "But Calvin comes of good stock, and I haven't heard Sally say one word about being bored or wishing she was back in the city since he arrived on the scene."

Jake took a swallow of the cold brew and lowered

the bottle. "What about you, Dr. Annie? Are you bored? Do you wish you were back in the big city?"

Annie flashed him a quick, startled glance and the color in her cheeks deepened. She dropped her eyes back to her work. "I'm happy here," she said.

"School starts in four weeks."

Annie lifted her eyes to his again. "Your point being…?"

"Sally might be smitten with Cal, but come September she'll be back at school and Amanda's going to be starting kindergarten."

"And the days will grow shorter and the foliage will turn and before you know it, winter will be here," Annie said, her voice carrying an edge and her eyes bright with an unspoken challenge. She was daring him to broach the subject more intimately, and he was prodding her to do the same.

"Daddy," Amanda called, pointing toward the pier. "Look, here they come. Can I go meet them?"

Jake pushed out of his chair and set the beer bottle down. "Wait for me, Pinch. I want to check this Cal dude out and make sure he's good enough for our Sally."

JIM ARRIVED PROMPTLY at 6:00 p.m. and he was not alone, a fact that surprised both Jake and Annie but didn't seem to fluster Lily at all. "There's plenty of everything," Lily said, checking on the salmon. "And even if there wasn't, we'd make do. It would be mighty poor behavior to turn the county sheriff away from the supper table."

Jake shot her an appraising glance. "Does the sheriff visit here often or is this a special occasion?"

"Well, Jim did mention something about Clyde

Sawyer wanting to meet you," Lily admitted, "but I didn't think you'd mind. Clyde's a good soul. Probably just wants a firsthand account of what went on here the other night."

Which proved a fairly accurate guess, though once the question-and-answer period had ended, the real reason Jim had brought Clyde Sawyer out to meet him was unveiled. "Jim told me you might be looking to stick around these parts, and that got me to thinking. After what happened here, I think now's the time for pushing the extra manpower we've been angling for, and it seems to me if we could use you to spearhead the position, we might gain some ground.

"If they vote in a new deputy sheriff's position, the job would start in November, right after election time, and I won't lie to you, it'd probably be kind of dull after what you're used to," Clyde admitted, forking down more of Lily's excellent cooking. He was stocky and balding, but his eyes were calm and kind and his character was salt of the earth.

"The sheriff's department is mostly rural patrol. Except during hunting season, there just isn't much to do with guns. Mostly domestic disputes, barking dog complaints, drunk driving, fender benders. But given what happened right here at Lily's, I'd like to push for a better police presence in our coastal waters, too, and work more closely with the harbor master and local police departments. I'd like to make drug runners think twice about using our particular stretch of coast, and our islands. The Coast Guard is stretched pretty thin these days, and I bet they'd be open to any help they could get. You'd need to learn how to drive a boat. And I should probably mention that the pay would stink, but the insurance benefits would be good. Great meal, Lily.''

''Thank you, Clyde.''

''I plan to pitch the idea as soon as possible in order to get the issue on the table. I'd also like to nominate you for the position, if you're agreeable. Think about it and let me know.''

''Sounds...interesting,'' Jake said, nodding.

''Boring, you mean,'' Sally said.

''Sally, start the salad around, please,'' Annie said with a warning glance.

After the supper dishes were washed and dried, they played poker until late, using matchsticks for money and making all sorts of rash bets. Lily was a quick study, picking up the rules of the game and maintaining the most inscrutable poker face that Jake had ever seen. The only thing missing was the sipping whiskey, but Lily surprised them all by producing a bottle of apricot brandy after the girls had gone to bed. She won the game, too, in one grand finale, with a total of sixty-eight matchsticks and a full house, kings over eights.

LATE, and the old cape was quiet. The loudest sound Annie could hear was the beating of Jake's heart as their breathing slowed and steadied. They were tangled up in the sheets and in each other's arms and Annie was drifting gently toward sleep when Jake murmured, ''That Lily's really something.''

''Mmm. Good card player.''

''No. I mean her inviting the sheriff.''

''Did she invite him?''

''Of course she did. She's scheming.''

"I think it's a wonderful scheme," Annie said, snuggling closer.

"Sally's right. I'd die of boredom after one week of being a deputy sheriff," Jake said, tracing a finger up and down her arm.

"Better than dying shot full of holes. Don't forget your promise to Amanda and your ex-wife."

Jake moaned. "Linda wants Amanda to be present at her wedding in September."

"In California?"

"Malibu."

"When?"

"September thirteenth. I asked her why a Thursday, and she made noises about the day being significant, the one year anniversary of their first date or some such thing, but the reception's being held in some kind of fancy mansion overlooking the Pacific and I think it's because Hans could rent it cheaper during the week."

Annie smothered a laugh. "Amanda's too young to fly alone."

"And I don't want to go, so I'm trying my damnedest to talk her out of making Amanda attend. I mean, Amanda and Hans don't exactly get along."

"But Amanda's her daughter, and on such an important day…"

"Linda wants Amanda to be the flower girl. There's a rehearsal dinner the night before, so we'd need to fly out two days earlier."

It was Annie's turn to moan. "California's so far away. Maybe you could play up the fact that Amanda would be missing school."

"Tried that already. Kindergarten doesn't hold much sway."

"Where will Amanda be going to kindergarten?" Annie asked pointedly.

"Where will Sally be going to seventh grade?" Jake's voice was as edgy as hers.

Annie hesitated. She hadn't realized she'd been holding her breath until she spoke and the words came out in a rush. "Not in New York City."

"You sure about that?"

"I'm sure, and so is Sally. She told me she wants to stay near her father and baby brother."

"And Cal."

Annie sighed. "Yes, him, too."

"What about your career?"

"I'll still have a career. I've already received two job offers, one from the hospital Ryan works at, and the other from the small hospital we took Matt to. They're revamping their emergency room and adding another operating room. They'd like to hire me as project consultant and then as director of emergency services or something along those lines."

"And?"

"I haven't made any decisions. I wanted to talk to you first."

"So talk."

"The only thing I know for sure is that I want to be with you, and you haven't said where you're going to be."

"I want to be wherever you are." Jake pulled her closer. "Annie, Annie. I'll take Clyde's new position if it'll make you happy, and if Linda okays it. We can rent a place somewhere near the farm so we can keep an eye on Lily, and the girls can grow up in a quaint coastal village where violence is something you only see on TV."

"Or down on Lily's stone pier after midnight," Annie reminded him.

They lay together in the darkness, discussing the logistics of moving their belongings from the city and contemplating the possibilities that life in Maine would offer.

"Oh, Jake," Annie murmured, holding him close. "I think we can make each other very, very happy."

"I promise I'll do my best."

BUT THE NEXT MORNING, as Jake drove to the Bangor airport to pick up Kathryn Yeager, he couldn't shake the feeling that he'd made a promise to Annie that he might not be able to keep. She was convinced that he could make her happy, but he wasn't so sure. He tried to picture how their life would be. Suppertime, the table set, the girls helping Annie get the meal on the table. His belly would no doubt be bigger from all those good home cooked meals and all that soft living. Maybe his hairline would have begun to recede, just like Clyde Sawyer's. "How was work?" Annie would ask, taking her seat and passing round the bowl of mashed potatoes.

"Quiet," he'd reply, taking a small portion. A man had to watch his calories when all he did was drive a patrol car down slumbering rural roads or a motor boat around a sleepy harbor in endless circles, dodging seagull droppings and picking up harbor trash. "Nothing happened again. It was another long, uneventful day."

"That's fine." She'd smile. "That's just what I like to hear."

Jake's hands tightened around the steering wheel with a surge of dread as he stared into that soft, sleepy future. No way. Even if the job was voted into existence in November, and even if Linda gave her approval, he couldn't live like that. And he couldn't sell used cars or vacuum cleaners, either. He didn't know *what* he was going to do, but he did know he couldn't promise Annie the peaceful, secure kind of happiness she craved.

KATE'S PLANE was right on time and she breezed out of the gate, smiling brilliantly when she caught sight of him waiting in the wings. "Jake!" She was pulling a little black carry on bag behind her and she let go of the handle and threw herself into his arms, much to the envy of every man present. "You look great." She held him at arm's length for a moment for a more searching up-and-down with those dark sparkling eyes and then hugged him again. "You look absolutely wonderful."

"So do you, Kate," he said, thinking that if she looked any more wonderful, this airport would cease to function. She was as beautiful and vivacious as ever, all long graceful lines and dark glossy hair. She could have been a runway model in Paris but had chosen instead to pursue a career as a trial lawyer, and woe to the poor fool who thought those gorgeous looks precluded a razor-sharp analytical mind.

In short order they were headed back toward Blue Harbor and Kate was talking a mile a minute, her words a bright, rapid-fire blur almost too quick to follow, explaining various litigations, court cases, criminal profiles, her conversations with Lily's physician, Dr. Elsa Morrow and Lily's son Lester. Finally she ran out of breath and sat for a few moments in silence, facing sideways and staring at him with a serious frown. "The last time I saw you, Jake, you were all hooked up to tubes and wires in that damn hospital. You didn't even know I was there."

"Somehow I can't imagine that."

"I couldn't bring myself to visit you again. I'm sorry. But I called every day to check on you, just so you know."

"It's okay. And just so you know, I've given it up. I quit the force."

"No way. Really? That's great, but I don't believe you for one moment. Oh, and by the way, I did some research on your doctor, Annie Crawford. Did you know she's one of the highest ranked trauma surgeons in the country...and you're in love with her, aren't you?"

Jake grinned. "Is it that obvious?"

"I read you like a book. And yes, it's that obvious. I'm happy for you. You deserve a good woman in your life. Love's the best medicine, Jake. It really is."

"How long can you stay?"

"One night, max. I had to sneak away and I'm hoping my husband doesn't notice I'm missing, though it's doubtful he will. Poor old thing, he's up to his eyeballs in politics, running for the senate. I'll fly out of Bangor tomorrow, after meeting with Lily."

"I appreciate you doing this for me, Kate. Lily Houghton's a great lady and she deserves all the help she can get."

She smiled, reached out and squeezed his arm. "I'd do just about anything for you, Jake Macpherson. You'll always be my number one hero."

ANNIE FELT A HEADACHE starting to form behind her eyes as she sat at the supper table that evening. The others were listening with bated breath to the lively courtroom stories Kate told over cold lobster salad. The girls had opted for hamburgers, which Jake had grilled out on the porch for them, sneaking generous portions of the raw ingredient to Rebel and Nelly when he thought no one was looking.

"Jake saved my life five years ago," Kate said in answer to a question from Lily about the origins of the unlikely friendship between the cop and the criminal defense lawyer.

"How?" Sally asked with a healthy dose of teen cynicism, poised to take a bite of her hamburger.

"That's an exaggeration," Jake said, refilling both Kate's and Annie's wineglasses. Lily held her hand over her own.

"Don't be so modest, Jake. They don't call you Fearless Macpherson for nothing," Kathryn said, raising her glass to him.

Annie poked at her salad, lifted her own glass for a sip and tried to suppress her anxiety. Not only was Kathryn Yeager riveting, she was dynamic and vivacious and so incredibly attractive that it was hard not to stare at her. She was keenly intelligent, and she wore her raven's wing hair swept into a twist on the back of her head, a hairstyle that would have proven disastrous to most women, but on Kate it was absolutely perfect. No other hairstyle could possibly have accentuated her bone structure so well. Her teeth were perfect. Her smile was perfect. Her nose was perfect. There was nothing about her that Annie could fault, including her manners, which were impeccable.

"Fearless Macpherson, huh?" Sally said, looking at Jake with grudging interest.

"Oh, yes, he was fearless then, and I'm sure he's

the same now," Kate said. "After all, a leopard can't change his spots. We were sharing a courtroom together. That was before we were on speaking terms, remember, Jake? In fact, you disliked me intensely and made no bones about it."

"You were putting the hardened criminals I worked so hard to arrest back out on the streets," Jake reminded her.

"Yes, but that's how the system works, Fearless. The accused is innocent until proven guilty. Can I help it if no one could prove beyond a shadow of doubt that my clients were guilty? Okay—" She raised a placating hand to ward off his anticipated protest. "So we're in court together, and Jake's champing at the bit, waiting to give his testimony on my guy, hoping it'll put him behind bars for life."

"He deserved nothing less," Jake said.

"Perhaps," Kate conceded, "though I might have gotten him off. But he definitely sealed his fate when Jake took the stand. All of a sudden my client, admittedly not the most intelligent of criminals, stands up, whips out this knife, which he'd managed to conceal from all that high-tech—but perpetually malfunctioning—security equipment, hauls me out of my chair with said knife at my throat and tries to make his escape past an impossible number of armed guards.

"*But* it wasn't all those armed court police who rescued me," Kate continued, dark eyes flashing with drama. "One moment Jake's standing up in the box with his hand on the Bible, being sworn in, and the next moment he's hurling himself over the railing and he's pulverizing this guy. Nearly killed him right in the courtroom in front of God and the judge." She picked up her glass and took a sip, gazing around the table. "You have to understand that no one else had moved a muscle. No one else even had time to blink, and then suddenly this brash young cop rushes in and saves my life." Kate brushed her blouse's collar back to expose the skin on the side of her neck.

Annie stared and felt a peculiar tightening in the pit of her stomach as she saw the ugly red scar. "My God."

"Yes," Kate said. "It was that close."

Annie abruptly pushed out of her chair and stood. "There's ice cream for desert," she said, gathering the nearest plates to begin clearing the table, "but it's in Blue Harbor, and we'll have to drive to get it."

AFTER THE DRIVE to Blue Harbor, after the ice-cream cones, after the drive back home and seeing the girls off to bed, after Lily had said her own good-night, Annie finally ceded the kitchen to Jake and Kathryn and retired to her own bedroom to nurse her growing doubts and fears. She read for a while before blowing out the lamp. In the darkness time stretched until she felt sure it must be almost dawn. She tossed restlessly in her bed, wondering if Jake was still downstairs in the kitchen with Kathryn, reminiscing over the last of the Chardonnay. Was it simply gratitude that Kathryn Yeager felt toward Jake for saving her life in that courtroom, or something more? And was that same powerful and mysterious *something more* the same thing that Jake felt when Annie had pulled *him* back from the edge of death after he'd been shot? Were the feelings he had for her real? Or had he mistaken gratitude for love?

Annie rolled onto her side and bunched the pillow

beneath her head. The last thing in the world she wanted to be was a jealous woman. Above all else there had to be trust in a relationship. Trust, respect, friendship and love. All those ingredients were vital. She trusted Jake. He was the kind of man who inspired trust. So why was she lying here even thinking about things like Jake and Kathryn sitting down in the kitchen finishing off that bottle of wine, or worse...

She heard a click and the barely audible sound of the doorknob turning and felt a surge of relief, all her dark imaginings swept instantly away. She lay still, feigning sleep, and it was quiet for so long that she thought she'd imagined the noise but then she heard him murmur, "You're faking."

She rolled onto her back and smiled into the darkness. "And you're late."

CHAPTER EIGHTEEN

KATE HAD REQUESTED that her official meeting with Lily take place at the nursing home, and she had also requested that Lester and Lily's doctor be present, plus both the ombudsman and administrator of the residence. Lily's doctor had sent word that he was indisposed, and Lester, though punctual, was visibly irate that he'd been asked to sit through a fact-finding interview in the administrator's office. "This is ridiculous," he said as he took a seat. "It's a waste of all our time."

Lily frowned at her son's words. "Lester, the very reason we're here is because you wouldn't take the time to look at the plans I've drawn up for the farm. I've been advised by my most excellent attorney, Kathryn Yeager, that as long as I'm of sound mind and body, I can take back my power of attorney, and if you push me, Lester, I'm afraid I'll have to do just that."

Kate laid her hand on Lily's arm and gave Lester a calm, level stare. "I'm surprised you didn't bring your own attorney, Mr. Houghton. I did tell you that this was a legal process, and the statements heard here today will be admissible in a court of law should you push this any further."

It was Lester's turn to sigh with exaggerated patience. "Being an attorney myself, I'm perfectly capable of representing my own interests in my mother's safety, and my position hasn't changed. She cannot remain at the farm. She needs to be where her health and well-being can be closely monitored.''

"But, Lester, my health and well-being are perfectly fine right where I am,'' Lily said, ignoring Kate's headshake. ''And if it's my future that's being decided here, I have a right to put in my two cents' worth.'' This last was directed toward Kate.

"You certainly do,'' Kate agreed, ''and you'll have an opportunity to do just that, but first let's clarify how the staff regarded your presence here. Mrs. Ridley, not only are you the official ombudsman, but you're also a registered nurse. What sort of interactions did you have with Lily during her stay here?''

Mrs. Ridley sat up straighter and folded her hands in her lap. ''Lily repeatedly requested that she be allowed to return home. At first, these requests were quite agitated and emotional.''

"Of course they were,'' Lily interrupted. ''At the time I thought Rebel was still at home, waiting for me to feed and water him. Can you imagine my distress?''

"Of course we can, Lily,'' Kate said, then glanced at Mrs. Ridley and tipped her head.

Mrs. Ridley composed herself and continued. ''Lily's request to return home didn't seem practical when she first arrived. She'd recently undergone hip replacement surgery and was just beginning daily physical therapy.''

"And in your opinion, how did she progress?'' Kate asked.

"Rapidly. She was, and is, in very good shape for

a woman of her years. She was walking with just the use of a cane in less than two weeks.''

''I've been walking all my life,'' Lily interrupted yet again. ''And I intend to walk for years more. I'm not ready for any nursing home, nor will I ever be.''

''Please, Lily,'' Kate said, laying her hand on Lily's arm. ''Let Mrs. Ridley continue.''

Mrs. Ridley nodded. ''I spoke with her son several times on her behalf about her wish to return home. He told me that the place she lived in was very remote, and that it would be dangerous for her to return there.''

''It *is* remote and it *would* be dangerous for her to return,'' Lester broke in. ''That farm is nearly a mile off the tarred road, and she lives there all by herself.''

''I'm *not* alone anymore, Lester,'' Lily said. ''As a matter of fact, I've never been less alone in my entire life. That old farmhouse has been filled to the guppers all summer long, and it's been wonderful.''

''Your son's fears seem to be based on what will happen when the current tenants leave,'' Mrs. Ridley pointed out.

Lily leaned forward intently in her chair. ''Yes, I understand that, and I'll address Lester's concerns. My plans are all drawn up and I've brought them with me. If you don't mind, Lester? I promise this won't take too much of your time.''

She adjusted her glasses, reached inside her canvas bag and pulled forth a scroll of papers, removing the rubber band and unrolling them carefully with her gnarled hands onto the caseworker's desk. ''As you can see, this is a blueprint of the farmhouse. The basic footprint of the building is the same, with the exception of a solarium here off the south side of the shed, but there are some major interior changes. In fact, the only thing that remains the same is the kitchen, which is my favorite room in that whole house and I wouldn't change it for the world.''

Jake, who was sitting in the back corner of the office, caught Annie's eye and raised his eyebrows, a questioning glance that generated only a small, mysterious smile in response. He stood and moved closer to view the plans, noticing that Annie didn't feel the need. Obviously she'd been part of the ground-floor planning committee.

Without further delay Lily proceeded to unveil her ideas for the old cape and its string of outbuildings. When she was done she sat back in her chair, gazed directly at her son with sharp eyes and nodded curtly. ''So you see, Lester, I have no intention of living there alone, and I certainly don't intend to leave. That farm is my home, and I love it. I intend to remain there, and God willing, I intend to die there. I hope you can understand my wishes, and give me my freedom the same way I gave you yours when you grew up and wanted to leave that very same place.''

Lily took a steadying breath and continued before Lester could respond. ''You don't remember the times you spent with me when you were just a babe. All the times I carried you in that pack basket when I would go out sketching. All the times you rode there, uncomplaining, rain or shine, to the places I had to see, first to sketch and then to paint. You were such a good baby, Lester. We climbed just about every mountain in this grand state, and covered just about every inch of its shoreline, just the two of us, because Ruel didn't care for camping and hiking. I was carrying you up Katahdin when this couple stopped me and said, 'Isn't he too heavy? You'll never make it to the top.'

"Well, we made it, Lester, you and I together, and I painted the canvas to prove it. It's hanging on the wall of your town house, isn't it? And though it seems like only yesterday we spent that triumphant hour on Katahdin's summit, me sketching like mad while you tried to find a word for those pretty blue wildflowers that clung to the cracks in the ledge, you grew up, as all babies do, and eventually I had to let you go." Lily shook her head, her eyes bright with tears.

"It broke my heart when you left, Lester. You were my only child, and I'd built my life around you. But I knew you had to find your own destiny, and you did. I'm very, very proud of what you've become and all you've accomplished, I truly am. But for the life of me I can't understand why such a smart man can't see that tearing me away from my home, and my beloved dog, and all the people and places I hold so dear, is a fate far, far worse than death."

Head held high, she sat back in her chair and folded her hands in front of her. "Be very careful which path you choose for me now, Lester, because while I admit that my mountain climbing days are long past, like it or not, you're walking that very same path behind me. You've grown up and I've grown old and frail, but the trail you blaze today might be the very one you yourself will have to follow in a few years. Think about that before you decide what's best for your old mother."

Lester stared, visibly taken aback by both the architectural drawings and Lily's calm yet poignant plea. "Mother, please understand," he finally managed to say. "I only want what's best for you."

"I believe you mean that," Lily said with a nod. "But what's best for me is what makes me happy, and what makes me happy is living the life I love. Please don't take that away from me. Growing old is hard enough without being torn up by the roots and put in a place I really don't care to be."

The room was quiet. Lester raised a hand and rubbed his forehead. "I honestly thought I was doing the right thing, the responsible thing, and I wanted you near me so I could see you more often." He dropped his hand with a sigh. "But if this is what you truly want, I guess I can get used to shuttle flights and rental cars."

"Of course you can," Lily said. "You're an attorney who flies all over the country at the drop of a hat to consult with your clients. You can certainly fly home once in a while to visit me." She gave her son an unexpectedly tender smile. "I do love you, Lester, even when you're being bullheaded. Come out to the farm for a visit before you go. I'll fix you lunch."

Lester shook his head. "I have to catch the next flight, but I'll take a rain check." He stood, crossed to his mother, and bent to give her an awkward hug and kiss on the cheek. "I love you, Mother," he said, his voice lowering and becoming rough with emotion. "And believe it or not, I do remember some of those times you carried me." Lily's frail, thin arms reached up to him and the embrace lasted another long moment before Lester straightened. Without another word or glance to anyone else in the room, he departed.

After his footsteps had faded into silence, Lily rolled her plans back up and tucked them into her canvas bag. She impatiently wiped the tears from her cheeks, pushed to her feet, picked up her cane and the handles of her bag and turned toward the door, where she paused to look back, eyebrows raised. "I trust that's the end of this?"

"Looks that way," Kate said, quickly brushing the heels of her hands across her own face before rising to her feet.

"It was good to see you again, Lily." Mrs. Ridley sniffed, fumbling for a handkerchief. "And I think the plans you've drawn up for your farm are wonderful."

THAT NIGHT at the supper table, over an impromptu meal of Colonel Sanders' Kentucky Fried Chicken that they'd picked up in Bangor after dropping Kate off at the airport, Lily unveiled her dream for the farm to the girls and to Jim, who had been appearing fairly regularly right around suppertime.

Her plans flew over Amanda's head, who was oblivious to everything except the greasy piece of chicken she was hungrily devouring. Sally gave Lily a thumbs-up gesture as she reached for another biscuit, whereas Jim cleared his throat, wiped his mouth on a napkin, and said, in an injured tone of voice, "Lily Houghton, nowhere in this vision of yours do I detect even the remotest hint that our lives might somehow be linked in the future."

"Why, they've always been linked, Jim," Lily said, staring at him with some surprise. "Why would you think I wasn't considering you in these plans?"

"Because you never once mentioned me, and I'd be proud to help in any way I can," Jim said.

"I never mentioned Annie, either, or Jake, or the girls, but you're all here, hidden in the drawings. I'm

surprised you didn't see yourselves. You're all here."
She tapped the blueprints and her face softened. She
reached out and clasped Jim's hand. "Jim, you're one
of the finest men I've ever known and I'd like for us
to be married, if you'd consider hitching your wagon
to an old woman like me."

Jim was visibly astounded by this unexpected dec-
laration of love. He blinked hard, squeezed her hand
and cleared his throat. "I'd be honored to be your
husband, Lily," he said in a solemn voice, "and
blessed to have you as my wife."

"Good." Lily smiled as he lifted her hand and
kissed it. "It's been way too long for us. We should
have married a long time ago. All those good years
wasted."

She turned her sharp gaze on Annie and said in her
firm, starched voice, "Now, then. The apartment
that's to be constructed in the ell has three bedrooms,
two baths, a living room and kitchen. A nice place
for a family to live, rent-free, in exchange for looking
in on an old lady from time to time. I planned that
apartment for you, Annie Crawford. It was selfish of
me, I know, but when I drew it, I was thinking of
you and Jake and the girls, thinking of how much I've
enjoyed your company this summer and wishing you
never had to leave. I know you probably feel that
Blue Harbor can't compare to New York City, but the
coast of Maine has its own calling. The people here
are good and it's a fine place to raise a child."

"It's a wonderful place to raise a child," Annie
said softly, her eyes stinging with tears. "But I
couldn't live here rent-free, Lily. I won't."

"We can fight about that later," Lily said. "Right
now I'm trying to get all my ducks in a row."

"Daddy?" Amanda said, her mouth full of fried chicken. "Does this mean we can stay here always with Lily and Dr. Annie, and this will be our home, and we can have ducks, too?"

Jake pushed out of his chair and paced to the door, to the sink, to the wood cookstove. He raised the lid of the fire box as if searching for the answers within, and then let it clatter down as he turned to face his daughter. "Finish your supper, Pinch. We'll talk about it later."

"Maybe everyone needs some time to think about this," Annie suggested.

"On the contrary," Lily said. "Time is short and decisions have to be made. Are you going to stay here, or are you going back to New York? You can't wait until September to decide. You know full well that I want you to stay, but if you choose not to, there are half a hundred people who would move into that apartment in a heartbeat. Either way, with Jim living here I won't be alone, but you need to make a decision."

Annie held her breath for a few moments, feeling a surge of excitement build within her. It was as if Lily were the catalyst she'd been needing to finalize her plans. Jake might drag his heels until the moon came over the mountain, and she simply didn't have that long. "Sally?" she said.

Her daughter's eyes widened. "Really? You mean, stay here? Live here? Go to *school* here?"

"Really. What do you think?"

Her answer was to bolt out of her seat and dash for the phone. "I've got to tell Cal right away!"

Annie met Lily's eyes and smiled. "Tomorrow I'll see about enrolling Sally in the Danfield school system.'' She reached out and grasped Lily's hand. ''Looks like we're staying.'' She glanced to where Jake stood by the stove, but he wasn't there. Somehow, in the space of a few short moments, he had vanished from the kitchen and his absence spoke louder to Annie's heart than any words ever could.

WITH JAKE AND AMANDA overseeing roofing of the cabin, and Sally spending her days on Joe's lobster boat, it was Annie and Lily who suffered the brunt of the disruptions as renovations on the cape and outbuildings got underway.

The construction firm that Lily had engaged for the project at the farm hailed out of Ellsworth and they knew their stuff. They met with Lily at the beginning of the week to discuss the plans, and within days truckloads of materials began to arrive on site to be stored in the huge barn. By week's end, the days were filled with the discordant cacophony of hammers banging, table saws whining, generators roaring, and what seemed like scores of carpenters, plumbers and electricians all busy at their respective trades. The old cape was in a state of chaotic transition that everyone, including Lily, took in stride, learning to live with the sawdust that flavored the air, the nails and wood scraps and pieces of wire on the floor and, hardest of all, the blatant loss of privacy.

Lily had engaged a solar engineering firm to install twenty photovoltaic panels on the south facing roof of the ell to provide solar power to the saltwater farmhouse and its outbuildings. The battery bank, fuse box and inverter were installed in a vented room in the ground floor of the shed that at one time had been an indoor two-holer. It was a sophisticated setup and

Jake temporarily abandoned the cabin's roofing project to assist in Lily's far more interesting solar-energy project.

Larry Garrison was the engineer and he and Jake hit it off immediately. Over supper Jake would enthusiastically recite blow-by-blow details of the process of harnessing the sun's energy and turning it into usable electricity, conversations that left everyone else cross-eyed with confusion. "I must admit that while I really love the idea of solar power," Lily said after one such lecture, "I don't begin to understand it. You're wasting your breath on me."

"I'll give you one of Larry's books to read," Jake said, reaching for the salt shaker. "You, too." He grinned at Annie.

"Oh, no thanks, really. It's enough just to know that eventually we'll be able to watch a movie without listening to the generator."

"Amen to that," Lily said.

Jim came over almost daily, looking sprier than ever and always bringing Lily a little something special. They planned to be married at the end of September, when most of the renovations would be completed. "Long engagements aren't wise when you're our age," Lily said.

Two weeks before school started Annie took the girls shopping for clothes in Bangor and visited with Ryan and Trudy and the baby. She also stopped in Ellsworth on the way home to touch base with the hospital staff there and to firm up her schedule. Her job officially began on the first Monday in September. She marked it on the calendar hung on the kitchen door. It was the same calendar Jake used to jot down his travel plans, Lily used to track progress on the renovation project, Sally used to mark her hours on Joe Storey's lobster boat, and Amanda had identified in red ink the first day of kindergarten. One calendar tracking five lives.

"Next year we're going to need a bigger calendar," Lily said as she tried to find space for her information one evening. "Girls, just two weeks and counting down to the first day of school."

"Like we need reminding," Sally moaned, slumping at the kitchen table. But her performance fooled no one. She was looking forward to seeing what school would be like in a small Maine town, anxious to share every spare moment with Cal, who was on the high-school football, basketball and baseball team.

That night Jake sat out on the porch long after everyone had gone to bed and Annie joined him there. The night was crisp and cloudless, the dark sky spangled with stars, and the quiet was a blessed gift. "I talked to Clyde Sawyer today, Annie," he said, reaching up and pulling her into his lap.

"And?" she said, stroking her fingers through his hair.

"Looks like the new deputy sheriff position is a happening thing. After what went down right here at Lily's place, everyone's all for it. They want to hold an executive meeting of all the enforcement agencies involved early next week to get the ball rolling."

Annie's fingers stilled. Jake's announcement had been made with all the enthusiasm of a man who'd just been told he had less than a month to live. She felt his remoteness, and a corresponding chill settled over her. "Just because it's a happening thing doesn't mean you have to be the one to make it happen," she said.

"Well, that's the hell of it," Jake said, staring into a bleak infinity. "Because of the way Clyde pitched me right along with the position, it really does. But it beats selling vacuum cleaners." He took one of her hands in his and squeezed it, dismissing the subject. "Listen, on Jim's advice, I made an offer on that old cabin, and the owners accepted. I let George and Walter go today. Good men, but I want the roof fixed before I take Amanda to California for the wedding. I figure if Amanda and I stay right at the cabin and I work at it steady, two or three days should see the job done."

Annie felt the chill deepen into an Arctic freeze, but she tried to sound cheerful when she replied, "Well, it will certainly be a lot more peaceful on that beautiful pond than it is here, with half a hundred contractors showing up at six every morning. I envy you. And I'll miss you."

His hand tightened reassuringly. "I'll work as fast as I can."

THE NEXT MORNING Jake and Amanda were gone by the time she awakened and, in spite of Annie's hopes, they didn't come back for supper that night, or the next. Although Jake called each evening to tell her how much he missed her, she sensed that he needed time alone to sort through his feelings about their future and about the deputy sheriff position he'd been offered. On the second night he put Amanda on the phone. "I caught my first fish, today," the little girl told Annie proudly. Then she lowered her voice to a whisper, "Dr. Annie, I think Daddy's sick. He doesn't want to eat anything. I think you should come and see him."

"Sounds like we're suffering from the same bug," Annie replied. "He'll feel better soon, sweetheart." But Annie knew that her own misery went far beyond a lack of appetite. She wondered if Jake's did, too.

"Mom, go see him," Sally urged at breakfast on the third morning as Annie listlessly pushed her scrambled eggs around the plate. "Tell him how you feel."

Annie shook her head. "Jake knows how I feel. I've made no secret about that."

"But he's a *man,* Mom, and men can be…"

"Thickheaded sometimes," Lily finished.

"They need…" Sally began, then paused, searching for the word.

"Prompting," Lily supplied.

"Jake's soooo in love with you, but he's *afraid.* Can't you see? He's scared." Sally leaned toward her mother, her expression earnest.

"You think Jake's afraid of *me?*" Annie said, raising her eyebrows.

"Yes! Of what he feels for you, and what your future together holds, and whether or not he can live the life you want him to live."

"Young lady, how did you gain all this wisdom?"

"It's not wisdom, Mom, it's common sense. I've been studying the two of you all summer. Go see him. Bring a picnic. Sit in the sun together. Talk a little and kiss a lot."

"Sally." Annie laughed in spite of her misery.

"Invite him to the fair this weekend," Lily suggested. "The Blue Hill Fair's a classic. Tell him to bring some betting money."

"There's gambling at a country fair?" Annie frowned. Lily smiled sagely. "Pig races."

THAT MORNING, after Sally had departed for the day on the *Glory B,* Annie packed a picnic and drove out to Jake's cabin. He was up on the roof hammering away, shirtless in the heat, his broad, powerful shoulders and back bronzed from the sun. Straddling the very peak and laying the last of the capping shingles, two days unshaven, hammer in gloved hand, he paused as she parked and climbed out. She raised the picnic hamper like a peace offering. "Hope you like cold fried chicken and potato salad," she said.

He squinted down at her through a sting of sweat. For several long moments he just stared, and then he nodded, a faint grin deepening the crow's-feet at the corners of his eyes. "They're two of my all-time favorites," he said.

"Lily thought I should invite you to the Blue Hill Fair this weekend."

His handsome grin broadened. "Last time I went to the Blue Hill Fair, I was sixteen years old and I won thirty bucks betting on a pig named Esmerelda. She had long legs for a pig, and boy, could she run."

"Dr. Annie!" Amanda's young voice piped up as she burst out of the cabin, her feet stampeding down the porch steps. "Daddy said the reason he wasn't eating good was because he missed you so bad."

"Oh?"

Amanda hugged her fiercely and looked up at her, beaming. "And he said when we finished the roof, he'd never let you out of his sight again."

"Is that right?" Annie said, stroking Amanda's hair and looking up at Jake with a slow smile.

"I was speaking figuratively," Jake said.

"Of course."

"I mean, we'd probably get pretty tired of each other's company after a while."

"You think so?" she asked.

He pondered for a moment and then shook his head. "No, actually, I don't."

"Me, either," Annie said.

They ate the picnic lunch on the shore of the pond in the shade of the big pines and afterward sat on the blanket, leaning into each other in the drowsy afternoon heat while Amanda, the cut on her hand long since healed, searched for frogs in the nearby shallow water. "I'm going to catch the biggest, bestest one in the pond," she announced.

"Stay right here by the dock, Pinch," Jake cautioned. "If you catch that lucky frog, try giving him a kiss and turning him into a prince."

"That's just a fairy tale, Daddy," she informed him before wading off on her mission.

"I was hoping you'd come home nights," Annie murmured, resting her head against his shoulder and twining her fingers with his.

"I wanted to, but I was scared," Jake confessed. "You need things to be safe and sane and stable, and I wasn't sure I knew how to provide that kind of life for you. I needed to figure out if I could become the man you wanted me to be."

Annie shook her head. "I knew the kind of man you were when I fell in love with you, and I'm sorry I ever made you feel like you had to change to please me. I'll stand behind you no matter what you decide to do, Jake. I mean that."

Jake raised her hand and kissed it tenderly. "I saw Clyde yesterday. He and Kyle Coffin came out here to meet with me. I've officially accepted the job."

Annie pulled back to look him in the eye. "But you don't have to, Jake. You can do anything you want, don't you see? That's what I'm trying to tell you."

Jake touched a finger to her lips to silence her. "I took the job because I *wanted* to, Annie. The job's going to be more than what Clyde envisioned. It involves this homeland security stuff, and they're pretty serious about it. They're giving me special training with the harbor patrol, the Coast Guard and the FBI. I'll be gone for six months starting in October, which brings me to the subject of Amanda…"

"Amanda will be fine here with us, but what about Linda?" Annie said, taken aback by Jake's unexpected announcement. "What if she wants Amanda back because you took another law enforcement job? I mean, all of a sudden this position is sounding a lot more complicated than it did…"

"I already called her, and she's okay with it. She's seen Blue Harbor and she thinks deputy sheriffing in Hancock County would be safer than selling vacuum cleaners. She's probably right."

"Six whole months of training?" Annie mourned.

"You know the saying, absence makes the heart grow fonder?" he said, tracing her lower lip with his thumb.

"Jake Macpherson, my heart couldn't possibly get any fonder," Annie said with a surge of feeling, her eyes stinging with tears. "I don't need a six-month separation from you to realize that. I've been dying of loneliness for the past three days. How long were you planning to wait before telling me all of this?"

"Well, the roof's about done, and I've been rehearsing what I wanted to say to you every moment I've been working on it. Carpentry work is good for that sort of thing. I was planning to tell you tonight. In person.''

"Well, I'm here, and you've told me, so now can we please go home?''

Jake shook his head and closed his hands firmly on her shoulders. "Not yet. There's something else. I haven't asked you the most important thing." The silence dragged out while Annie waited. His expression intensified until at length he shook his head. "Damnation," he blurted, frustrated. "All those fancy words I memorized just flew out of my head.''

"Just ask," Annie prompted. "Plain words work for me.''

He gathered himself again. "I love you.''

"That's a good start, even if it isn't a question," she encouraged. "I love you, too, in case you hadn't already guessed. Keep going.''

His grip tightened on her shoulders. "Annie, would you consider marrying a low-paid deputy sheriff like myself?''

Annie's heart leaped and she blinked back tears. "I just might, if you'd consider marrying a low-paid country doctor like myself.''

"Is that a yes?''

"Of course it's a yes," Annie said, giving over to the smile that lit up her heart. Her breath left her in a happy rush as he pulled her into his arms and kissed her long and passionately.

"Annie, Annie," he said when at last they pulled apart. "You've just made me the happiest man on earth.''

"I'll do my best to keep you that way," Annie promised as he bent to kiss her again.

"Daddy, Dr. Annie, look!" Amanda's excited voice squeaked. "I just caught the bestest one in the whole *world!*"

"So did I," Jake and Annie murmured simultaneously as they sealed their future together with a kiss that just might have turned any frog into royalty.

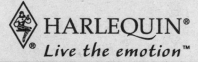

He's a man on his own, trying to raise his children.
Sometimes he gets things right. Sometimes he needs a little help....

Unfinished Business
by Inglath Cooper
(Superromance #1214) On-sale July 2004

Culley Rutherford is doing the best he can raising his young
daughter on his own. One night while on a medical conference in
New York City, Culley runs into his old friend Addy Taylor. After a
passionate night together, they go their separate ways, so Culley
is surprised to see Addy back in Harper's Mill. Now that she's
there, though, he's determined to show Addy that the three of
them can be a family.

Daddy's Little Matchmaker
by Roz Denny Fox
(Superromance #1220) On-sale August 2004

Alan Ridge is a widower and the father of nine-year-old Louemma,
who suffers from paralysis caused by the accident that killed her
mother. Laurel Ashline is a weaver who's come to the town of
Ridge City, Kentucky, to explore her family's history—a history
that includes a long-ago feud with the wealthy Ridges. Louemma
brings Alan and Laurel together, despite everything that keeps
them apart....

Available wherever Harlequin books are sold.

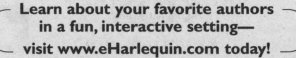

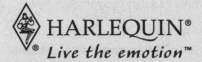

It's all about me!

Coming in July 2004,

Harlequin Flipside heroines tell you exactly what
they think...in their own words!

WHEN SIZE MATTERS
by Carly Laine
Harlequin Flipside #19

WHAT PHOEBE WANTS
by Cindi Myers
Harlequin Flipside #20

I promise these first-person tales will speak to you!

Look for Harlequin Flipside
at your favorite retail outlet.

HFFPT

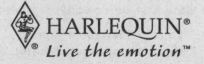